COURTSHIP AT SHADOWCREST

A Regency Duet
The Strongs of Shadowcrest
Book Five

Alexa Aston

ARE YOU SIGNED UP FOR DRAGONBLADE'S BLOG?

You'll get the latest news and information on exclusive giveaways, exclusive excerpts, coming releases, sales, free books, cover reveals and more.

Check out our complete list of authors, too!

No spam, no junk. That's a promise!

Sign Up Here

www.dragonbladepublishing.com

Dearest Reader;

Thank you for your support of a small press. At Dragonblade Publishing, we strive to bring you the highest quality Historical Romance from some of the best authors in the business. Without your support, there is no 'us', so we sincerely hope you adore these stories and find some new favorite authors along the way.

Happy Reading!

CEO, Dragonblade Publishing

Additional Dragonblade books by Author Alexa Aston

The Strongs of Shadowcrest Series
The Duke's Unexpected Love (Book 1)
The Perks of Loving a Viscount (Book 2)
Falling for the Marquess (Book 3)
The Captain and the Duchess (Book 4)
Courtship at Shadowcrest (Book 5)

Suddenly a Duke Series
Portrait of the Duke (Book 1)
Music for the Duke (Book 2)
Polishing the Duke (Book 3)
Designs on the Duke (Book 4)
Fashioning the Duke (Book 5)
Love Blooms with the Duke (Book 6)
Training the Duke (Book 7)
Investigating the Duke (Book 8)

Second Sons of London Series
Educated By The Earl (Book 1)
Debating With The Duke (Book 2)
Empowered By The Earl (Book 3)
Made for the Marquess (Book 4)
Dubious about the Duke (Book 5)
Valued by the Viscount (Book 6)
Meant for the Marquess (Book 7)

Dukes Done Wrong Series
Discouraging the Duke (Book 1)
Deflecting the Duke (Book 2)
Disrupting the Duke (Book 3)
Delighting the Duke (Book 4)

Destiny with a Duke (Book 5)

Dukes of Distinction Series
Duke of Renown (Book 1)
Duke of Charm (Book 2)
Duke of Disrepute (Book 3)
Duke of Arrogance (Book 4)
Duke of Honor (Book 5)
The Duke That I Want (Book 6)

The St. Clairs Series
Devoted to the Duke (Book 1)
Midnight with the Marquess (Book 2)
Embracing the Earl (Book 3)
Defending the Duke (Book 4)
Suddenly a St. Clair (Book 5)
Starlight Night (Novella)
The Twelve Days of Love (Novella)

Soldiers & Soulmates Series
To Heal an Earl (Book 1)
To Tame a Rogue (Book 2)
To Trust a Duke (Book 3)
To Save a Love (Book 4)
To Win a Widow (Book 5)
Yuletide at Gillingham (Novella)

King's Cousins Series
The Pawn (Book 1)
The Heir (Book 2)
The Bastard (Book 3)

Medieval Runaway Wives
Song of the Heart (Book 1)
A Promise of Tomorrow (Book 2)
Destined for Love (Book 3)

Knights of Honor Series
Word of Honor (Book 1)

Marked by Honor (Book 2)
Code of Honor (Book 3)
Journey to Honor (Book 4)
Heart of Honor (Book 5)
Bold in Honor (Book 6)
Love and Honor (Book 7)
Gift of Honor (Book 8)
Path to Honor (Book 9)
Return to Honor (Book 10)

The Lyon's Den Series
The Lyon's Lady Love

Pirates of Britannia Series
God of the Seas

De Wolfe Pack: The Series
Rise of de Wolfe

The de Wolfes of Esterley Castle
Diana
Derek
Thea

Also from Alexa Aston
The Bridge to Love (Novella)
One Magic Night

Tempted by the Earl

Part 1 of
Courtship at Shadowcrest

Alexa Aston

PROLOGUE

Oxford—November 1803

S TERLING AYLES FLIPPED the woman onto her back, climbing atop her and thrusting in and out, hearing her call his name as she writhed beneath him.

He couldn't recall hers.

He buried himself in her a final time and then quickly pulled out, spilling his seed in the handkerchief which lay nearby. Sterling had no interest in fathering any bastards. Actually, he had no interest in being a father to legitimate children, either. Being the heir apparent to his father, the Earl of Carroll, he supposed he would have to think about providing an heir of his own someday. That day would be a long way off, however. He was only twenty years of age. Even if his father dropped dead tomorrow, Sterling wouldn't think of taking a wife for another twenty years. It was far too much fun to tup a woman and move on.

Wives meant taking responsibility. That was the last thing he cared about now. He still had two years left at university, where he'd spent more time gambling and bedding women than he had with any Oxford don. He planned to continue this pattern, living in the moment and only one day at a time.

He knew he was incredibly attractive to women and took

pride in being the rogue he was. He was charming and smooth-talking. A great raconteur. A man others—both men and women—wished to be around. His life was about seeking pleasure and enjoying himself, knowing his smile was irresistible and able to get him whatever he wanted.

Besides, why should he settle down and become responsible? He was young and selfish, not caring what others thought. Especially his parents. While Sterling believed no one knew the true him, the people who knew him the least were the pair who had brought him into the world. Both the Earl and Countess of Carroll still seemed surprised when they came across him on the rare occasions they were in the same household at the same time. The couple was self-centered and hated country life. They had abandoned him to be raised by nannies and tutors and the household servants at Carrollwood, only coming home for a week around Christmas to East Sussex. They were parents in name only, and he refused to acknowledge them as thus.

Sterling believed he had raised himself. He had no other siblings and had gone away to school when he was but eight years of age. Holidays had usually been spent at the country estates of friends, though he had come home to Carrollwood each Christmas, in part to see if his parents still recognized him or might wish to apologize for abandoning him as they had. While they would speak to him briefly, they had little to do with him during their brief respite at home. Finally, he had stopped bothering to speak to them. He came home and did as he pleased and then returned to school, and now university.

At Oxford, he had made a few friends, though he wasn't truly close to anyone. Everyone found him amusing and charming, but it seemed no one saw the true Sterling Ayles. Of course, he did try to keep the real Sterling hidden from the world. He had done so for so long, even he wasn't quite certain who that man really was.

The widow in bed with him stroked his arm. "That was love-ly, my lord," she said, giving him a come-hither look.

But he was done with her. They had coupled several times. He had no need of becoming involved with one woman or seeing to her needs. Even though he admitted he was selfish in that regard, women still flocked to him.

"Fools," he said under his breath, shaking his head.

"What was that?" she asked.

He smiled, knowing it would distract her. "Nothing. I must be going, though."

"When will I see you again?" she asked, her hand still moving along his arm.

"You won't," he said bluntly. "We are done."

Her bottom lip trembled as she sat up. "Did I do something wrong, my lord?"

"No, nothing at all," he assured her, smiling again to reassure her. "I simply must dedicate more time to my studies. I want my father to be proud of me, you know."

That was so far from the truth, he bit the inside of his mouth to keep from bursting into laughter. Fortunately, he was a good actor, and he saw from her face that she believed the outlandish lie.

"I know you work hard," she said. "You must have so much to read."

"I do." He brushed the hair back from her face. "I have neglected my studies for you. I must remedy that now. You will find someone else."

She sighed, moving close and kissing his shoulder. "No one like you, Ayles. You are a lover like no other."

Rising from the bed, he pulled his shirt over his head. "Well, I am glad that I have satisfied you."

He finished dressing and then blew her a kiss, which she pretended to catch.

"Good luck with your studies," she called as he exited the bedchamber and hurried down the stairs.

Sterling pulled his greatcoat tightly about him, trying to ward off the damp chill in the air. The wind had picked up, making it seem colder than it truly was.

He stopped in a pub for a quick meal, and then returned to his rented rooms. Of course, his father paid for them, but the man had never asked Sterling one question about his time at Oxford. Where he lived. What he studied. Who his friends were. Instead, the family solicitor took care of any bills Sterling acquired, along with paying tuition and the rent for the rooms. Most of his fellow students shared rooms with one or two others, but he was a loner, despite seeming so social and affable. He preferred total silence when he came home, using the quiet to pen poetry and plays. Now *that* would surprise his fellow students if they learned of those endeavors. Everyone knew Sterling was smart, but he brushed that aside, pretending he didn't care for his studies or anything related to academics.

Writing fulfilled something inside him, something unspoken. He had accumulated stacks of his work but would never share them with anyone. It was for his eyes alone, an expression of who he was, the man no one knew.

Using his key, he unlocked the door to his rooms. As he stepped over the threshold, he saw someone had pushed a letter under it. He bent to retrieve it and took it to the table, where he lit a candle. It was only a little past four in the afternoon, but dark had already fallen.

He broke the seal, curious as to who had written him since this was the first letter he had received since he had come to Oxford to study. The letter was dated but carried no salutation, which Sterling found odd as he begin to read.

12 November 1803

There is no easy way to say this, so I will be blunt.
You are now the Earl of Carroll.
Your parents passed away this morning at his lordship's London residence. A sudden fever struck them both a few days ago. The doctor was called, and he did all he could. Unfortunately, the countess succumbed to it first around four

this morning, quickly followed by the earl at five-thirty.

Having prepared your father's will, I know they wanted to be buried in town. I assume you will wish to be at their burial. I will share the contents of Lord Carroll's will with you afterward.

I took the liberty of borrowing his lordship's carriage and coming to Oxford to retrieve you. I am staying at the Deerfield Inn, which is near your rented rooms. I suggest you return with me to town tomorrow morning, after you have spoken to your tutors, informing them of your parents' deaths. Certainly, they will be sympathetic to your situation and grant you a leave from your studies, at least until the beginning of the new year.

Please contact me once you have read this to confirm these plans. I am here to serve you, Lord Carroll, and will answer any questions you might have regarding the estate and your inheritance.

Sincerely,
Mr. Potter

Folding the letter, Sterling slipped it inside his coat's pocket. He paused, thinking the only family he had left was now gone.

And he felt absolutely nothing.

He wondered if there might be something wrong with him, or had the fault been with his parents? While he knew from talking with other boys at school that many parents had little to do with their children, his seemed especially distant.

It didn't matter. They were gone. Good riddance to them. He was now the Earl of Carroll. While he believed he would one day wed and produce the expected heir apparent, that day was far into the future. No reason to make him and a woman miserable by shackling themselves together now. No, he would remain at Cambridge and finish his time here, and then he would carouse to his heart's desire, staying in London most of the year. Carrollwood had seemed a prison to him all those years growing up. He would only go to the country when absolutely necessary.

For now, he would live life as he saw fit and enjoy his wealth and status in Polite Society. Sterling would choose to look forward—and never back to his unhappy childhood.

CHAPTER ONE

Shadowcrest—Kent—August 1810

Allegra Strong came down to breakfast with her twin Lyric. They were the last of the family to arrive this morning. Her cousin James and his wife Sophie were present, along with her aunt and two cousins. Aunt Matty was not present, but she usually ate quite early.

"Good morning, everyone," she said as she and Lyric took their seats.

After a footman poured tea for her, she looked to Effie and asked her cousin, "Would you like to go riding this morning?

Effie shook her head. "No, I won't have time. We will be packing."

"Packing?" Lyric interjected. "Where on earth would you be going? The house party begins the day after tomorrow."

James and Sophie were hosting a house party in honor of Allegra and Lyric. The party would serve as their introduction into Polite Society, albeit a small portion of it. It had been Allegra who balked against her and Lyric making their come-outs this past spring in town. While they were at the modiste's shop being measured for an entire new wardrobe of gowns to be made up for the upcoming Season, she had overheard that James would be paying entirely for her and Lyric's expensive wardrobes. Usually, a girl making her come-out had no less than sixty ballgowns sewn, as well as countless other gowns for other social events and receiving callers.

Her father, who was James' uncle, had never really paid much attention to his daughters. He was close with his older son Theodore, and moderately interested in his younger son Caleb, who now served as the Shadowcrest steward. Their mother had died after producing Allegra and Lyric, and Adolphus Strong had no interest in having female twins in his nursery. Her father had let their aunt, the Duchess of Seaton, take over the responsibility of raising them. Eventually, the twins moved permanently to the Seaton household.

Allegra looked to Aunt Dinah now, the only mother she had ever known. "What is going on, Aunt?"

Her aunt was planning the entire house party. After learning of James footing the bill for their come-outs, Allegra had discussed things with her twin, and the two of them had gone to Aunt Dinah, explaining that unless their father owned up to his financial responsibilities to them, they would not make their debuts as planned. Unfortunately, the twins learned that neglect of them was only one of their father's faults. It came out that her father and Theodore had schemed to kidnap Sophie and hold her for ransom. Adolphus Strong was bitterly disappointed that James had appeared after having vanished when he was a small boy seventeen years earlier. Adolphus had believed he would become the new Duke of Seaton when his brother died, and he would eventually pass along the title to Theodore.

When James did return to London and assumed the ducal title shortly after his father's death, it had driven her father to the brink of despair. Fortunately, the kidnapping was foiled. James had banished his uncle and cousin to the other side of the world, with only the clothes on their backs. Allegra felt a deep shame that her relatives had conspired against James and Sophie, who were lovely to her and Lyric.

Still, Allegra did not want to remain in their household forever, dependent upon James, no matter how much he loved her and Lyric. That was why the twins had agreed to Aunt Dinah's idea of a house party held at the end of the Season at Shadowcrest in their honor. Her aunt was managing the entire event, planning all the activities and inviting the guests, since Sophie had little interest in social affairs. She was the owner of Neptune Shipping, an active owner who ran her business. Sophie was also increasing and would give birth to her and James' first child in about five weeks' time, so she had been happy to turn over all aspects of the house party to Aunt Dinah.

Hopefully, now that Aunt Dinah had wed Captain Andrews recently and he had been placed in charge of the London office, he would help ease Sophie's burden. The duchess said she would be counting on the captain to help in the daily running of her business, but she reserved the right to make critical decisions as she taught him the ropes.

Aunt Dinah said, "I think I will allow Mirella to explain since it was her idea." She looked to her daughter.

Mirella cleared her throat. "You know that I had to delay my own come-out this spring because of the broken elbow I suffered. I still prefer to make my debut into Polite Society in a traditional fashion and will do so at the first ball held next spring. I want to experience the full slate of social activities in a Season."

That made sense to Allegra. Mirella was mad for dancing and would most likely dance every set at each ball come next spring.

Her cousin smiled. "Besides, this house party is being given in your honor, Allegra. Yours and Lyric's. Since I am not officially out in society, Aunt Matty is taking Effie and me on a tour."

Effie's eyes lit up. "We are going to the Lake District," she shared. "It is supposed to be the most beautiful part of England. Aunt Matty said that we will enjoy the scenery, and Mirella can take her paints with her, painting various landscapes."

"We will also be able to visit some of the larger estates in the area and tour their houses," Mirella continued. "Aunt Matty said you can often call at a house, and the housekeeper will give you a tour of it. Effie and I are excited to not only spend time together, but with Aunt Matty, too. She has a few friends in this area, and so we will be staying with them, as well as stopping at various inns during the three or four weeks we will be gone."

"Your trip sounds very exciting," Lyric said enthusiastically. "In a way, I am a bit jealous and wish I could go along with you. I know, though, that Aunt Dinah has been hard at work on this party for us. I am eager to meet the guests coming and partake in all the activities which are planned." Her twin smiled mysteriously. "Who knows? Allegra and I might actually find someone to call our own when all is said and done."

Allegra knew house parties took place often at the end of a Season or during Christmastime. She had been looking forward to making her come-out this spring alongside her cousins Georgie and Mirella, as well as Lyric. Georgie had experienced a most successful Season, marrying a former army officer who was now the Marquess of Edgethorne. They had wed in June, and August had taken Georgie to Scotland for an extended honeymoon. They were supposed to return sometime in early September to August's country estate. Edgefield was in Surrey and not far from Shadowcrest in Kent.

She had seen how happy her cousin Pippa was when she married Seth, Viscount Hopewell, and Georgie looked just as joyful when she wed August. Aunt Dinah had continued to have a glow about her since her wedding to Captain Andrews, and so Allegra was quite aware of the love matches being made within the Strong family. She wondered if Lyric was right and that the possibility of finding love during this upcoming party at Shadowcrest might exist.

She knew these type of parties were held in order to give people a way to come to know one another in a small, intimate setting. The Season was full of meeting dozens of gentlemen, but because of the sheer numbers of guests at events and the rules enforced by the *ton*, it was difficult to truly get to know someone.

Aunt Dinah had said she had invited five eligible bachelors to the house party, along with three unwed ladies. That would keep the numbers even at five men and five women, now that Mirella and Effie would not be taking part.

"I hope you have a lovely time with Aunt Matty," Allegra said. "When will you return?"

"Aunt Matty believes we should be home by the end of the second week in September or early in the third week," Mirella explained.

They finished their breakfasts, with Mirella and Effie going upstairs to pack. Allegra assumed Aunt Matty had already breakfasted and was now packing, as well. While she would miss her cousins, she could understand Mirella's desire to be brought out in a more formal manner. After all, she was the sister of a duke. As for Effie, she would not even make her come-out until a year after Mirella did. Allegra wondered if Effie would ever wish to settle down in marriage. Her cousin was quite nurturing, but it involved animals. Effie had often remarked that animals were better friends than people. Allegra only hoped Effie would mature a bit more and change her mind, since she believed her youngest cousin would make for a wonderful wife and mother, nurturing her family as she did her strays.

Aunt Dinah asked if she and Lyric would like to come to her sitting room, and both girls quickly agreed to do so. Allegra had always liked spending special time with her aunt, who had made her and Lyric feel wanted and loved. The four daughters of the Duke of Seaton were more like sisters to them than cousins since they had all been brought up in the same household.

When they arrived, Aunt Dinah handed each girl a small, wrapped present. Allegra's heart sped up, guessing what it was. She and Lyric opened them and held up the gold lockets.

"You know I have given the same locket to Georgina and Pippa," their aunt said. "It is inscribed with the initial of your first name, and inside is a lock of your baby hair which I snipped many years ago."

"Thank you, Aunt Dinah," Allegra and Lyric said in unison.

"You are my girls just as much as the four I gave birth to," Aunt Dinah said, wiping away a tear. "But enough of that. Shall we talk about the house party?"

Aunt Dinah handed each of them a list. "These are the activities which I have decided upon. Please look over them and see if there is anything you might wish to add."

Allegra perused it carefully, eager for the house party to begin.

"The only thing I think we should add, Aunt Dinah, is a picnic," Lyric said. "Pippa has always been fond of us holding ones by the lake. If we did so, it would remind me of her, as if she were here at the party with us."

Her aunt smiled approvingly. "I agree. Of course, the two of you will have to step up and play the pianoforte for our guests. I am hoping to have everyone gather around and sing together as one of you play."

Allegra and Lyric both played very well, but nothing like Georgie and Mirella did. Since both of them would be missing from the party, she knew she and her twin would need to perform for their guests, most likely on more than one occasion.

Her twin laughed. "If that is the case, I will abandon my gardening today in favor of practicing." She looked to Allegra. "Will you also be practicing?"

She grinned. "I'd better. At least Mirella won't be here to show all of us up." She looked to her aunt. "Do any of the other ladies attending play the pianoforte or another musical instrument?"

"I have no idea, Allegra, but I expect they do. Every well-bred lady takes musical lessons of some sort."

"Who is coming to the house party?" Lyric asked. "I have been curious about our guests."

"I can provide you their names. Even tell you a bit about them. But I believe you should form your own opinions of our guests instead of having preconceived notions," Aunt Dinah explained. "All I will say is that all five men are bachelors, well known to the *ton*. A few are more outgoing than others, and one is a bit shy. One among this group is a widower, and he has a two-year-old daughter. That is all you will get out of me regarding these gentlemen."

"Then at last tell us a bit about the ladies," Allegra pressed. "Lyric and I have always had the advantage of having our four cousins as our constant companions, and they have been our closest friends. One of the reasons I looked forward to making my come-out—and now this party—is to be able to meet other ladies our same age, besides the gentlemen who will attend."

"I will tell you a bit about our three female guests, then," her aunt said. "Lady Lida and Miss Markle are cousins who were brought up together. They come from Somerset, and Lord and Lady Crowell, Lady Lida's parents, will be here to chaperone them. Lady Lida made her come-out the previous Season, while Miss Markle made hers this past spring."

Allegra wondered why this Lady Lida was not betrothed after two Seasons. Although not every girl made a match by the end of her come-out Season, a majority did by their second. She was extremely curious about Lady Lida and also looked forward to meeting Miss Markle, the cousin.

"The third lady attending is Miss Bancroft. She became friends with Georgie during this Season. I am certain Georgie will continue to pursue her friendship with Miss Bancroft. And her aunt, another Miss Bancroft, will be her chaperone."

If her cousin liked Miss Bancroft, that was good enough for Allegra. Georgie was both kind and level-headed. She must have seen something special in Miss Bancroft since she had made friends with her.

"If that is all, Aunt Dinah, I think I will go to the music room to begin my practice," Lyric said. Looking to Allegra, she said, "Unless you would rather practice there."

"No, go ahead. I will practice in the drawing room."

They left Aunt Dinah's sitting room, discussing which pieces they would practice, so that neither of them would play the same number for their guests.

"We should prepare at least three each," Lyric suggested. "We will be retiring to the drawing room after dinner each evening. While I know Aunt Dinah has us playing games and cards and even dancing some, there will still be plenty of time for music to be played for our guests."

"You're right," Allegra agreed. "We should each prepare five different pieces. I would rather be overprepared than caught unprepared."

She went to the music room with Lyric, combing through the sheet music, each one of them selecting the composers they enjoyed most.

Allegra retreated to the drawing room, where she practiced for a good two hours. She usually practiced a couple of times a week, unlike Georgie and Mirella, who practiced daily. She chuckled, thinking even if she practiced as much as those two, neither she nor Lyric would ever attain their level of skill.

Satisfied with the progress she had made, Allegra took the sheet music back to the music room.

"I am exhausted," Lyric said. "I do not see how Mirella and Georgie stay at it for so long. I think I would like to stretch my legs. Would you care to take a walk with me?"

"I would indeed," she said, linking her arm through her sister's as they left the house.

As they strolled through the gardens, she couldn't help but think that after tomorrow, Shadowcrest would be full of guests.

And perhaps she and her twin might be fortunate enough to find love.

CHAPTER TWO

STERLING HAD NO idea why he had been invited to a house party hosted by the Duke and Duchess of Seaton. He had never even met the pair, who had been the talk of last Season. The duchess, formerly Mrs. Josiah Grant, had shocked Polite Society after her husband's death. Not only had Mr. Grant left the shipping empire to his widow, but she actually also ran it herself. When she married the duke, many a tongue had wagged, especially since Seaton's family owned Strong Shipping Lines, chief competitor to Mrs. Grant's Neptune Shipping.

While the *ton* assumed the duke wed the widow merely to get his hands on her company, Seaton had shocked London by deliberately allowing his bride to keep her business in the marriage settlements. According to gossip, the ducal heir would inherit Strong Shipping, while any other children—male or female—would own Neptune Shipping.

Even though Sterling didn't know the couple personally, he was eager to speak to both. People who refused to play by the rules of Polite Society interested him, especially since he took delight in breaking as many as possible. Still, house parties were notorious for producing multiple betrothals between couples. The Seatons hosted this party in honor of the duke's cousins, twin girls who had yet to make their come-outs.

One of the duke's sisters, had, though. Sterling had thought Lady Georgina Strong a diamond of the first water. She was beautiful, calm, and intelligent. They had danced once, but she only had eyes for the scarred Marquess of Edgethorne. He didn't really know the former officer, but he had seen Edgethorne at events and heard the vicious gossip about him. The fact that Georgina Strong had ignored it and followed her heart intrigued him even more about these Strongs. Perhaps Lord and Lady Edgethorne might be in attendance at the house party and would agree to spend some time with him.

He only came today because one simply did not turn down the invitation issued by a duke. From what he gathered, however, even though the Seatons were the nominal hosts, it was the former Dowager Duchess of Seaton who had planned the activities. She was as much a beauty as her daughter had been, and Sterling had seen the wedding announcement in the newspapers of her recent marriage. To his shock, the former duchess had wed a sea captain.

Yes, the Strongs of Shadowcrest were a most unusual lot. Though Sterling had no desire to make a match with either of the Strong girls, he thought this house party would prove to be quite entertaining.

He glanced to his companion in the carriage. Silas Chase, Viscount Blankenship, had been a boon companion of his for a few years. Though the viscount was a Cambridge man and Sterling an Oxford one, they had been cut from the same cloth. When Blankenship arrived in town after finishing his university years, he had been as wild as they came and a perfect friend for Sterling. They had cut quite a swath through London society, gambling and rutting, until Blankenship had a sudden change of heart.

This past Season, his friend had cut ties with Sterling and their crowd of rakes. Instead, he had entered the Season with his eye on the Marriage Mart. At one point, Sterling thought Blankenship might have made a match with Lady Georgina, but it proved not to be the case. He wondered if the viscount would pursue another Strong female at this house party. His gut told him it was likely the event would end with a betrothal announcement regarding his former friend.

"I am surprised you wished to share a carriage with me," Sterling said. "You haven't wanted a thing to do with me in months."

"When I heard you were invited to Shadowcrest, I thought I might try and make amends with you, Carroll. I am afraid I did not do a good thing, cutting you from my life so abruptly. For that, I apologize."

"Apology accepted," he said breezily. "I am not one to hold grudges, Blankenship. What happened to you?"

Sadness filled the viscount's eyes. "My uncle died. It left me truly on my own. I decided it was time I began acting my age and assuming the responsibilities I should have long ago."

"Does that include finding a wife?" Sterling pressed.

"Yes, it does. I am eager to wed and have children. The Season did not play out quite as I expected. This house party will give me an opportunity to get to know a few young ladies in a better setting. Hopefully, my future viscountess will be amongst those in attendance."

"You already lost one Strong female," he said, seeing if he would get a rise out of his former friend. "Let's hope you can hang on to one here."

Blankenship didn't take the bait. "I had thought to make a match with Lady Georgina Strong," he admitted. "But I was delighted when Edgethorne stole her heart. You see, we were the closest of friends at Eton and Cambridge and even shared rooms while at university. Edgethorne is the brother I never had." He smiled. "We were randy as they came and had many good times together before he left for the war. I am only glad that he is home again and has the love of a good woman."

He hadn't known the viscount and marquess were longtime friends.

"I will leave the matchmaking to others," he said airily. "I hope you find what you are looking for, Blankenship. As for me, I do not plan to wed until I absolutely have to."

They fell silent again. At least the air between them had been cleared. He didn't think Blankenship wished him ill. His friend had simply moved on to another chapter in his life, one which did not interest Sterling in the slightest. He had many more years of adventures to write in the story of his life before he thought of settling down.

As for him, he would be polite and charming to the other guests, male and female. He doubted any of the young misses invited would be suitable bed partners, but there were always their chaperones. When the house party ended, he would proudly stand with his freedom intact and head back to town.

Their carriage turned onto a lane and about five minutes later, they reached the main house itself. As it came to a halt, he noticed neither the duke nor duchess were present to greet their guests. The beautiful dowager duchess was present, though, along with two other women who resembled one another. They were of a similar height, though the one with sable hair was slightly taller than the woman with russet hair. They favored one another closely in the face, but the shorter one was small everywhere, including her breasts and waist.

It was the dark-haired one who drew Sterling's attention now.

She had curves in all the right places and a ready smile. He had always been attracted to a woman with curves. Being that she stood with the dowager duchess, she had to be either Allegra or Lyric Strong. He knew enough not to get caught in an embrace with an innocent, but Sterling definitely planned upon kissing her. At a house party, he would have plenty of opportunities to pull this Miss Strong into some nook or cranny and at least enjoy the taste of her.

Glancing to Blankenship, he saw the viscount also looked out the window, his gaze fixated on the other Strong girl. He liked

Blankenship and the good times they had spent together. If he were interested in the russet-haired woman, then Sterling would keep his hands off her as a courtesy.

The vehicle rolled to a halt, and a footman quickly placed stairs down, opening the carriage door for them. He allowed Blankenship to descend first and then followed.

"Lord Blankenship," the dowager duchess said, giving the viscount a warm smile. "How good it is to see you again soon. Thank you again for coming to the wedding."

"Thank you for having me, Your Grace," Blankenship replied. "It did my heart good to see my friend and Lady Georgina marry. Are they still honeymooning in Scotland?"

"They are. And I am Mrs. Andrews now, my lord." She looked to Sterling. "Good afternoon, Lord Carroll. Thank you for accepting our invitation."

He greeted the former duchess. "I am honored to visit Shadowcrest," he said smoothly, finding it a shame that this woman had recently wed because she was still quite the beauty. He would have enjoyed a romp in bed with her.

"May I introduce you to my nieces?" she asked. Turning, she indicated one. "This is Miss Lyric Strong. And Miss Allegra Strong."

So, the one he was attracted to was Allegra. Because of that, Sterling deliberately greeted the other one first.

"It is lovely to make your acquaintance, Miss Strong," he said, taking her hand and kissing it. Then turning, he added, "And you, as well, Miss Strong."

When he took her offered hand, though, something struck him. An awareness rippled through him as she looked at him with those large, cornflower eyes.

"I am happy to make your acquaintance, Lord Carroll," she said, her voice low and musical, causing desire to shoot through him. "But please, address me as Miss Allegra. Aunt Dinah said it would be too complicated for Lyric and me to both be Miss Strong."

He still held her hand. She tugged on it, but he wasn't ready to release it yet.

"Miss Allegra," he repeated, bending and kissing her fingers a second time.

When he looked at her, he saw how flushed her cheeks had grown, making her even more attractive.

"I am partial to this hand, my lord," she said lightly, tugging again, causing him to release it.

"You may have it back. For now," he flirted, already wanting to kiss her.

"Come inside," Mrs. Andrews told them. "Miss Forrester will see you to your rooms. Hot water is already being sent up now for you to freshen up after your journey from town. Once you are settled, make your way to the drawing room. You are the last to arrive, gentlemen. It is almost teatime. You can visit with the other guests there."

"Thank you, Mrs. Andrews," Blankenship said. "Come along, Carroll."

They went inside the house, and while he saw Miss Lyric escorting Blankenship up the stairs to a bedchamber, Miss Allegra motioned to a footman and asked that he take Lord Carroll upstairs to his guestroom. The servant did so. Already, his trunk had been placed in his room while he spoke with his hostess, and his valet awaited him, unpacking it. He untied his cravat and stripped off his coat, waistcoat, and shirt.

"Have fresh ones ready once I have washed," he instructed.

Sterling did so, glad to have new clothes after the heat of the carriage. He then redressed with his valet's help. When he stepped into the corridor, he saw Blankenship had done the same, emerging from the bedchamber across from him.

A waiting footman said, "I will escort you to the drawing room, my lords."

The two lords followed the servant. When they entered the room, his eyes swept over the women present. He had met Lady Lida and Miss Markle but had no idea who the plain woman was who spoke with them. Miss Lyric was speaking to Lord Lamkin and Lord Tillings, two men he knew from White's.

Miss Allegra was engaged in conversation with Lord Motley. The earl was a widower, about two years Sterling's senior. Miss Allegra laughed at something Motley said.

And Sterling didn't like that one whit.

He moved in the general direction of everyone, but his goal was to separate Allegra Strong from Lord Motley, the sooner the better.

Because he was reacting to this woman in a manner he never had before—and Sterling was determined to figure out why.

ALLEGRA SENSED LORD Carroll's presence before she saw him. She kept her attention focused on Lord Motley, nodding encouragingly so he would continue with the story he told her.

But her skin prickled and her breath quickened as she saw Lord Carroll cross the room from the corner of her eye.

"Good afternoon," the earl said, joining them.

Coolly, she said, "Have you met Lord Motley, Lord Carroll?"

"It was quite a while ago." Carroll offered Motley his hand, and the two men shook, though Allegra noticed Motley's frown and wondered why the earl would disapprove of Lord Carroll.

Turning, she wanted to introduce Lord Motley to Lord Blankenship, only to see the viscount had approached Lyric and Miss Bancroft.

"You will have to wait a moment to make Lord Blankenship's acquaintance, Lord Motley," she said to the earl.

"I know of him," Lord Motley said. "Blankenship was at Eton when I was, but he was several years behind me. I believe I read in the newspapers where he lost his uncle before this past Season started."

Aunt Dinah claimed everyone's attention, making the necessary introductions, and then said, "We are so happy to have you here with us at Shadowcrest for this party."

Just then, James and Sophie entered, Sophie moving slowly because of the size of her belly.

"And here are your true hosts, the Duke and Duchess of Seaton," Aunt Dinah proclaimed.

A shuffle began, with guests moving in small groups to meet their hosts and the others present. Once several teacarts were rolled in, Sophie asked if they would all find a seat. While the drawing room easily seated everyone present, they could not all sit together, so people began moving to the smaller seating groups scattered about the room. Aunt Dinah had already told her nieces when this situation occurred to make certain they split up so that there would be someone from Shadowcrest to pour out within each group.

Allegra moved to her right and found Lady Lida, her mother, Lord Motley, and Lord Carroll joining her. She didn't quite know how he did it, but Lord Carroll maneuvered everyone into sitting so that the two of them wound up together on a settee.

"Oh, these sandwiches look delicious," Lady Crowell exclaimed. "And these teacakes! I cannot wait to sample them, as well."

She poured out, giving Lord Carroll his serving last and then filling her own cup. By now, Lady Lida and her mother were discussing gardening with Lord Motley, leaving her to entertain Lord Carroll.

She swallowed, her insides racing. Never had her heart beat quite so fast.

"You did not make your come-out this Season," the earl observed. "If you had, I would have noticed you."

"I did not. Plans changed. There were to be five of us from this household doing so—and only one actually did."

Curiosity filled his face. "What happened?"

"My cousin Pippa and our neighbor, the new Viscount Hopewell, fell in love even before the Season began. Lord

Hopewell is a former sea captain, and Pippa has always had an adventurous spirit. Their honeymoon is one which is taking them around the globe."

"How interesting," Lord Carroll said, sipping his tea, his gaze burning into her, making her cheeks heat.

"Pippa and my cousin Georgie are twins. Georgie did make her come-out as planned."

"And wed Lord Edgethorne. I think the entire *ton* witnessed them falling in love."

Allegra nodded. "Their honeymoon has taken them to one of Edgethorne's properties in Scotland. As for my cousin Mirella, she broke her forearm and elbow just before the Season began. If anyone enjoys dancing more than Mirella, I have yet to meet them. Since the doctor forbid my cousin to dance because the plaster would have her off-balance, she has chosen to make her come-out next spring. She, my youngest cousin Effie, and Aunt Matty are now touring the Lake District."

"It is a large family. Full of females," the earl noted.

"Well, there is Seaton," she pointed out. "He is head of our family."

"I find I enjoy the company of women," he said, his voice warm and seductive, despite them being in a drawing room full of others. "I hope you and I will be able to enjoy one another's company during this house party, Miss Allegra."

Now she understood why Lord Motley had been cool to this man. From his elegant dress and smooth talking, she realized that Lord Carroll was a rake. Why Aunt Dinah had invited such a rogue to this house party puzzled her, though. Yes, she and Lyric were eager to meet all kinds of people, but at the same time, it was understood that this house party would give them the advantage of getting to know a small group rather quickly. Rakes weren't known for committing to any woman, much less offering marriage.

Allegra decided to call him out and be done with him.

"Have you always been a rake, my lord?" she asked softly, not wishing for the others to hear their conversation.

His eyes widened in surprise, but he recovered quickly. "Have you always been so bold in speaking your mind, Miss Allegra?" He paused. "Especially when speaking to a rake such as myself?

"I am outgoing," she said. "A bit impulsive at times. But not so careless as to want to be bedded by the likes of you underneath Shadowcrest's roof."

With that, Allegra turned to the others present, knowing she had stunned the earl into silence. "Tell me more about your daughter, Lord Motley. I believe you said her name is Viola?"

She knew the girl's name, of course, because she had spent time in the nursery showing her various dolls the Strong girls had played with during their own years there. But she knew allowing Lord Motley to talk of his daughter would be a new topic of discussion and would easily draw in the others in their grouping.

Except for Lord Carroll. A rogue wouldn't be one to talk of children. By intentionally introducing this line of conversation, she deliberately excluded the earl.

And she knew that he knew exactly what she did.

"Yes," the earl said with enthusiasm. "And I cannot thank His and Her Grace enough for allowing me to bring Viola and her nursery governess with me to Kent. My daughter has just turned two and is quite attached to me."

Allegra continued to converse with Lord Motley, Lady Crowell, and Lady Lida. She made no effort to draw Lord Carroll into the conversation once they began talking of the various activities in the coming days, and he made no attempt to enter it. She had already crossed the rogue off her list of potential suitors—and would warn Lyric and the other ladies present of the wolf in their midst.

But first, she would confront Aunt Dinah about her reasons for asking such a man to Shadowcrest.

CHAPTER THREE

ALLEGRA WENT TO Aunt Dinah's rooms a quarter-hour before they were due in the drawing room, knowing her aunt would be leaving soon in order to be present to make their guests feel at home.

Sure enough, Aunt Dinah emerged just as Allegra arrived, closing her door behind her. "Oh, hello, Allegra. Did you have need of me?"

"May I walk to the drawing room with you?"

"Why, certainly, my dear. What do wish to speak to me about?"

She had never been able to hide anything from this woman. "I wanted to ask your logic behind inviting certain guests to the house party," she began, not ready to name names.

"Miss Bancroft was the first I thought of when organizing this event for you and Lyric," Aunt Dinah explained. "I met her this Season through Georgie and found her to be utterly delightful. She is a woman who has much to offer—if the right man actually looks for it."

Knowing her aunt referred to Miss Bancroft's plain appearance, she said, "I agree. I do like Miss Bancroft."

"As for Lady Lida and her cousin, they both are spirited girls, with a Season or two of experience. They are pleasant and interesting. I believe Lady Lida has had offers of marriage, but she is reluctant to accept one until her cousin also has a betrothal lined up. They are close, possibly as close as you and Lyric are."

That covered the women, so Allegra pressed on. "And the gentlemen you decided to invite to Shadowcrest?"

"Lord Blankenship was the second name I jotted onto my list. He is a gentleman in every way possible, and his strong connection with August certainly was in his favor. I recalled Lord Motley wedding his wife during the last Season I went to, the one before your uncle's fit of apoplexy."

That had been a dark time in the Strong household. Uncle Seaton had lain paralyzed, unable to speak, for three years. It had been the catalyst which had set her own father on the path to claiming the dukedom in all but name. While he and her brother Theodore had flitted about town without a care in the world, Papa had restricted all the Strong women, forcing them to remain inside the London townhouse that entire time. They neither called upon nor were allowed to have others call upon them. No rides or walks in the park occurred. They were housebound the entire time, with Aunt Dinah ministering to her husband until his death.

Allegra had never understood her father's reasoning in keeping them away from others, only knowing he wanted to be the Duke of Seaton so badly that he could taste it. When an adult James appeared out of nowhere after being missing since he was a boy, it had knocked the winds out of Adolphus Strong's proverbial sails, leading to Papa hatching the scheme to hold Sophie for ransom. James had one of his ships dump them unceremoniously in Australia with no funds.

She hoped none of them would ever see the two again.

"I recalled how good a man Lord Motley was and how devoted he was to his betrothed," her aunt continued. "When I read about her passing in the newspapers, I jotted a note to him and had Powell deliver it for me."

"That was bold of you, Aunt Dinah, considering Papa did not

want us in communication with anyone in Polite Society."

"I am glad I asked Lord Motley to come to this house party since he is out of mourning," her aunt said. "And when he told me he would only be able to attend if he could bring Viola and her nursemaid with him, I thought all the more of him for the request."

They had reached the drawing room now. Thankfully, no guests were waiting. She wanted to finish this conversation with her aunt in privacy.

Trying to hurry things along, she said, "I can understand why you asked Lord Lamkin. He is the most amiable of men. And while Lord Tillings is quiet and new to his title, he is intelligent and unfailingly polite." She paused, wondering how to introduce the topic of Lord Carroll.

"You are curious as to why I added Lord Carroll to the mix," Aunt Dinah said knowingly.

"Well, yes. I am. He is quite handsome. Irresistible, in a way. But I believe him to be most arrogant."

Her aunt touched Allegra's shoulder. "The earl's reputation is quite wicked, but my intuition tells me there is much more to him than he wishes others to see. He is amusing and incredibly charming, but I believe he hides his true self. I was hoping being in the company of interesting, intelligent men and women would help him either discover his nature or open up more to the possibility of being who he really is."

"So, you do not think him a handsome shell with little to no substance to him?"

Aunt Dinah studied her carefully. "I think he wears the label the *ton* has placed upon him with pride and enjoys playing the rake. Perhaps he will understand himself—and others—better by the end of this house party."

Aunt Dinah looked over Allegra's shoulder and smiled. "Ah, Lord and Lady Crowell, it is so good to see you again. I hope you have everything to your liking."

Her aunt engaged in conversation with the earl and countess, and the drawing room began filling with their guests and various Strongs. Allegra made the effort to circulate through the room, making everyone feel at home. James and Sophie made their appearance and warmly conversed with their guests.

Lord Blankenship escorted her and Lyric in to dinner. Afterward, the men stayed behind to smoke their cheroots and drink a glass of port, while the ladies retired to the drawing room. During that time, Aunt Dinah asked their three young female guests if they would be willing to entertain everyone with their musical talents this evening. The three spoke briefly, all deciding on what numbers they would perform, so as no two would play the same piece.

The gentlemen joined them again, led by James. Allegra chose the closest seat and before she had sat in it, Lord Carroll took up the remainder of the settee.

"You look rather irked," he quipped.

Arching her brows, she said, "Possibly because I am? I wish you would go pester someone else, my lord. I have had more than enough of your company."

He frowned slightly. "I am sorry to have made such a poor first impression upon you, Miss Allegra. Might I have a second chance?"

She had no intention of giving him one, but she did know that they would need to coexist in this house for the next ten days. The least she could do is be polite and represent her family well. Unlike Aunt Dinah, she didn't believe Lord Carroll had any redeeming qualities.

Smiling graciously, she said, "I do not wish to quarrel with you, my lord. I am happy that you accepted the invitation for this house party."

He looked almost relieved, which caused her to chuckle. She coughed into her hand to cover it.

"Might I fetch you something to drink, Miss Allegra?"

She waved him away. "No, my lord. That will not be necessary." Glancing up, she saw that Miss Bancroft was seating herself at the pianoforte. "What I would like is to focus on Miss Bancroft's performance at the pianoforte. That means I require your absolute silence and no distractions."

Looking to their guest, Allegra concentrated on the piece the woman played, all the while conscious of the handsome devil beside her. It bothered her greatly that her pulse continued to pound, especially when she caught a whiff of the cologne he wore. Neither her father nor James ever wore any, yet on this man it seemed not only right—but tempting.

She couldn't help but imagine what it would be like to kiss him. Neither she nor Lyric had ever been kissed. There simply hadn't been an opportunity for that experience to occur. They had spent three years locked away from Polite Society, and then she had imposed her own imprisonment on herself and Lyric, upset that their father had squandered their dowries and would not offer up the coin it would take to clothe his daughters appropriately for the Season.

When they had gone to Madame Dumas' dress shop to be fitted for their come-out wardrobes, Allegra had been shocked at the number of gowns required during a Season, not to mention the dozens of other gowns to be made up for the routs, card parties, musicales, and garden parties. That did not even include day dresses to greet suitors during morning calls the day following an evening social event.

She had put down a firm foot, not wanting her cousin to pay such an exorbitant amount for both her and Lyric. It had led to many discussions between her and Lyric about what they were to do with themselves. Lyric had thought they might teach music lessons to young ladies to earn their living, while Allegra had toyed with the idea of them becoming governesses.

In the end, it was their brother Caleb who told them to go ahead and make a quieter debut into Polite Society. He was the one who had suggested the idea of a house party to Aunt Dinah as a way for her nieces to make their appearance in the *ton* in an understated manner. After much discussion, she and Lyric had agreed with Caleb. A house party would allow them to get to know a small, select group of others close to their age. Aunt Dinah had said to place everything in her hands, from the guest list to the activities.

So far, Allegra liked the three women in attendance, as well as the gentlemen. Except for Lord Carroll. He irritated her in a way no one ever had. The earl was far too self-assured and smug for her taste. She would stay the course and be unfailingly polite, but she had no reason to get to know him on a deeper level.

They listened to Miss Markle play, and she did as admirable a job as Miss Bancroft. Lady Lida, on the other hand, played abominably, but she had the voice of an angel, so her inept playing could be forgiven.

Lord Carroll leaned closer, which was hard for him to do since he took up most of the settee, and said, "You will be much better than any of them."

Frowning, she turned to him. "You could not possibly know well I do or do not play."

"I overheard Her Grace—Mrs. Andrews, that is—speaking of your talent to one of her friends."

Allegra snorted. "Now I know you are untruthful, as well as being a conceited rascal. If Aunt Dinah were bragging about any of us, it would be Georgie or Mirella. They are the true musicians in the family. While I play well, I cannot hold a candle to either of them."

His gaze pinned her. "You have that wrong, Miss Allegra. No one can hold a candle to you."

She shook her head, fighting to tamp down the attraction that continued to grow. "Every time you open your mouth, you prove me right. Save your flattery for the women you wish to fall under your spell, my lord."

"You think me a warlock, Miss Allegra?" He chuckled. "I can guarantee that I am not one, so it is impossible for me to cast a spell upon you."

Allegra almost growled at him. "You are vexing me, my

lord." Picking up that the others were ready to turn in, she stood and smiled sweetly. "Good night, Lord Carroll."

He rose. "I thought you were going to give me a second chance."

She heard his annoyed tone and wanted to celebrate. "No, my lord. You said I *should* give you a second chance. I did not agree to do so, however. In fact, you never would have had a chance with me because you are merely looking for stolen kisses and a good time. I, on the other hand, am looking to broaden my horizons and make new acquaintances—and hopefully, find someone who appeals to me. A gentleman who appreciates family and the sanctity of marriage. You are not a gentleman, despite your manner of dress and title. You are a rakehell. You couldn't care less about being faithful in a marriage, much less being an involved father to any children you sired with your wife."

Allegra glared at him. "You are the antithesis of what I want in a husband. Frankly, even though it would unbalance our numbers, I think it best if you return to town to get into whatever mischief you might be up to. I am certain you left behind friends who have as little substance as you do. Besides, your mistress probably misses you. Why, I could not guess."

Allegra quickly moved away from him, saying her good nights to their other guests, her heart pounding so fiercely that she prayed it would not spring forth from her chest.

When she slipped her arm through Lyric's to go upstairs, she sensed Lord Carroll's eyes upon her. She only hoped he would follow her recommendation and excuse himself from the house party.

Before the overwhelming urge to kiss him did her in.

CHAPTER FOUR

STERLING HUNG BACK as the other houseguests and the Strongs left the drawing room.

Who did the chit think she was?

He still did not understand why he had been invited to the house party the Seatons hosted, having never met the duke or duchess, much less if he were going to be able to survive the entire ten days. He would not capitulate, however. Miss Allegra Strong had all but ordered him to leave. Just because this party was being given partially in her honor did not mean she could uninvite an earl.

If anything, Sterling could be stubborn. He would dig in his heels and show her he was having the time of his life. Without her. Four other unwed ladies were present at this party. While he understood he could not become overly involved with any of them—much less bed one of them—he could still be his most charming self. Perhaps even steal a kiss or two from all of them, including Miss Lyric Strong. Wouldn't that stick in her sister's craw?

The room now empty, he paced it, not ready for bed at such an ungodly hour. That was one of the things he did not enjoy about the country. Not only was it boring most of the time, but people stuck to what they termed country hours. Why, the clock had barely chimed ten times before people were saying they had to go to bed because of the busy day tomorrow and how tired they were from today's travels. To Sterling, ten o'clock in the evening was about the time he dressed to go out. He was a night owl, used to being up all night, every night.

Dread filled him as he thought about how he might get through these next ten days and maintain his sanity.

At least he knew a little about Lady Lida and Miss Markle. They were both lively, vivacious women and pleasant to be around. He wouldn't mind passing a bit of time in their company. On the other hand, Miss Bancroft was as plain as they came. Though she had played the pianoforte well enough tonight, her looks alone—or lack of them—put him off.

As for the gentlemen present, he no longer seemed to have anything in common with his old friend Blankenship. The death of the viscount's uncle had affected him greatly, and Blankenship was buckling down and taking his responsibilities seriously.

"That is what stewards and solicitors are for," he said aloud to the empty room.

What good was it to be a wealthy, titled gentleman if he couldn't enjoy himself fully? It wasn't as if he neglected his country estate or its tenants. He had hired a capable steward. He also had a solicitor in town who handled any pressing matters which might arise, as well as paid his bills. Carrollwood had plenty of servants to see to its care and upkeep.

Looking about the drawing room, he saw nothing to drink and decided to make his way to the library, hoping he would find a sideboard of either brandy or whisky. He wasn't sleepy in the least, so he might as well read. Or compose some verse.

When troubled or bored, Sterling turned to his writing. He wasn't quite sure why he had hid his intelligence from others, much less his talent for writing. It was one thing he held in common with Blankenship, though. His old friend was smarter than he let on. He supposed Blankenship had his own demons which he chose to keep secret.

Over the years, Sterling had penned two plays and countless poems. He wrote with no plans of ever sharing them with anyone, but writing had soothed him many a time when he was out of sorts. Deciding he would be continually out of sorts during his time at Shadowcrest, he would ask to be provided with paper and ink tomorrow. If they thought him writing letters to his mistress, so much the better.

Retreating to the library now, Sterling took a candelabra from the drawing room to light his way. As he suspected, the library, which a footman had pointed out to him earlier, was dark. He perused the large room, finding what he was looking for, and poured himself a large amount of brandy in a snifter. Taking it to the far end of the room, he sat in a chair and blew out the candles, preferring to sit in the dark and brood, drink in hand.

The brandy blazed a trail of warmth from his mouth to his belly as he reflected on the day since his arrival in Kent. At least the food had been quite good, both at tea and dinner. He would simply need to put himself in a set frame of mind, telling himself he could endure anything, even a dull house party. When he received invitations to ones in the future, however, he would remind himself of this one. Duke or no duke, he would turn down invitations to any event held in the country.

As he sipped the brandy, lost in thought, he was surprised to hear the door open. It was a woman who entered, holding a single candle high, her incandescent beauty shining even from afar.

"Bloody hell," Sterling cursed softly to himself.

Allegra Strong wore a dressing gown, and he assumed her night rail was beneath it. The thought of her wearing something filmy that he could see through caused his cock to stir. Her curves were in all the right places, and his hands longed to roam her luscious body. He wanted to be angry at her, but he admitted to himself that he actually liked the feistiness she had shown in dressing him down. No woman had ever turned away the Earl of Carroll, much less stood up to him, until Miss Allegra Strong had tonight.

A deep need filled him, and he knew he had to have the taste of her, despite her sharp tongue and stinging words. He would not force her to kiss him. Somehow, he would cajole her into it. It seemed important to him all of a sudden that he hadn't lost his touch where a woman was concerned. He would charm her. Kiss her. Then be done with her.

Or so he told himself.

Draining the remainder of his brandy, he quietly set down the snifter and rose, moving toward her silently. She had set her candle down and was pulling a book from the shelves. He did not speak until he stood directly behind her.

"Having trouble sleeping, Miss Allegra?" he asked, his voice smooth as silk, the tone he used when he was ready to seduce a woman.

She startled, dropping the book, peering at him. "You!" she hissed.

He could see enough of her face in the shadows to know she could also see his, and Sterling gave her his most enticing smile, one he knew even this resistant woman could not resist.

"Were you not tired?" he asked. "Greeting and entertaining so many guests?"

Her mouth set stubbornly. "I decided to claim a book and read for a bit. Of course, reading is something you have not done since your schoolboy days. Or did you have another read it for you and share the highlights of it?"

For some reason, he wanted this woman to have a better opinion of him and said, "Actually, I enjoy reading very much. I even write a little myself."

She snorted. "Oh, so you pen love letters to your mistresses?"

"No," he said defensively. "I would not waste my time engaged in such an activity. A mistress is paid for her time. She is not someone who requires a man to court her and woo her with love poems."

She looked taken aback. "Do you speak of such things so

openly with others?"

"Whether or not I keep a mistress is my business alone, so no, I usually do not mention things of that nature to men or women."

Her eyes narrowed. "And yet you blithely talk about your mistress with me."

"I did not say I had a mistress, Miss Allegra. You are the one who assumed I did. Frankly, a mistress can be more trouble than she's worth. Expensive, too."

Curiosity filled her face, and she said, "This conversation is already inappropriate enough, but I would not mind hearing why you believe a mistress might not be a good investment."

He chuckled, knowing she must be extremely naïve when it came to this topic. Despite her finding him to be disagreeable, she still wanted information about a topic forbidden to young ladies such as herself.

"First of all, the women who wish to become a gentleman's mistress are of a higher class than other women who give their favors more freely. While a mistress is a certainty, to maintain her loyalty, you must compensate her adequately. That means setting her up in her own house, usually in St. John's Wood. She will need a staff to wait on her and someone to cook for her and the servants. So, renting or buying her a house and providing her with that staff turns out to be quite a financial drain."

"I had no idea," she said breathlessly, and he noted the pulse in her throat jumped.

"Oh, yes," he continued. "And then she will expect gifts from you. Expensive gifts."

"Such as?"

"Jewelry is a favorite. A diamond necklace. Emerald earrings. A sapphire bracelet. Most mistresses anticipate these gifts."

Understanding filled her face. "Because those are items which might be easily sold when the affair comes to its conclusion."

She was clever, he would give her that. "Exactly. Not every man wishes to keep the same mistress for a great length of time. A year. Two, at most. Items such as jewelry can be easily pawned.

While I have heard of the odd man here and there allowing his mistress to keep her house as a parting gift, many remove her from the residence—and replace her just as quickly."

She wet her lips, and desire flared within him. Sterling focused on them as he said, "And then there are other gifts you can bring to her. Most men also set up their mistress with an allowance, along with paying her bills at the dressmaker or greengrocer. So you see, Miss Allegra, having a mistress can be quite draining on a man's coffers, along with his time."

"I suppose you are the type who would tire easily of a woman and wish to move on to the next," she said astutely.

He nodded. "It is the very reason I have never had a mistress," he revealed. "Yes, I do bore easily. Besides, there are always women within the *ton* willing to have a short affair with a handsome young buck such as myself."

Her eyes hardened. "An affair is wrong," she said. "Men and women take vows during the wedding ceremony. They should be faithful to one another."

He clucked his tongue, marveling at her innocence. "And yet so many in Polite Society stray from those vows. Your head is filled with stars, Miss Allegra. Marriages are business arrangements between families. They are done for financial and social purposes. It is the rare couple which makes a love match. For the most part, a man and woman abide by their marriage settlements. Heirs are provided, pin money is provided, and life goes on, usually separately from one another."

She shook her head. "You are so callused. So unfeeling, my lord. I could never live that way. I have seen what marriage is like when it is a business arrangement. My aunt was forced into such a marriage as that, with the Duke of Seaton, when she was quite young. They led the so-called separate lives you refer to. They barely spoke to one another, especially after she disappointingly produced four daughters and no heirs. Aunt Dinah has told us how miserable she was in her marriage and that we will never be made to wed someone strictly as business."

"Ah, you are one of those rare creatures who believe in love."

"Of course, I do," she said sincerely, her face open. "My own cousin made a love match with Sophie, and they are two of the happiest people I have ever seen."

Grudgingly, he had to agree with her. Sterling had observed his hosts throughout the evening, seeing the fond looks the Duke and Duchess of Seaton had exchanged, even a heated one when it was suggested that all retire early.

"Their Graces are fortunate they made such a match," he told her.

Her eyes, a distinct cornflower blue, drew him in now, as she said, "But it wasn't merely James and Sophie. I have grown up in this household, my lord, and the daughters are as sisters to Lyric and me. I have already spoken to you about my other cousins and the marriages they have made. Pippa wed Seth, and love shines in both their eyes when they see or speak of one another. The same is true for Georgie and August. You merely say her husband's name, and Georgie lights up."

"Of all the recent marriages, the one my aunt Dinah made perhaps is the greatest love of all. Captain Andrews is a remarkable man. He will come to Shadowcrest in a few days. You will see when they reunite just how much love there is between them. So do not tell me that love does not exist. Perhaps in your jaded world, it never will, but the Strongs know love abounds. That love is worth every risk."

He shook his head. "You are so very naïve, Miss Allegra, spouting about love. Why, I will wager you have never even been kissed."

A hot blush stained her cheeks, letting him know he was right.

"Not that it is any of your business, Lord Carroll, but I have yet to be kissed. I do plan to try it at this house party, however. I understand enough to know that love is a feeling. An ephemeral emotion which grows deeper over time. I also realize, however, that there must be some attraction between a man and woman for the seed of love to be planted."

She studied him intently, and he could have sworn it made him blush.

"*You* will not be anyone I will be kissing, however, my lord. I have no interest in being one of your conquests, seduced by your actions and words. I have made no secret as we have spoken that I am looking for love—and marriage. We both know those things are an anathema to you."

Oh, she was a bold beauty.

"While I would not think to offer you love or marriage, Miss Allegra, what I can do is tutor you a bit in the art of kissing," he offered.

He almost laughed aloud at the shocked expression which crossed her face and quickly said, "You know, people can kiss without being in love. If I bestow a kiss upon you, it will give you an idea what to do when you do kiss some gentleman at this house party," he reasoned. "You are a novice. I am an expert. I am happy to share my expertise with you."

Without giving her time to think—or even protest—Sterling framed her face with his long fingers and bent, their lips grazing one another's.

What surprised him, however, was the instant spark that flared between them. He had not been prepared to experience that.

Because he never had before. Not with a single woman.

Knowing she was inexperienced, he did not rush the kiss. Taking his time, he brushed his own lips softly against hers and then broke the kiss, immediately fusing their mouths together again. He kissed her for several minutes that way, the kisses become a little harder and more demanding. His hands left her face, sliding down her arms until he clasped her elbows. For her part, Allegra Strong grabbed on to his coat's lapels, holding on for dear life.

He decided to up the stakes, outlining her mouth with the tip of his tongue. She stiffened a bit as he coaxed her mouth open and slipped his own tongue inside, but then she relaxed as his tongue stroked hers in a gentle caress.

Sterling leisurely explored her mouth, and she responded to his kiss. The problem was, he liked what they did together too much. He had never been affected by a kiss in such a way.

It frightened the hell out of him.

Breaking the kiss, he tried to pull away, but she was having none of it. She jerked him back down to her, their mouths colliding. Greedily, he drank from her nectar again, losing himself.

Then he realized he must stop. Now. Not only because anyone might walk into the library and see she wore her nightclothes, but because he was in danger of jumping off a cliff he had never even come close to approaching before. Sterling had never gone looking for love because he did not believe it existed.

But he was sorely afraid love might have found him. In the form of Miss Allegra Strong.

This time when he broke the kiss, he clasped her elbows tightly and pushed her away from him, keeping her at arm's length.

His tone light, he said, "That is how you kiss, Miss Allegra."

For a moment, he drank her in. The dazed expression on her face. The darkening of her irises. The feel of her.

Then Sterling released her and exited the library without a goodbye. He had played with fire, wanting to teach the little chit a lesson.

Instead, he was the one who had been burned.

CHAPTER FIVE

THE DAY HAD been busy, with a long ride led by Caleb Strong. The group had stopped at a local inn for refreshments. Sterling deliberately avoided looking at Miss Allegra and did not converse with her once. The same held true at tea, which was held al fresco on the terrace since the day was beautiful. He had chatted with Miss Lyric and Lady Lida, along with Mrs. Andrews, Lord Tillings, and Lord Lamkin. Never once did he even glance in Miss Allegra's direction, though he could hear her merry laugh numerous times throughout the day.

He was the most miserable he had ever been.

Sterling's valet readied him for dinner now. He knew he must get Allegra Strong by herself. When he did, he would have to give her a stern talking to. His original intention had been for her to use the lessons he had taught her on kissing with other men. How he was to explain to her why she wasn't to do so was another matter.

He had been on his own for so long, hiding who he truly was even from himself. Truth be told, he pretended to be bored most of the time, and that façade had now come to pass. He *was* bored with his hedonistic life. With his friends and what he did. His life was empty and meaningless. Though he had never admitted it to himself—possibly he had never even realized it before now—

Sterling yearned for connections. True, deep, human connections, not merely superficial ones. And especially not a quick dalliance in a woman's bed or a night of drinking and gambling with men who pretended to be his friends but neither cared for him or about him.

Being around these Strongs for even so short a time had shown him how others could care for one another and how important those relationships could be. Just because he had come from two people who had spent their whole lives as strangers to him did not mean he was forced to follow in their footsteps and make those same mistakes. No, Sterling was ready to make deeper connections with those around him.

Above all, that meant Allegra Strong.

It wasn't merely her beauty that appealed to him so much, though she had that in abundance. She had an aura about her which drew him and others to her. Vivaciousness filled her, a zest for life that he was desperate to attach himself to. Yes, he had been physically attracted to her from the moment he laid eyes upon her, but he felt something more had been established between them, an intangible that he found hard to put into words. He knew she did not think highly of him, but he was bound and determined to change her opinion of him.

Because he wanted her in his life. As his wife.

That thought would have sent him running into the arms of the closest, willing woman before he had arrived at Shadowcrest. It was almost humorous how the pendulum had swung in an entirely different direction. Sterling was suddenly enthralled with the idea of a wife. Children. Even possibly spending more time in the country. He did not know if Allegra preferred town or the country, but it truly didn't matter to him. He merely wanted to be with her. The place did not matter.

And that was when he knew just how much he had changed. Like his friend Blankenship, Sterling's priorities had shifted monumentally since he had stepped from the carriage upon his arrival at Shadowcrest.

He decided the best chance he had of changing Allegra's mind about him would be through her twin. He had spoken to Miss Lyric some already, and he had observed how close the twins were. While he knew without a doubt that Allegra had told her sister about her ill opinion of him, Sterling believed Lyric Strong might very well be the key in helping him win over Allegra. He determined to get Miss Lyric alone and plead his case to her, seeing if she might be willing to help him.

His valet finished helping him dress for dinner, and Sterling left his room. Lord Motley emerged from his bedchamber, and he waited for the earl so that they might walk down to the drawing room together.

"Your daughter is delightful, Motley," he began.

Motley looked surprised. "I did not think you were in the habit of noticing children, my lord."

"Lady Viola is quite exceptional," Sterling said, knowing the way to Motley's good side would be through his daughter. Besides, he had found he liked this man, someone he hadn't bothered getting to know previously. He found himself not only interested in courting Allegra, but he knew if he were to truly change, he would need a new circle of friends.

"Viola is the light of my life," Motley told him. "Her mother was, as well. While I have mourned my wife's loss deeply, she left the greatest gift entrusted to me. I take the raising of my daughter most seriously. I am attending this house party in order to find a mother for my girl, but I also hope to find a wife again that I can grow to love. She needs to be one who can accept how much I love Viola."

"There are good candidates here that I believe would be more than suited to that task," he said earnestly, hoping Motley wasn't considering Allegra as a choice.

"I believe the same myself, Carroll. But house parties are notoriously known for betrothals. Why are you here? You must admit that your reputation proceeds you."

"Reputations often lie in the hands of gossips," he said crisply.

"I do not believe I am everything those gossips say. That there is more depth to me than they would ever willingly acknowledge."

Surprise showed in Motley's eyes. "Might *you* be searching for your countess, my lord?"

"I am open to that possibility," he said cryptically, not wanting to tilt his hand.

They reached the drawing room and took drinks from a tray which a footman offered. He parted from Motley, going to speak with the Duke of Seaton and Lord Crowell. There had been much talk during the Season about where Seaton had been for years, but Sterling would never ask the man about his lengthy absence. All he knew was that Seaton had accepted his dukedom with an air of confidence that few men possessed.

Lord Crowell excused himself, leaving the two of them alone.

Sterling decided to take advantage of this rare opportunity in having the duke to himself, hoping his reputation for being unconventional would allow for a bold question.

"Might I ask something rather personal of you, Your Grace?"

Seaton studied Sterling a long moment, to the point he was about to squirm. "You can ask—but I reserve the right not to answer, my lord."

"Fair enough." He hesitated now that he had this man's attention. Working up his courage, he asked, "How did you know that Her Grace was the one for you?"

The duke grew thoughtful. "I suppose it was an accumulation of bits and pieces. So many things about her appealed to me. Her confidence. Her intelligence. The kindness she exhibited when she dealt with others from all walks of life." Seaton paused. "A day quickly came when I knew in my heart I must have her in my life always. That I loved her beyond measure and would be miserable if I did not make my feelings known to her—and win her heart."

Seaton's brows knit together. "Are you in the same boat I was, Lord Carroll?"

He smiled wryly. "My boat is like a small rowboat cast out to sea, Your Grace. I have been tossed about so much in every kind of element that I am not quite certain which way is up or down. I have always been secure in myself—some even calling me arrogant—and led what I will admit is a hedonistic life. This house party has turned everything I believed about myself on its ear."

The duke smiled broadly. "I doubt it is the house party itself which has caused such a maelstrom, my lord. I do believe in these cases that it is one woman who has you in such a quandary. Might you share the name of that young lady?"

Sterling hesitated a moment, wondering how Seaton might react to the news that his niece was the one causing a known rake to try and change his stripes. Then decided he should clue this man in. If he convinced Seaton of his worth, the duke might be a helpful ally in Sterling's quest.

"I am not ready to offer for her, Your Grace, but I will make my intentions known to you since you are head of the Strong family. Your cousin Miss Allegra has quite stolen my heart." He hesitated before adding, "The trouble is, she has a low opinion of me at this point."

The duke burst out laughing, causing heads to turn in their direction.

"Oh, Carroll, you have hooked an extremely slippery fish on your line. Allegra is one of my favorite people in the world. Feisty. Opinionated. Loved by all because she puts everyone at ease. I will tell you that my cousin is worth whatever she puts you through. I wish you the best of luck in winning her heart."

At that moment, the Duchess of Seaton and Mrs. Andrews joined them, with Her Grace asking, "What was so amusing, my love?"

Sterling wasn't quite ready for his suit to be known publicly. He met the duke's gaze. Understanding passed between them.

"Something only gentlemen would find humorous, my sweet Sophie." Seaton lifted his wife's hand to his lips and kissed her fingers tenderly. "Perhaps you and I should circulate among our other guests now."

Their Graces excused themselves, leaving him with Mrs. Andrews. He decided to quell his curiosity and ask her the question which had been burning within him.

"Mrs. Andrews, may I be so bold as to inquire why I was invited to this house party? It is known by all your guests that Her Grace has little interest in planning these types of affairs. That lets me know that not only have you established which activities would occur during our stay, but you also are responsible for the men and women present here at Shadowcrest."

She studied him a long moment, and Sterling felt himself almost blushing under her scrutiny.

Finally, Mrs. Andrews said, "I saw potential within you, Lord Carroll. And before you ask, I know of your wicked reputation within the *ton*. That you are a rakehell above all others. But I found myself thinking you might possibly want more out of life than the empty existence you have been leading."

He prickled at her description and said, "I never asked you or anyone else to pass judgment upon me. What if I am more than enthusiastic about the life I lead?" he countered, playing devil's advocate.

"Have you found yourself questioning things about you while you have been here, my lord? Have you seen the closeness the Strong family shares—and you wish you could be a part of it?"

She placed her hand upon his sleeve. "You must remember that I have been in Polite Society for many years, my lord. Two decades. I knew your parents. The kind of people they were. I can tell they never realized the gem of a son they had. Call me a meddlesome matron, Lord Carroll, but I have always seen something in you that perhaps you have never seen in yourself. I invited you here to help you understand more about who you are and what you truly want out of life."

His throat grew thick with emotion, hearing her speak so frankly to him, and the faith she, as a stranger, had in him.

Mrs. Andrews squeezed his arm and dropped her hand, saying, "I believe you could find someone here who might be the perfect partner to go on life's journey with you, my lord. All five young ladies present possess wonderful qualities."

"I agree with your evaluation of them, Mrs. Andrews. And yes, I will admit that I have been rethinking my life, thanks to my presence and observations at this house party. In fact, one particular lady has acquired my attention. Unfortunately, I made a poor first impression upon her."

Mrs. Andrews smiled knowingly. "Then you will be scrambling to show her the new you. The *true* you. If you need my help in any way, I am willing to assist you."

"Even if it turns out to be one of your nieces?"

"Especially if it might be one of my nieces." She smiled warmly at him. "I know you can be quite amusing and incredibly charming, Lord Carroll, but it will take more than that to win one of my girls. Being in the company of interesting, intelligent men and women will help you discover what you truly have to offer to others. Be open to the man you have kept hidden all these years. By being who you truly are, you will find happiness within yourself. I firmly believe that can then lead to happiness with another."

He sighed, thinking this former duchess had more insight into him than anyone he knew.

"Go and join the younger people now, my lord," she encouraged.

Sterling gazed at her a long moment. "Thank you for asking me to come to Shadowcrest, Mrs. Andrews. If you had not, I doubt I would be on this new path, taking an unexpected fork in the road."

He joined the closest group next to them, not deliberately wanting to seek out Allegra. He spent several minutes talking with Miss Markle, Lady Lida, and Lord Lamkin before they were given the notice to go into dinner.

Unfortunately, Allegra was seated at the far end of the table from him. Each night they entered the dining room, they had a new seat, in order for them to be able to converse with different guests at each meal. He only hoped he and Allegra might partner for the card games to be held later this evening.

The ladies withdrew to the drawing room after dinner, while the men sipped brandy and smoked cheroots. Sterling abstained from the cigars, not wanting the stench of it on his breath.

Because he hoped he would have the chance to kiss Allegra Strong tonight.

When they finished and joined the ladies again, Mrs. Andrews told the group, "Only the young people will be playing cards this evening. There are enough of you for us to have six partners, which will make up three tables of play. Tonight's game will be whist, but we will also play other card games in evenings to come, including faro and commerce."

She picked up a small crystal bowl and continued. "The names of the five gentlemen are here on slips of parchment. I will ask each young lady to draw for her partner. Their Graces will also play as partners. Miss Markle? Would you do the honor of drawing the first name?"

Miss Markle rose and went to the bowl, pulling out a slip. "Lord Motley," she read aloud.

"Lady Lida?" Mrs. Andrews called. "Your turn."

Lady Lida followed in her cousin's footsteps and announced, "Lord Blankenship."

Sterling's heart beat faster, hoping he would partner with Allegra. He now had a one in three chance of doing so.

That was not to be, however.

Miss Bancroft was asked next to draw for her partner. She did so, her gaze meeting his.

"Lord Carroll is to be my partner," she told the group.

He smiled as if he did not have a care in the world, as he heard Miss Lyric would play with Lord Tillings, leaving Allegra to be Lord Lamkin's partner.

"We may not win the tournament this evening, Miss Allegra," Lord Lamkin said. "But I guarantee you we will have a wonderful time trying to do so."

"Get with your partner for a moment and strategize," Mrs. Andrews told the group. "Remember the rules of whist. No conversing about anything related to the game itself once you are at your table. No tipping your hand to your partner. And certainly no signaling your partner."

Sterling rose and joined Miss Bancroft, who retreated to the far corner of the room.

"Shall we make the most of this evening?" he asked, looking over her shoulder and watching Allegra putting her head close to Lord Lamkin's as they discussed their gameplay.

"My lord?"

He turned back to the plain woman who stood before him, suddenly not finding her plain at all. She was smiling at him brilliantly. It amazed him how much a smile could change her features.

"Yes, Miss Bancroft?"

"I know I am not the partner you would have wished for." She held up a hand when he tried to protest. "I have seen you looking at Miss Allegra when you believe no one is watching. I am a great watcher of others, Lord Carroll. It is a habit of wallflowers, I suppose. If you feel the need to impress her this evening, then let us combine to outplay everyone at the tables. I am quite good at maths, my lord, and easily keep track of the cards which have been played. You have a reputation of being a skilled card player. Together, we will be unbeatable."

He returned her smile, suddenly liking this honest, open woman. "Then what shall our strategy be?"

"Whichever of us opens, play the highest card in your dominant suit. That will signal to the other which suit you have the most cards in, and we can play appropriately. If we win that trick, go for the lowest card in your hand next."

Quickly, she continued to outline a strategy that showed how shrewd she truly was.

"Why, Miss Bancroft, if I took you to the gaming hells with

me, you would conquer your competition. They would be calling you a cardsharp because you would win at the tables so frequently."

She looked pleased at his unusual compliment. "Thank you, my lord."

"Is there anyone here who has drawn your attention?" he asked. "Perhaps I might be in a position to sing your praises to this gentleman."

A furious blush spread across her cheeks. "You would do that for me?"

"I would do anything for the partner who has all but guaranteed we will demolish our competition," he teased.

"Lord Tillings," she blurted out.

Sterling could see her and the shy viscount as a couple. "Then I will play matchmaker when I can," he promised. Offering her his arm, he said, "Come, Miss Bancroft. Let's go and triumph over our competition." He grinned. "And see if two certain people notice."

CHAPTER SIX

ALLEGRA HID HER disappointment when Miss Bancroft called out her partner's name. She had wanted to play with Lord Carroll, simply to show him how little she cared about him. She had been afraid that he might heed her advice and leave the house party.

If he had, she might have hopped on her horse and ridden after him.

She couldn't understand why she was so taken with the man. Yes, he was the most handsome devil she had ever laid eyes upon. He dressed exquisitely, taking far more care with his wardrobe than many women did. She feared it was his kiss which had her so discombobulated. The things that man could do with his tongue. Why, he was certainly no gentleman.

She had heard how men could sometimes become addicted to strong drink, their need for it so vast that they would do anything to get it. Was she the same, obsessed with this arrogant rake and yearning for more of his delicious kisses?

Aunt Dinah recommended they strategize with their partners before play began, so she made her way toward Lord Lamkin. Now, why couldn't she like a fellow such as Lamkin? He was goodhearted. Outgoing. Intelligent. It made her all the more determined to use the kissing lesson Lord Carroll had so thoughtfully provided her with. Who better than her card partner this evening?

"Do you have a specific way in mind in which you would like us to play?" Allegra asked the earl.

He chuckled. "Never. I let the cards fall where they will. I do know enough to understand I should never trump my partner. Other than that, I say we should simply enjoy ourselves tonight." He paused. "And perhaps even stroll along the terrace when there is a break in play."

Oh, she knew what that meant. He was informing her that he was interested in her—and planned to kiss her if she would allow him to do so.

"I would enjoy a brief stroll," Allegra replied, letting him know she was perfectly willing to accompany him. And kiss him.

"I look forward to it," Lord Lamkin said, a gleam in his eyes.

Suddenly, Lyric appeared at her elbow. "I must speak to you. Now," she said firmly, not waiting for Allegra to even excuse herself from Lord Lamkin.

Her twin led her swiftly away, into the corridor, away from the others.

"What is going on?" she demanded.

"He kissed me. Lord Blankenship. He kissed me. Again." Her twin beamed. "And it was a kiss like you received, Allegra." Lyric sighed. "Oh, it was everything I might ever want in a kiss."

"You are in love," she said, seeing the look on her sister's face.

Grinning, Lyric nodded. "I might very well be. You were right. Kissing is . . . magical. I have no other way to describe it."

She hugged her twin. "I am glad Lord Blankenship gave you a proper kiss."

"He still asked permission," Lyric revealed. "And you were right. He didn't want to scare me off and gentled his first kiss. But oh, my! The kisses we exchanged? I simply must have more of them." She bit her lip. "Do you think he will offer for me?"

Allegra laughed. "If he doesn't, I will box his ears."

"You wouldn't!"

"Try me," she said. "I will not have a rogue dally with my sister and then drop her." Seeing Lyric's alarmed look, she quickly added, "That will not happen with Lord Blankenship, though. He is a good man. Just think—he asked permission to kiss you, as a gentleman should—and then he kissed you like a rogue. I think you will be very happy together."

Lyric frowned. "I hated when Lady Lida called his name. She is the nicest girl, but I simply wanted to claw out her eyes."

They both laughed, and Allegra said, "We should return to our guests."

Her twin touched her arm. "How are you feeling about Lord Carroll?"

She shrugged. "I want to kiss him again. Desperately. But I believe I should kiss a few other gentlemen instead. Simply to have something to compare his kiss to. Lord Lamkin has already asked me to stroll with him on the terrace later. I think it means he wishes to be alone with me in order to kiss me."

Lyric grew thoughtful. "I do like Lamkin, Allegra. Actually— except for Lord Carroll—I like all the men Aunt Dinah invited to our party. And I probably would have liked Lord Carroll if you hadn't told me what an arrogant rake he is."

"Don't judge him too harshly," she begged. "He even asked me for a second chance, saying he knew he had made a poor impression upon me."

"Be careful," her sister warned.

"I will."

They returned to the drawing room just as Aunt Dinah said, "We are ready to start play. The pair who wins the most points by ten o'clock tonight will receive the crystal bowl we used to draw names."

"Which means I will be giving it to Miss Allegra," Lord Lamkin quipped.

The others laughed, including Aunt Dinah, who continued, saying, "We will abide by the usual deck of fifty-two cards, with each player receiving thirteen. After all hands have been played, the partners who won more tricks will score a point each for every trick they took in excess of six. The game will conclude at a table when one team reaches five total points."

"Just assign us to our tables, Mrs. Andrews," Lord Motley said. "Miss Markle is already eyeing that crystal bowl."

The group laughed again, and Aunt Dinah instructed them as to which table each pair would start. Allegra found her and Lord Lamkin seated with Lady Lida and Lord Blankenship. She looked at the viscount.

"I hope you have had an interesting evening so far, my lord," letting him know that she knew what he had been up to with her twin.

His ears pinkened slightly. "What I am up to now is claiming victory over you and Lord Lamkin, Miss Allegra."

They began play, and it took almost half an hour before she and Lord Lamkin attained their victory. The earl pulled Allegra from her seat and danced her about the drawing room in a victory lap, causing her to laugh aloud.

Then she caught Lord Carroll glowering at them, and she sobered.

"Since you are the first table to finish," Aunt Dinah said, "you might wish to go to the library. I had refreshments set up there so that you might mingle between games. Lord and Lady Crowell are there now to chaperone."

"I would like something cool to drink," she told the earl.

"Perhaps we could get some punch and then take it outside and stroll in the evening breeze," he suggested, his voice in a normal tone, so she knew others heard what he said.

Allegra refused to look in Lord Carroll's direction as Lord Lamkin, along with Lady Lida and Lord Blankenship, accompanied her to the library. The other couple claimed some punch and went to sit with Lady Lida's parents.

"Shall we stroll?" the earl asked, leading her from the library and to a door which opened onto the terrace.

They moved slowly along the length of the terrace, chatting

about the archery contest planned for tomorrow afternoon.

"Have you shot a bow and arrow before?" Lord Lamkin asked her.

"Actually I am fairly good at it. I may simply watch to give the other ladies a chance to shine," she replied.

"No, you need to participate. There is nothing wrong with winning. Besides, my archery skills are excellent. Why don't I give you a lesson before the competition begins? I am a patient teacher, and you might pick up on something which will help improve your aim."

"That would be very kind of you, my lord," she said demurely, seeing his eyes drop to her mouth.

They reached the end of the terrace, and he removed her cup from her hand, placing it and his on the stone wall.

"I am very glad I came to this house party," he said, his voice low.

"We are delighted to have you here."

"But are *you* delighted I came, Miss Allegra?"

She took a deep breath. "I am glad you came, my lord."

He took a step toward her, his hands cupping her cheeks. Her heart sped up. Then he bent, pressing his lips to hers. She kept her mouth closed, waiting to see what he might do. He kissed her a moment and then used his tongue to ease her mouth open. Sliding his tongue against hers, he caressed it.

She stood stock still, waiting for something to happen. A rush of warmth to flood her. A tightening of her nipples.

Nothing.

Because of that, Allegra did not return his kiss. She let him do all the work.

When he stepped back, he said, "You are a very nice lady, Miss Allegra. Very nice, indeed. But I think you understand that you are not the lady for me."

"I do, my lord. Thank you for the kiss, though."

He took her hand and raised it, pressing his lips to it. "I will still help you in archery, Miss Allegra. If you will allow me to do so, that is."

"Only if you wish to, Lord Lamkin. If you feel a pull toward another guest and wish to help her learn the sport better, I will understand."

"Well, there is Miss Markle," the earl said. "She has interested me for some time."

"Then I suggest you kiss her," Allegra said. "I believe it is the only way to know for certain."

They reclaimed their punch and returned inside, finding Lord Carroll and Miss Bancroft in the library, along with James and Sophie.

"We are celebrating our victory," Miss Bancroft said. "Lord Carroll is quite the cardplayer."

"Oh, but it is you who carried us to victory over Their Graces," Lord Carroll said.

"I have a head for business. Not cards," the duchess bemoaned. "Miss Bancroft, you must teach me your secrets."

"I would be honored to, Your Grace. Just as soon as Lord Carroll and I have claimed the crystal bowl."

Aunt Dinah appeared. "We are ready for the second round."

They returned to the drawing room, where Allegra found them going against Lyric and Lord Tillings. She had to hide her smile, seeing how distracted Lord Tillings was. He spent more time looking to his left—the table Miss Bancroft sat at—than focusing on his cards. Tillings and Lyric lost quickly to them.

They faced Miss Markle and Lord Motley next. It proved to be the first time Lord Lamkin was distracted. In fact, at one point, Allegra kicked him under the table to gain his attention. He jumped, their gazes meeting, and he smiled sheepishly.

"Woolgathering," he said simply, though she knew he was focusing more on Miss Markle than gameplay.

They narrowly won that round.

"We only have time for one more game," Aunt Dinah told them.

"Count us out," James said. "My duchess' eyes are drooping,

and we are out of contention at any rate." He scooped his wife off her feet. "We are headed for bed. Where we may sleep—or not."

Allegra heard the others tittering. James' declaration had not surprised her. She had come across the couple kissing in various places throughout the house and thought it sweet how affectionate they were.

Aunt Dinah announced the final groupings, and Allegra smiled as Lord Lamkin seated her. Lord Carroll and Miss Bancroft took their places at the same table.

"I hear that we are the only sets of partners who have not suffered a loss," Miss Bancroft said. "How exciting that this last game will determine who wins the crystal bowl."

"We will," Lord Carroll said arrogantly. "They have nothing on us, my dear Miss Bancroft."

She wondered when these two had gotten so chummy. Miss Bancroft was not the type of woman Lord Carroll would be attracted to. While Allegra enjoyed the woman's company and knew exactly why Georgie liked this friend so much, she was not the type of woman the earl noticed. Of course, Miss Bancroft was most likely the most intelligent woman here, not counting Sophie. Winning would appeal to Lord Carroll. Allegra only hoped that Miss Bancroft would not get her hopes up with the attention Lord Carroll seemed to be paying her.

As Lord Lamkin shuffled the cards and asked Miss Bancroft a question, Lord Carroll turned to her.

"You seem jealous, Miss Allegra."

"Jealous?" she sputtered. "Of . . . what?"

"The fact that Miss Bancroft and I make for such a remarkable team," he said smoothly.

Her eyes narrowed. "I hope you won't think of taking advantage of her."

His seductive smile made her gasp. Which made him chuckle. Which made her angry.

"So, you don't wish for me to kiss her? Who should I be kissing? You?"

Allegra tamped down her anger, biting back the retort on her lips, because the other two turned toward them.

"Ready to play?" Lord Lamkin asked.

"I am ready for us to win," she told her partner, smiling charmingly at him just to rankle Lord Carroll.

They were still playing when the other two tables finished. The others came to stand around them in order to watch the proceedings. Allegra concentrated deeply, not wanting to see Lord Carroll gain victory. She was angry at him, as well as being angry at herself for allowing him to get a rise from her.

Then she caught Lord Tillings watching Miss Bancroft, his face one of adoration. Suddenly, beating Lord Carroll was no longer important to Allegra. Instead, she wanted Miss Bancroft to shine for the viscount.

Deliberately, she played a lower card of the same suit when she could have taken the trick. Lord Lamkin frowned at her. She met his gaze and then turned her eyes quickly to Lord Tillings and back. Lamkin did the same, and he seemed to understand because when he played his next card, she knew they would lose the last trick of this hand.

And the game.

As Miss Bancroft took the trick, she smiled, her face flushing from the victory.

"I do believe that is game and match to Miss Bancroft and Lord Carroll," Aunt Dinah proclaimed.

Those gathered around them applauded loudly, with Lord Tillings saying, "Well done!" above the din.

It was Tillings who quickly pulled Miss Bancroft's chair back and assisted her to her feet. She went to Aunt Dinah, Lord Carroll following, and received the crystal bowl.

"Thank you so much, Mrs. Andrews," Miss Bancroft said. "I must acknowledge Lord Carroll, who is the best whist player I have ever partnered with."

The earl bowed his head slightly and smiled at his partner. "I would say the same, Miss Bancroft. We make quite the team."

A few declared they would take a last cup of punch or snifter of brandy in the library, while a few more announced they were going to bed. Allegra followed that group upstairs, only to find someone tugging on her elbow when she stepped onto the landing. Turning, she saw it was Lord Carroll who held it.

"You deliberately let us win," he said. "I knew what cards you—or Lamkin—held. Why did you lose to us?"

Her pulse was leaping at his touch. "Because I wanted Miss Bancroft to win. Lord Tillings had been watching her all night. I thought her victory was important for him to see. She is an excellent card player and most intelligent. More importantly, she is one of the kindest ladies I have ever met. I wanted her to have her time in the sun. She is a lovely person and deserves to receive her due after so many years of being cast aside by others."

His eyes darkened. "That was very generous of you, Allegra," he said huskily.

She noticed he called her by her Christian name but did not want to correct him.

All she wanted to do was kiss him.

"I was proud of how well you accepted her as a partner," she told him. "When she drew your name, I was worried you would . . . well, that you might . . ." Her voice trailed off because she couldn't finish the thought.

He reached for her hand, slipping his large one around hers. It felt so right—and yet she knew this rake was so wrong for her.

"I am not quite the arse you believe me to be. Somehow, I am going to convince you of that before this house party ends."

The thought of it ending and him leaving Shadowcrest left her feeling bereft. Tears swam in her eyes and she glanced down, not wanting him to see them.

His fingers touched her chin, however, raising it until their gazes met.

"I asked for a second chance with you, Allegra. I cannot force you to give me one, but I hope you will, all the same. I have been contemplating many things since we met, chief amongst them how I have been living my life and how unsatisfying it has been for longer than I care to admit."

Hope sprang within her that he might truly be changing.

"You wish to leave your roguish ways behind?" she asked lightly.

He smiled wryly. "Once a rogue, always a rogue," he replied lightly. "But even rogues can have a good heart." He swallowed visibly. "I want you to see that I am more than my blackened reputation. Will you give me a chance to prove to you that there are honorable parts within me?"

"Yes," she said, the word coming out a whisper.

He smiled, looking pleased. "Then that is all I can ask from you. That—and perhaps a kiss."

This time she swallowed, her heart beating wildly at the thought of kissing him again.

Lord Carroll glanced over his shoulder. Then he bent, softly pressing his lips to hers, lingering for a moment before breaking the kiss. It had been sweet and tender, something totally unexpected.

"I will see you tomorrow, Allegra."

With that, he released her hand and hurried back down the stairs again.

He had surprised her. She had expected a much different kiss from him. Instead, he had intrigued her, leaving her wanting more. Not just his kisses, but wanting to know more of him.

Lord Carroll just might prove himself to be the man Allegra was looking for after all.

CHAPTER SEVEN

ALLEGRA FELT FLUSH from her triumph at archery, not because she beat all the other ladies who were participating.

But because she wanted to show off for Lord Carroll.

She knew it was wrong to be attracted to him. She had even questioned Aunt Dinah as to why the earl had even been invited to this house party. Rakes weren't known for commitment and betrothals. Allegra had thought the invitation a waste and that a better candidate should have been invited.

Her aunt had surprised her, though, telling Allegra that she believed there to be good within Lord Carroll and perhaps he wasn't the wicked man Polite Society's gossips made him out to be.

Could that possibly be true?

With Aunt Dinah having been a duchess for almost two decades, she had moved freely through the *ton*. Her aunt was also an excellent judge of character. If she saw potential in Lord Carroll, it was there. Did that make him good husband material for her, though?

Allegra supposed she needed to find out.

He had asked her for a second chance. Instead of listening to the gossip, which Aunt Dinah had said for years often proved to be untrue, as well as unkind, Allegra would set out to do what this house party was for and get to know the Earl of Carroll a bit better. She wouldn't kiss him again. His kisses clouded her judgment. No, she would refuse any kiss and try to find out more about him. If he were willing to do so and get to know her better in return, they might possibly have a future together.

She entered the drawing room alone. Lyric had been fussing with her hair and wasn't pleased with any of her efforts. She had encouraged Allegra to go downstairs without her. Now, as her eyes scanned the room, she saw disappointment on Lord Blankenship's face.

He crossed toward her as she accepted wine from a footman.

"Is anything wrong with Miss Lyric? Is she ill? Does she have a headache?" he asked worriedly.

"No, my lord. She was merely taking too long to get ready. Primping for someone special, I suppose," she said, seeing if she might draw a reaction from him.

He flushed, and she knew he had feelings for her twin.

"She will be here soon," she reassured the viscount. "After all, the two of us are to play this evening for our guests." Taking a sip of the wine, she continued, "Might you have feelings for my sister, Lord Blankenship?"

"I most definitely do, Miss Allegra," he said fervently.

When he did not elaborate, she asked, "The kind that lead to an offer of marriage?"

"Yes. That kind," he said, glancing toward the door again.

Oh, Lyric was going to be so pleased. Allegra planned to prepare her sister for when the viscount offered for her. She thought him quite a decent fellow.

"Do you have an idea when you might make your offer?"

This time, he looked her in the eyes. "That is between the two of us, Miss Allegra. Please, do not spoil things. I promise you that it will be soon."

"I can only hold a secret for so long," she teased.

"And I can only keep from asking for her hand for so long," he glibly replied.

"Touché, my lord," she said, laughing. "I promise I will say nothing to Lyric tonight."

"Thank you. There she is," he said. "Excuse me."

Allegra watched him head toward her twin. She would enjoy having Lord Blankenship as a brother. She already felt sisterly toward him.

The exact opposite of her feelings toward Lord Carroll.

She joined Lord Motley, Miss Markle, and Lady Lida. She was seeing the earl and Lady Lida together more and more and wondered if a betrothal between them might occur before the house party ended. She was certain Lord Tillings would ask for Miss Bancroft's hand, knowing Georgie would be pleased that her friend became engaged while at Shadowcrest. She hoped a letter from Georgie would arrive soon, letting them know when she and August would be returning from Scotland. Allegra had a feeling her sister would be increasing when she arrived back in England from her extended honeymoon.

Lord Carroll joined them, claiming a drink from the footman. His dark brown hair had been tamed somewhat, but those hazel eyes seemed to continually change color according to his mood. Physically, everything about him appealed to her. He was about six feet, with an athletic frame, his muscles in all the right places, shown off by the fit of his superfine coat and tight breeches. She looked at his sensual lips, remembered how they felt on hers, and found a blush start to heat her cheeks.

Quickly, she took a sip of her wine, hoping it would cool her. Their gazes met, and he smiled, as if he knew exactly what she had been thinking. Most likely, he had been thinking the same thing. Didn't men who were rakes always think of kissing—and other sensual pleasures?

Allegra had no idea what those involved. Aunt Dinah had told all the girls that when they were betrothed, she would share with them a little of what occurred in the bedroom. Whatever it was, Pippa and Georgie positively glowed with love for their new husbands. Pippa and Seth had been off quickly on their world tour, else Allegra would have asked her cousin about the mysteries of the marriage bed. The same occurred with Georgie. She and August had left Shadowcrest in a rush, going to spend a few nights at August's country estate, Edgefield, before heading for Dalmara in Scotland.

But Allegra also knew not all women experienced love with their husbands, nor did they wear the glow that Sophie had before conceiving, one which had grown in magnitude since she had announced she was increasing. Aunt Dinah was a perfect example of that. She had been made to wed the Duke of Seaton at ten and seven. Though they lived in the same house, Allegra had rarely seen the couple together, much less conversing. Yet Aunt Dinah had done her duty as a wife and spent three, long years nursing her ill husband before his death.

Thank goodness Captain Andrews had appeared in her life. Aunt Dinah practically sparkled like the stars now that she had wed her sea captain. Allegra wanted that. She wanted to love and be loved.

Or would it be enough if she merely enjoyed bed sport with her husband? Did she have to be in love to be happy?

When the butler announced that dinner was ready, Lord Carroll immediately claimed her arm, escorting her into the dining room. The entire way, Allegra's heart pounded as if she had just run an extremely long race. She wished she could think straight around the man, but found it literally impossible.

She found tonight was the night they had been placed together at dinner. Miss Markle was on her right, but she only saw the back of her head because she was engaged in conversation with Lord Motley. That left Allegra the entire time with Lord Carroll.

"You performed even better than I expected at archery today, Allegra."

"You should call me Miss Allegra, my lord."

He glanced around. "No one is listening. You could call me Sterling, you know."

"That is your given name?"

"Yes. Apparently, it was the only thing my mother got out of the marriage to my father. Her father was named Sterling. I overheard our housekeeper telling the story one time to the cook. She said Mother shrieked at the top of her lungs that if she were going to carry a babe for almost a year *and* ruin her figure over it, the infant would be named what she wanted. It seems that my father agreed. He merely wanted an heir. Sometimes, I think he couldn't even remember my name."

"I am sorry your childhood was so difficult," she said, her tone sympathetic.

"Actually, it was quite nice. It wasn't gloomy in the slightest. My parents were never at Carrollwood, which turned out to be a blessing. The servants were more relaxed and happier caring for the house when they were gone. I was able to roam freely and do whatever I wanted."

He smiled, and she caught a glimpse of the mischievous boy he had been.

"I was a handful, but I was never mean or spiteful. Merely high-spirited, as one tutor called me."

"Tell me more."

"Carrollwood is in East Sussex. The estate is large. If the weather was pleasant, I was outside. I couldn't abide being cooped up in the house."

He told her about wading in the stream, catching frogs with his hands and fish with his rod. The head footman had taught him how to fish. The head groom had given him riding lessons. He talked of climbing trees and learning how to patch fences and shape iron, thanks to the local blacksmith.

"The nearest village is only two miles away. I would walk there many a day and visit with the shopkeepers. I even ran errands for some of them. The baker would have me take items back to Carrollwood with me. The haberdasher taught me quite a bit about numbers and how to record sales in a ledger. I suppose you could say the entire village had a hand in raising me, along with the Carrollwood servants."

He told several more amusing stories throughout the meal, and she found herself laughing aloud several times. He had a way about him, an easy manner that put others at ease. Allegra wondered if it might be because he was always trying to win the affection of those around him since he received none from his parents.

The ladies left for the drawing room, and she and Lyric went to collect their sheet music from the music room. They decided between them who would play which piece and even sat and played one each to warm up their fingers. They agreed two songs apiece was plenty, and then Allegra would play the final number, but they both would sing.

By the time they returned to the drawing room, the men were arriving. Lyric had asked if she might play first, and Allegra readily agreed. She noticed as her twin set out her sheet music, Lord Blankenship joined her. Most likely, he was offering to turn the pages.

"Will you play or also sing?" Lord Carroll asked, coming to stand next to her.

"We should sit," she said, taking a seat on the nearest settee. "I will do both this evening."

"I see Blankenship is assisting Miss Lyric. Might I perform the same service for you?"

"I have my pieces memorized. So does Lyric, but she gets nervous sometimes and likes to have the music before her, in case she stumbles."

"You are too confident to stumble," he declared. "But I will go and stand beside you anyway so no other gentleman claims the post."

"You are not asking," she noted. "You are telling me."

"Yes, I suppose I am." He gazed at her longingly. "I do not want any other man present to be close to you, Allegra."

She liked how he was bold enough to tell her this. Her first impression of him had been a false one. The more time she spent around the earl, the better she liked him. Allegra thought of the amusing stories he had told her during dinner, which had kept her laughing. He had a way about him, an easy manner that put others at ease when in his company. It made her wonder if he did so because he was always trying to win the affection of those around him since he had received none from his parents.

Suddenly, things were crystal clear to her. Allegra realized that she had already made up her mind. She wanted Lord Carroll—and no other—as her husband. She would play no more games.

"May I turn the pages to your music?" he asked.

"You may," she agreed, secretly pleased that he did ask to do so.

Lyric performed the numbers she had selected, and Allegra replaced her at the pianoforte, Lord Carroll joining her. When the other three ladies had performed, they had all played from memory, no doubt practicing many hours in order to be able to do so. She still thought she and her twin did a better job, however.

"You may sit," she told Lord Carroll. "Lyric and I are going to perform together now."

Her sister joined her as the earl took a seat nearby. They harmonized beautifully together, Lyric singing soprano, while Allegra took the alto part. The guests applauded thunderously when they finished, causing her to beam. Lord Carroll caught her eye and mouthed, "Bravo."

"Perhaps more of you would like to sing along," Aunt Dinah suggested. "Allegra, would you continue to play? Gather around if you enjoy singing."

Suddenly, she was surrounded by all their guests except for the chaperones, who looked on indulgently. She played several folk songs, the entire group joining in. It was easy to distinguish Lady Lida's voice because she clearly was the most talented with her high, sweet soprano. Allegra even suggested Lady Lida sing a ballad alone and accompanied her.

They finished with "The British Grenadiers." It was obvious

that Lord Blankenship had the best voice of the men, and as the final verse began, the others fell silent. In his rich tenor, the viscount sang:

Then let us fill a bumper, and drink a health of those
Who carry caps and pouches, and wear the l`looped` clothes.
May they and their commanders live happy all their years.
With a row, row, row, row, row, row, for the British Grenadiers.

Allegra finished with a flourish up and down the keys, and everyone clapped.

"You have an excellent voice, my lord," James complimented from where he sat next to Sophie. "I might have to teach you a few songs you aren't familiar with."

"No!" said the duchess, turning red at the suggestion. "My husband knows several songs sung by sailors. He has even taught some of them to the girls. They are *not* fit for guests, however."

Lord Carroll leaned down and said in her ear, "You will have to teach *me* some of these."

Thinking of the lyrics that James and Captain Andrews sang, she vigorously shook her head. "I think not, my lord. Those lyrics should stay within the family."

He gazed at her intently, and she grew hot all over. If she wed him, he would be family.

But that was a big *if*. She couldn't get ahead of herself. While she might have made up her mind, she did not know if he were serious about her. A rake could utter tender words, but the earl would have to prove to her that he had truly changed. If he had, she believed he would ask for her hand in marriage.

"I think I might persuade you to share a bit of the lyrics with me later, Miss Allegra."

The chaperones decided to make their way to bed as couples began splitting up. She heard Lyric say something about cooling down with a stroll in the gardens, and her twin left with Lord Blankenship. Other couples disappeared, one by one, until she and Lord Carroll had the drawing room to themselves.

He took her hand, threading his fingers through hers, and led her to the far corner. The area was not lit, and he took a seat in a wing chair, pulling her into his lap.

"Oh!" she exclaimed, toppling into him, feeling the hard muscles of his chest.

"I like the feel of you against me, Allegra," he said, his voice smooth as silk.

She peered at him, his face covered in the shadows. Swallowing, she said, "I will not be seduced, my lord." Her words seemed weak and ineffectual.

"I promise not to seduce you. But I want you to make a choice." He paused. "Choose me, Allegra. Choose us."

"How?" she asked. "I am so confused. What do you want of me?"

He chuckled, low. His hands came up, cradling her face. "I want you to willingly take a leap into the unknown. Let me show you what pleasure is."

Oh, this earl certainly tempted her.

When she didn't reply, he added, "I know exactly what to do to make you mine. A few kisses. A few caresses. I can have you writhing in my arms."

"But?" she asked.

"I do not want to touch you if you are unwilling. I want you to want me. As much as I want you. Please, Allegra. Let me show you what can exist between a man and a woman. I promise I will not steal your virginity. I will merely let you sample what it could be like if you agreed to wed me."

She sucked in a quick breath. "You are . . . *offering* for me?"

"Yes." His thumbs caressed her cheeks. "I can think of no other woman I would wish to make my wife. But you are the one who decides your fate—and mine. I want to kiss you. Touch you intimately. No one is here. No one will ever know what passes between us. When we are done, you will have all the control. You can seek pleasure—even marriage—with another man.

"Or you can become my countess."

He had not mentioned love. Allegra wanted to press him on that, but her natural curiosity won out. No man had ever moved her—or infuriated her—more than Lord Carroll.

Sterling . . .

"I do want to learn from you," she admitted.

"I am not asking for any promises from you now. You will be free to decide if you still would like a future with me. Just give me a few minutes to convince you we belong together."

Allegra gazed at him, catching a gleam in his eyes, the rest of his face hidden in shadow.

"Yes. Take as long as you need, Sterling."

His fingers stilled. "Thank you," he said softly, touching his lips to hers.

CHAPTER EIGHT

STERLING KNEW HE wanted this woman. Desperately. He had to show her that he had changed. Of course, in doing so, he would use the lessons he had learned over the years to do so. If anything, he knew how to please a woman. What would make her melt in his arms. It didn't matter. He would do whatever he had to in order to convince Allegra Strong they were meant to be.

He kissed her gently at first, not wanting to rush things between them. No one would be returning to this drawing room tonight. Couples had scattered throughout Shadowcrest, most likely doing the very things he would do with Allegra now.

He smiled against her mouth. Well, some of the things. He doubted any of the other four gentlemen would go quite as far as he would tonight in his pursuit of the lively, vivacious woman sitting in his lap.

"Something is humorous?" she murmured against his lips.

Sterling didn't bother replying to her question. Instead, he kissed her harder, wanting to increase the passion between them.

It worked. She didn't ask him anything else, instead becoming consumed by the kiss. While he knew he was an excellent kisser, he had never kissed any woman for the length of time he did with Allegra. It was just another way he knew how special she was. The electricity between them was powerful. Even dangerous.

Just how he liked things.

But this was not a woman he would bed and walk away from. No, he was different now. Sterling saw how empty his life had been. He was ready to begin anew, and this fresh start must include Allegra. No one could replace her.

He eased back on the kiss, giving her small, quick ones now, lulling her. Then he sank his teeth into her full, bottom lip, hearing her gasp. A rush of excitement filled him—and he believed it did her, as well.

He tongued the place, soothing it, outlining her mouth with the tip of his tongue. She readily opened to him, already knowing what he wanted. Sterling leisurely explored her mouth, and as he did, his hand went to her breast, kneading it. She moaned. It swelled in his palm. He raked his fingernail over the taut nipple, hearing her breath hitch.

"You like that," he murmured against her lips.

"Yes," she admitted. "Do it again."

"I will do better than that, love."

He broke the kiss, his lips trailing down her throat, to where her bosom swelled above the gown. His tongue outlined the rise of each breast, and he could hear her breath quickening. His fingers went to the top of the gown, easing it from her shoulders, pulling it down to her waist, Her corset still imprisoned the pair, though, and he lifted them to freedom.

Sterling kneaded the left one as he kissed the right, allowing his mouth to take it in. His tongue flicked against her nipple, causing her to cry out. She pushed her hands into his hair, tightening her fingers, holding him to her breast. Greedily, he devoured it, sucking, laving, grazing his teeth against the nipple, delighting in her whimpers.

He moved to the other one, causing her to mewl with a repeat performance as she writhed against him. Oh, Allegra Strong was definitely one who would bring him pleasure for many years to come. How ironic that he, who had bedded countless women, was even entertaining the thought of being faithful to one woman. Sterling wasn't sure if he could do so or not.

Yet Allegra made him want to try.

Moving his hands to her waist, he lifted her so she straddled him. He wanted her to feel his enlarged cock hard against her. He would not take her virginity tonight.

But he would tempt her beyond measure.

"Better," he told her, his hands cupping her breasts as her head fell back. "You are beautiful, Allegra. So very, very beautiful."

He slipped her breasts back into the corset and brought her gown up again. Then he seized her mouth, the kisses enflaming them. He tilted her in his arms, moving her head back so he had better access, and deepened the kisses. He had never felt desire as strongly as he did now, nor had he ever reined it in. Sterling would do so, but he still needed Allegra pushed over the edge so that she would want him as much as he did her.

And he knew exactly how to make that happen.

Rising, Allegra still in his arms, he turned and placed her in the chair. Though they were in the far corner of the drawing room, the lighting dim, he could see enough of her face to know she was experiencing the rush of desire.

Kneeling before her, he raised her gown and the undergarments below it, pushing them to her waist.

"What . . . are you doing?" she demanded, trying to push them back down.

He grabbed her wrists and kissed each palm, sensing her shudder.

"Doing exactly what I told you I would do. Giving you the greatest pleasure I can without fear of making a babe. Now, let me do what I wish to you, Allegra," he commanded.

"All right," she said meekly, and he released her wrists.

Sterling pushed her skirts back up again, wishing he had more light and could see her beauty. He could taste it, though, sampling her sweet nectar.

Kissing her knee, he nibbled at it, causing her to giggle. He ran his tongue up her inner thigh, seeking the heat of her core. When his tongue made contact, she jerked, pushing his shoulders away.

"What on earth do you think you are doing?" she demanded.

"If you are going to stop me every time, this is going to take much longer than it should, Allegra," he reprimanded, as if she were a naughty schoolgirl caught at mischief. "No more talking. And *no* more interruptions."

He didn't wait for her reply. He moved to her core again, licking the seam of her sex, feeling her start and hearing her gasp. He did so again, slowly, already tasting her juices because she was ready for him. Still, he took his time, enjoying the sounds she made, the little whimpers and gasps of an innocent receiving pure pleasure for the first time.

Without warning, he pushed his tongue inside her, and she almost came off the chair. By now, though, he had taken her waist with both hands, anchoring her to the spot. As he devoured her, she writhed, groaning, calling out his name. A powerful feeling passed through him, knowing he was the only man who had tasted her.

With tongue and teeth, he pleasured her, finding her sweet nub and teasing it unmercifully. Then her orgasm erupted, and she bucked beneath him, riding the wave of passion for longer than any woman he had ever been with. Her fingers had fisted in his hair, holding him close to her, and he experienced the orgasm with her, smiling as it rocked her safe, innocent world.

Finally, she stilled, her hands falling from his hair. He lifted his head, the urge to kiss her uncontrollable. He rose, pulling her along with him, until they stood locked together, their mouths fusing. His tongue pushed into her mouth, allowing her to taste herself. She clung to him, and their hunger was fed through their kisses. He wrapped his arms about her for support, knowing her legs were about to give out, kissing her with everything he had.

Her hands went to his face, touching him, and he gentled the kiss. A wave of tenderness for this woman swept through him.

Sterling gathered her in his arms again and sat once more in the chair. Allegra snuggled against him, her head resting upon his shoulder.

They sat this way for some minutes. He wondered what it would be like to make love to her. He wasn't one to remain in bed with a woman after the act, leaving as soon as it was done, never wanting to commit. Would he go to her bed to make love to her when they wed—and then return to his own? Or would he bring her to his bed and keep her there?

Of course, she had yet to give him an answer.

Stroking her hair, he asked, "What did you think?"

Her palm moved against his chest. "What you did to me made it hard to think," she admitted. "The ways you touched me. Especially . . . well . . . I mean . . . I did not know you would kiss me . . . *there*."

"But you enjoyed it, didn't you?" he asked.

"Very much," she said, and he heard the satisfaction in her voice. "I simply had no idea that kind of thing was done."

"Would you like me to do it again to you?"

Her breath hitched. "No. As much as I would enjoy it, I am so weary, I fear I will not be able to put one foot in front of the other in order to make it to my bed."

"I could carry you to my bed," he said.

She gasped. "You will not!"

"Then I will carry you to your bed," he teased.

"No, Sterling. There will be no carrying me. Anyone could see us."

He decided to press his suit. "Since you enjoyed what we did together, you only have to say yes to me. To my offer. And we can do all kinds of forbidden things when we are man and wife."

Her head came off his shoulder, and she peered deeply into his eyes. "Are you being flippant—or do you really wish me to be your wife?"

"I want you in my bed and as my countess," he replied huskily, pressing his lips against hers in a soft kiss.

When he broke the kiss, he saw he had won. Even in the dim light, he could see she was his.

"Yes. I want you as my husband."

Sterling kissed her again, sweet, tender kisses. Her passion, for now, was spent.

"I love you," she told him after he broke the kiss. "I cannot believe we have found what other Strongs have."

He might be a rake, but he was an honest one. Not a man given to lies. Especially with this woman whom he wanted to make his wife, the mother of his children.

"Do not speak for me, Allegra," he warned softly, knowing the stickiness of the situation.

She frowned. "What do you mean?"

They gazed at one another a long moment, and the realization obviously hit her.

"You do not love me."

She scrambled off him, coming to her feet. He stood, reaching for her, but she swatted his hands away.

"How could we have done what we just did and you not love me?" she demanded.

Calmly, he said, "I told you before. Men and women can couple. They can experience a great depth of passion in their physical attraction to one another. Love does not have to be a part of marriage, Allegra. In fact, it rarely is."

She stomped her foot. "But *I want* love in my marriage," she insisted. "I told you of how Strongs wed for love. You knew that, Sterling. You knew that and . . . did what you did to me."

His patience waned. "I gave you the choice. You accepted it. I also told you that you would hold no obligation to me afterward. I still want us to wed, Allegra. I think we would suit one another quite well."

She thrust out her hands, slamming them into his chest, causing him to stumble backward. He caught himself.

"I do not wish to wed *you*, my lord. I will settle for nothing less than a love match."

His eyes narrowed. "You would give up what we experienced just now between us? Love is simply a word, Allegra. Even those who believe in it knows it fades after time. I want you. You want me. We would have a good marriage."

She fisted her hands, placing them on her waist. "Why the bloody hell would I want to wed a man who does not love me? I am certain you would get me with child and then rush into the arms of another woman." She paused. "No, many women. You are a man with a voracious appetite. One woman would never be enough for you. I would be a fool to shackle myself to you."

Her tears began to fall, and she angrily wiped them away. "Marriage without love—and commitment—is no marriage at all. Find some other woman in the *ton* who is willing to look away from your many liaisons with other women, all just to be called your countess. I would rather die a spinster than spend one day as your wife."

She whirled, rushing from the drawing room. Sterling watched her, stunned that she had rejected his offer.

That she had rejected him.

Determination filled him. He was no puppet on a string who would dance to the tune Allegra Strong played. He could easily have any other woman he wanted. He would leave this damned house party and return to town. Lose himself in the arms of as many lovers as he could find.

He returned to his bedchamber, anger boiling inside him. Sterling had behaved in the most ungentlemanly manner possible. Disappointment in himself now flooded him. He had ruined the best opportunity he had ever had to change his life and have the future he had thought would be impossible.

All because he refused to admit—both to himself and Allegra—that he *did* love her.

CHAPTER NINE

ALLEGRA AND LYRIC went to breakfast later than usual the next morning, trying to avoid the two men who had upended their lives and broken their hearts. In a cruel twist of fate, Lord Blankenship had offered for Lyric. He, too, wanted marriage, but could not bring himself to love her twin. At least they had each other, because Allegra knew they would need one another more than they ever had.

She had returned to her bedchamber last night, stunned by what had transpired between her and Sterling. To have given so much of herself to him—even to declare her love for him—had made her feel small and worthless when he adamantly insisted they did not need love to wed one another.

How she had wanted him to have changed his roguish ways! Allegra had believed Aunt Dinah when she had told Allegra she thought Sterling had more substance to him than he readily allowed Polite Society to see. She had been dazzled by his kisses, hoping they were building a friendship which would blossom into love. It had for her.

It never would for him.

She supposed a majority of gentlemen in the *ton* were cut from the same cloth, not wanting or believing in love. Marriage was, after all, a business transaction within most families, with dutiful—or even rebellious—daughters accepting their parents' wishes and entering a marriage without love.

Allegra wanted more. She wanted what her Strong cousins had found. What even Aunt Dinah, at her age, had found. Of course, her aunt had suffered through almost two decades being married to a man who used her to get an heir and when no heir was produced, completely ignored his wife. If she did wed Sterling, she did not think he would ignore her. At least at first.

No, she was wrong to think that. He was a rake. He might have changed a bit, realizing he needed to own up to the responsibilities required by his title and produce an heir. That meant marriage. Even though physically things were incredible between them, she doubted it would last. The newness of her would wear off, and he would discard her as he had countless lovers. Of course, they would always be bound by matrimony, but she could never live a separate life, knowing the man she loved was going off to be with his current lover. Allegra was proud she had stood her ground and turned down his offer.

Even if she was in pure misery now.

They entered the drawing room, and she was relieved to find no Sterling present. Lord Blankenship was also absent. Only a handful of others were there. They split up, Lyric joining the elder Miss Bancroft, who was sitting alone, as Lord Lamkin was excusing himself from her company. Allegra went to sit with Lord and Lady Crowell and Lord Motley. She wondered if the earl would offer for Lady Lida.

They welcomed her presence, and she determined she was not interrupting any serious conversation. Lord Crowell was looking forward to today's hunt, which Allegra learned that her brother Caleb would be leading. Aunt Dinah had tried to include him in the house party, but Caleb was having none of it, telling everyone he had too much work to do as Shadowcrest's steward, even affirming he had no interest in marriage now or in the future.

Aunt Dinah came and told those left in the dining room about the ladies painting at the lake at noon today, while the gentlemen would be hunting in the forest. She knew this would be the perfect time to approach her aunt, and she excused herself.

"May we speak, Aunt Dinah?"

"Certainly, Allegra. A few ladies are using my sitting room now. Is this a more private conversation to be had?" she asked hopefully, and Allegra knew her aunt thought she would be revealing that a marriage offer had been made and accepted.

"It is. We could check the library and see if it is available," she suggested neutrally, not wanting to tip her hand until they were in private.

They went there, finding it empty. Allegra closed the door and took a seat next to her aunt.

"Did Lord Carroll offer for you?" her aunt asked eagerly. "Though you are perfectly capable of accepting his offer, I do think it would be good if he spoke to James. Even Caleb."

"He did offer for me," she confirmed, wincing when Aunt Dinah smiled radiantly at her. "But we will not wed." She swallowed, watching her aunt's face fall.

"In fact, Lord Blankenship also offered for Lyric last night. Like me, Lyric accepted him at first. We both changed our minds, however."

Sympathy filled her aunt's face, and it took everything Allegra had not to give in to the tears. Her throat was thick with emotion, and she took a moment to compose herself.

"Lyric and I find ourselves in the same circumstances. We have fallen in love with men who do not love us in return."

Aunt Dinah's jaw dropped. "But . . . they both made offers of marriage to you."

"Yes. And my twin and I unwisely professed our love to the pair, giddy with the idea we would be wedding our soulmates as other Strongs have."

Understanding filled the older woman's eyes. "They could not speak the words to you. Is that correct?"

"Yes," she said, her voice breaking. "Both Lord Carroll and

Lord Blankenship wanted to make us their wives, but they wanted nothing to do with love."

Aunt Dinah brushed her fingers against Allegra's cheek. "And you two will settle for nothing less."

She nodded, unable to speak further. Her aunt enveloped her in an embrace, and Allegra wept softly. How she still had tears within her was beyond her. She told herself she must quit shedding them for a man who did not love her and never would, but it was so very hard. She had always been such a positive person, yet her future appeared so very bleak at the moment.

"I know this is hard for you, Allegra, but I must ask you if you would consider marriage with the earl. Obviously, he feels strongly enough about you to have extended an offer. Do you believe he could grow to love you?"

"I doubt it, Aunt. I know you believe there is more to him than what he presents to the world, but at heart, he has been a rake for so long, I doubt he would ever change. Yes, there is passion between us. I never knew a kiss could be powerful—but I believe Lord Carroll would tire of me quickly. He is not a patient man. He would not give love a chance to grow. That would leave me in an intolerable marriage, watching him leave to go to a series of lovers."

Allegra shook her head, reaffirming her position. "No, Aunt Dinah. I love him. But I must take care to protect my heart. I will not enter a marriage with a man who cannot love me the way I love him."

Her aunt cradled Allegra's cheeks and kissed her brow. "You are making the right decision. It is the most difficult one you have ever made, but it is one which impacts the rest of your life. I will need to put the same question to Lyric, however."

"She will express to you that she feels the same as I do," she said stubbornly.

"Most likely, she will, but I will ask her all the same if there is a chance she believes Lord Blankenship could grow to love her."

Clearing her throat, she said, "Obviously, Lyric and I want

nothing to do with these two men. We would like to ask you to help us keep our distance from them. I know you have several other activities planned for the house party, and some of those might include partnering with a gentleman. If there is any way you can keep us from matching with them, we would appreciate it. We do not wish to make the other guests uncomfortable, but we will not see ourselves deliberately hurt further."

"I understand, Allegra. Let me go and find Lyric and speak with her. Would you go with me and entertain the other young ladies while I do so?"

She agreed, replacing her twin in Aunt Dinah's sitting room. Lady Lida and her mother had joined Miss Bancroft and Miss Markle, and the five of them talked about a variety of things before Aunt Dinah appeared again. She signaled to Allegra that she might leave, telling her as she passed that her twin was in the library. She was grateful her aunt understood they might need some time alone together.

When she got to the library, Lyric explained she wanted to be alone for a few minutes.

"I will go to the lake and paint with the others, but for now, I prefer sitting by myself. Perhaps I will go and play the pianoforte for a while. Georgie and Mirella always seem to lose themselves in music. I thought I might try to do the same."

"That is an excellent idea, but we are to go to the lake in half an hour to paint with the others."

Lyric swore softly.

"Lyric Strong!" said Allegra. "I have never heard you utter such a foul oath before."

Her twin grinned. "Actually, it made me feel better. You should try it."

Allegra did—and they both burst out laughing.

"It feels good to laugh, doesn't it?" Lyric asked.

"No wonder men go about swearing. At least I think they do. Why, the next time either of is feeling blue, I think that will be the remedy to change our mood."

"Can you imagine if we did so in front of the elder Miss Bancroft?" her twin asked.

She giggled. "Why, her heart would stop! Oh, I know we should not jest about such a serious matter, but I was afraid we might never laugh again."

Lyric's eyes narrowed. "I will not let Lord Blankenship rule my life. I am over and done with him. I will laugh. Sing. Dance. Why, I might even flirt," she said saucily. "Just not with any of our guests. I would not want to interfere with the budding attachments which are forming."

"We should go and retrieve our bonnets," Allegra suggested. "The sun is bright today. Then we can take our time walking to the lake."

They returned to their bedchamber, freshening up and choosing straw bonnets to wear. Allegra tied the ribbons under her chin and then did so for Lyric, who never seemed to be able to manage a decent bow. Arm-in-arm, they went down the stairs. As they reached the final landing, the foyer in sight, she froze in her tracks.

Both Lord Carroll and Lord Blankenship stood there, hats in hand, talking with Viscount Tillings.

Her grip tightened on her twin's arm and she hissed, "I would have thought at least one of them would have left Shadowcrest by now."

"Cheer up and chin up," Lyric advised. "And be extremely polite."

They moved down the stairs, both their former suitors glancing up. Allegra looked straight ahead, refusing to make eye contact.

As they reached the bottom, Lord Blankenship said, "Good afternoon, ladies."

"Good afternoon," Lyric replied coolly. "I hope you enjoy your hunt."

"I am quite looking forward to it," Lord Tillings said, oblivious to the undercurrent in the air.

"We are off to paint," Allegra said breezily. "Good day."

They sailed out the front door, a footman opening it for them, and continued down the lane.

"We did it," she said. "We met the enemy and yielded no ground."

"Poor Lord Tillings had no idea what was going on," Lyric said. "He is intelligent when it comes to academics and politics, but his social skills are lacking. I hope Miss Bancroft, as his viscountess, will put a bit of polish on him."

She chuckled. "Lord Tillings' head is in the clouds. His thoughts are reserved for Miss Bancroft and not deciphering what is going on between the other guests."

"They do make a delightful pair, don't they?" Lyric noted. "Miss Bancroft and the viscount."

"Georgie will be so pleased when she and August return from Dalmara and finds not only her new friend is also our friend now—but that she is engaged to be married."

"Let us hope that is the case," her twin said. "Lord Tillings still has yet to ask her. He might even wait and accompany the Misses Bancroft back to Somerset and speak with Miss Bancroft's father."

"He might," Allegra agreed. "I still believe they will announce their betrothal here at Shadowcrest, however."

The thought of that announcement—and not one of her own—quickly sobered Allegra. As she and Lyric walked to the lake and the waiting paints and canvases, she told herself that life would go on once the house party ended and Lord Carroll left.

She just didn't know how she would manage to make it through each day.

CHAPTER TEN

STERLING WAS UTTERLY miserable throughout the hunt. Usually, he was at home in the saddle, any worries melting away. Today, however, he could not concentrate on anything.

Because thoughts of Allegra swirled throughout him.

He had gone to breakfast as early as possible, hoping to avoid both her and her twin, and then remained in his bedchamber until just before it was time to leave for the hunt. He had gone downstairs, where he had run into Blankenship and Tillings and stopped to visit with them a moment, trying to play the role of an affable guest. Tillings had been waiting on Lord Lamkin, and Sterling agreed to remain with the pair, waiting for the earl.

That had been a mistake—because he had seen Allegra.

She had been wearing a gown of periwinkle, which made her eyes a rich shade of blue. The sweet curves he had caressed only the night before called out to his fingers. She had barely said a word, avoiding looking at him. He had not realized how hard it would be.

Why wasn't she like all the other women? Why could he not get her out of his mind? He was Sterling Ayles, the Earl of Carroll. He could have any woman in the whole of England.

But the one woman he wanted no longer wanted him.

Her head was full of fairy tales. Life did not guarantee a happily ever after. She believed in love, where he only believed in the pleasures of the flesh.

Yet Sterling knew he lied to himself. Because he suspected he *did* love her. Very much. And he was too afraid to tell her that he did.

He should leave the house party. Yes, that was the best action to take at this point. No sense in staying and prolonging his misery—and hers. He would leave first thing in the morning. In fact, he would leave the hunt now since he had no taste for it. Besides, every time he looked forward, he saw Caleb Strong, Allegra's brother. They favored one another far too much, especially with those Strong eyes. It irked him to no end.

The group slowed a bit, Strong raising his hand as they searched the area for their prey.

Not spying it, Strong said, "We should ride on."

Sterling took that opportunity to say, "I must return to the house, Mr. Strong. Please continue without me."

He gave no further explanation, merely nodding brusquely at the Shadowcrest steward before he wheeled his horse, riding away from the group and returning to the stables.

Once he left the woods, he galloped at full speed, wishing he could ride until his problems ceased. Never had he experienced heartache. He was a man who coupled with a lover and never became emotionally involved with her. This time, however, he had lost his heart.

Swinging from the saddle, he tossed the reins to a groom, and turned. Much to his surprise, he saw Blankenship also coming this way. He did not want to engage in conversation with anyone at present, least of all a man who had been a former friend and who seemed quite cozy with Miss Lyric Strong.

As he strode off, the viscount steered his horse toward Sterling, stopping mere feet from him. He dismounted.

"We must talk," Blankenship said crisply.

"We have nothing to discuss," he said flatly.

A pained expression crossed the viscount's face. "Then let me talk and you listen. I am in need of advice."

That surprised him, and he nodded. "Very well."

Blankenship rode the short distance to the stables, giving his horse over to a groom before returning to where Sterling stood.

"Would you walk with me?" asked the viscount. "This is not something I would wish to be overheard by guests or servants. The gardens are nearby. They would give us privacy. I suggest we go there."

Curiosity won out, and he agreed to accompany Blankenship to the gardens. Once they entered them, his old friend led them to a bench and sat.

Sterling took a seat. "What is this about?"

"I need your advice," Blankenship said. "You are, without a doubt, the last person I should turn to because of your rakehell ways, but I am desperate." He swallowed. "I have totally ruined my chances with Lyric. And I haven't a bloody clue how to win her back."

He stiffened. "What are you saying?"

Blankenship raked his fingers through his hair, his frustration obvious. "I am a fool. A coward. That is what Lyric accused me of being—and she was right."

The viscount braced his elbows on his knees, dropping his head into his hands.

Sterling kept quiet, keeping a tight rein on his own emotions, waiting for Blankenship to speak.

Finally, he lifted his head, and Sterling saw tears brimming in Blankenship's eyes.

"Good God, man. What is wrong?"

"We are two men cut from the same cloth, Carroll. From the little I know of your background, you had parents much as my own. Ones who practically abandoned us at birth. We had to find our own way—and we did so—becoming two of the most notorious rakes in all of London. I know I have hidden who I am from the world, my true self, because I have been confused about who I might be. My uncle's death greatly affected me, however.

Uncle Oscar was the only one who ever showed me any kind of affection. I have never ever taken my responsibilities seriously, but I wanted to be a better man to prove to myself that his faith in me was not in vain."

Blankenship shook his head sadly. "That is why I went into last Season looking for a bride. I thought if I settled into marriage and produced my heir, it would be a start. Fate had other plans for me, though. Not a blessed woman appealed to me enough to offer marriage, and it was because I was meant to come to this house party at Shadowcrest and meet Lyric."

Understanding filled Sterling. "You love her," he said simply.

The viscount nodded. "Yes, I love her. And was fool enough not to be able to voice those sentiments to her."

He could not believe how much his own situation with Allegra paralleled that of Blankenship and Lyric Strong.

"What happened?" he prodded.

"We walked in these very gardens just last night," Blankenship said morosely. "I offered for her. I cannot begin to explain to you what it is like being with her. She is different from any woman I have ever known. Yet being the hard-headed idiot I am, I could not say the words she wanted to hear. Words I have never spoken to any woman."

Blankenship raked his hands through his hair again, his frustration growing. "I offered. She accepted. You would think all would be well in my world after that. But no, she went and told me that she loved me. And she does, Carroll. I saw the love for me shining in her eyes, and suddenly, I knew I was not worthy of such a creature."

Suspecting what had occurred, Sterling asked, "What did she say when you did not echo the same sentiment?"

"She is a Strong, through and through. She believes in the power of love because she has seen the incredible love matches her family members have made. Lyric took me to the woodshed, so to speak. And yet I still could not give her what she wanted."

Blankenship looked Sterling in the eyes. "Why? Why can't I

say the words? Even if I muster the courage and do utter them, what if she will not take me back?"

It surprised him when tears misted his own eyes. He saw the quizzical look on his friend's face when he spotted them.

"Tell me, Carroll. What is going on with you and Miss Allegra?"

He laughed harshly. "The story you just poured to me, Blankenship? It mirrors ours in every way."

Sterling rose from the bench and began pacing. "I also offered for Allegra last night. It is magical being with her. I—unlike you— have not been searching for a wife. I had no idea why I was even invited to this house party until Mrs. Andrews pulled me aside and gave me a heart-to-heart talk. She told me that she believed there was more to me than what Polite Society saw. That a good man lay beneath the façade the *ton* knew."

He stopped and gazed intently at Blankenship. "And I began to believe her. I began to believe in myself for the first time. The feelings that Allegra stirs within me are hard to put into words."

"Yes, I understand exactly what you mean."

"I offered for Allegra, and she, too, accepted. That is where our stories are identical, for she also spoke those words which I have never understood, much less wanted to speak myself."

"Did she take it badly?" asked Blankenship.

He smiled ruefully. "Allegra Strong is a fiery beauty, and she was having none of me not declaring my love for her. I was so confused, Blankenship. I do not even know if I could ever be faithful to one woman."

He began pacing again and stopped. "No, I am even lying right now to you. I *do* love her. I would never stray from her. But because I was too cowardly to voice aloud these strange, new feelings, I lost her. As you did Miss Lyric. You saw how frosty she was when she and her twin passed us in the foyer earlier. I have no hope of reclaiming her."

Plopping on the bench again, he sighed. They sat in silence, each lost in his own thoughts, mulling over their despair.

Finally, Sterling said, "I am going to leave Shadowcrest first thing in the morning. I have no reason to stay. I do not wish to make Allegra or anyone else uncomfortable."

He rose. "I wish you the best with Miss Lyric."

Blankenship shot to his feet. "Are you mad, man? From what you have told me, your feelings for Miss Allegra echo mine for Lyric. How can you walk away from the woman you love without even trying to see if she will forgive you?" He shook his head. "I sought advice from you, despite the fact you are a rake, only to learn that you are a sad, sad man. Go back to town, Carroll. Rut your way from one end to another. I guarantee you that no woman you couple with will make you forget Allegra Strong. No amount of drink will cause her memory to fade. You should be fighting for her—not walking away."

Sterling knew what the viscount said was true, and yet he was terrified of rejection.

"What are you going to do?" he countered. "Are you going to try and change Miss Lyric's mind?"

"It may be too late for that," the viscount admitted. "Lyric, though not as vocal as her sister, is even more stubborn than Miss Allegra ever could be. I have no idea what to do or how to persuade her that we are meant to be together. But I will stay at this house party until the end, trying to find a way. Even though, in my heart, I know I am not worthy of such a wonderful creature."

Blankenship strode off, leaving Sterling in the gardens. He thought of the lonely, empty life that would be ahead of him if he did not pursue Allegra.

But how could he make her understand that he *did* love her?

If he told her now—if he said those words—she would think he was merely giving her lip service. No, it would take some grand gesture in order to have a chance to make Allegra his once more.

Then it struck him. God only knew how many poems he had penned over the years. What he would now do is write the greatest love poem he could, pouring his heart and soul onto the page. He would gift Allegra the poem, hoping it would move her. That she would recognize the depth of his feelings.

With this plan in mind, Sterling returned to the house.

CHAPTER ELEVEN

STERLING SCRIBBLED THE final words of the last verse and set the quill down. He raked his fingers through his hair, emitting a long sigh.

It was done.

He glanced to the top of the parchment and re-read the words which he had penned. Words of love on a page to the woman he held dear. They read well to him, but then again, he was so exhausted, his brain would probably tell him anything sounded perfect just to get a bit of sleep. He decided to leave it as it was for now and review it again when he awakened. He could make any adjustments needed when he was feeling more refreshed. As it was, midnight had come and gone a long time ago.

Rising from the chair, he hadn't even the strength to extinguish the candle, which sputtered on its last legs. Instead, he stumbled to the bed, collapsing upon it, falling into a deep sleep.

He awoke with a start, his eyes still gritty from lack of sleep. He had not bothered to summon his valet last night, and the curtains were still open. The faint light of the morning dawn, which would come shortly, already seeped through the windows. The candle had long gone out.

There it was again. A light tap. He had not rung for his valet, so he had no idea why the servant would be knocking upon his door at such an ungodly hour. Irritated, Sterling pushed himself off the bed and strode to the door, opening it.

Lyric Strong stood before him, wearing her dressing gown and holding a candle. Her eyes went wide at the sight of him, and he realized he was stripped to the waist, wearing only his breeches. Even his feet were bare.

"What are you doing here?" he hissed.

"I needed to speak to you in private, with no prying eyes or ears around, my lord. Are you going to ask me in?"

Before he could close the door in her face, she pushed past him, giving him no choice. He quickly closed the door to the bedchamber and spun, hurrying to the bed, slipping into his banyan and belting it.

"I am not going to be trapped into marriage—and that is exactly what will happen if someone sees you leaving this bedchamber, especially dressed the way you are. They will believe we have spent the night together, no matter how much we protest."

Horror filled her eyes, and he saw she realized how foolish her actions had been. Then her jaw set, steely determination filling those cornflower blue eyes. He recalled what Blankenship had said about her and decided Miss Lyric Strong had the same stubborn core as her more outgoing twin.

"I am not asking—I am telling—you to leave Shadowcrest this morning, Lord Carroll," she began. "You stole my sister's heart, and then you shattered it almost beyond repair."

Sterling liked how protective this woman was of her twin. He even wondered if Allegra might be bold enough to have the same heart-to-heart talk with Blankenship.

"I know Allegra can heal, but it is going to take some time. That healing process cannot begin with you at Shadowcrest. I see no reason for you to stay, my lord. I learned you left the hunt early yesterday. You did not bother to show for tea, nor did you send an excuse. You barely arrived in the drawing room before dinner was announced, and then you were silent throughout the entire meal. Then once more, you slipped away, not coming to the drawing room after dinner for charades. If you are not going to participate in the activities my aunt has planned, you should return to town."

"I can't," he said flatly. "I love Allegra too much to do so."

That got her attention. Those lovely Strong eyes widened. "What? What did you just say?"

Then her eyes fell to the ground, and Sterling knew what she saw. The far half of the bedchamber was littered with balled-up pieces of parchment. She pushed past him and walked to that side, turning her head as she took in his numerous failed attempts. Bending, she picked up one and unfurled it, her eyes skimming the page.

Her gaze met his. "You are writing . . . love poetry to Allegra?"

Frustration filled him. "Yes. I have written poetry—even a few plays—for years. It is one of those secret activities I harbor. No one knows. I am trying to put my feelings for your sister on the page."

Confusion clouded her eyes. "Why don't you simply tell her that you love her?"

He sighed. "It isn't that easy. You, of all people, should know that."

She drew in a quick breath. "What are you saying?"

Gazing at her steadily, Sterling said, "I know of what happened between you and Blankenship. He offered for you, and you accepted him. Then you told him that you loved him, and he could not say the same in return. It caused you to cry off. The same happened to Allegra and me."

He began pacing the room. "I did not come to this house party looking for a wife, and yet Allegra is everything I want in one. Yes, I love her. No, I could not bring myself to tell her that for some reason I cannot even explain to myself. She wants a declaration of love from me, yet if I gave one to her now? She would question it. Doubt that I meant the words. Allegra would believe I only said them in order to persuade her to wed me."

Lyric nodded sadly. "Yes, I do understand, my lord. If Lord Blankenship were to tell me now that he loved me, I know he wouldn't mean it. That he simply was trying to convince me to marry him."

Sterling knew just how much his friend did love this woman, but it was not for him to solve their problems when he had ones of his own.

"The only way I thought I could tell Allegra of my feelings was to write her a love poem." He waved his arms about the room. "You see how many times I started and failed to convey that message. But I believe that I finally have done it."

He went to the table where he had worked so diligently and picked up the poem.

"I finished this in the wee hours of the morning. I was so bleary-eyed, I hoped I had finally captured my feelings. I think my heart is on the page, however. If this does not allow Allegra to understand the depth of my feelings for her, then it is hopeless. I will leave Shadowcrest."

Offering the page to her, he added, "Read it. See if you believe this will be the answer to my unspoken prayers."

She accepted the poem from him and held her candle close to it. He watched the expressions on her face as she read it, his heart beating fast.

Lifting her eyes, she met his gaze. Tears swam in them. "You will win Allegra over with your heartfelt words," Lyric declared. "And you are correct. If you had merely told her that you loved her, I doubt she would have believed you. She *will* believe this, my lord."

Swallowing, she added, "I have misjudged you. I thought you were nothing but a shallow rake, trying to add another lady's heart to your vast collection, but your words convey the depth of your love for my twin."

She handed the page to him. "Forgive me for not attempting to get to know the true Lord Carroll. I will help you in any way I can to bring you and Allegra together."

"Thank you, Lyric," he said fervently. "I know she wants nothing to do with me. Just as you feel about Blankenship." He paused, not wanting to meddle, but added, "I believe that you, too, should give the good viscount a second chance."

That was all he would say. The rest would be up to his friend to figure out how to let this lovely creature know just how much he loved her.

"We are to have a picnic by the lake today," she told him. "I will do my best to steer Allegra in your direction, my lord. I hope you meet with success."

They hatched a brief scheme, which he hoped would grant him uninterrupted time with Allegra. Then Lyric surprised him, coming toward him and kissing his cheek. He escorted her to the door and opened it. Stepping out, he saw no one in the corridor.

"Hurry back to your bedchamber. And thank you."

"I only want my sister's happiness. I believe she will find it with you."

Lyric Strong exited the room, and Sterling felt hope swell within him.

ALLEGRA STIRRED, COMING awake. She felt Lyric's warmth next to her and was grateful for her sister's presence because the raw hurt engulfed Allegra again.

How was she to get over Sterling if he dominated her every waking thought?

She thought about pretending to be ill but decided that would be unfair to Aunt Dinah and their guests. The bulk of entertaining had been placed upon her aunt since Sophie was dealing with business matters, especially now that Captain Andrews had arrived. She also was trying to rest as much as she could. The fact Sophie even allowed this house party to take place when she was due to give birth in a month was so decent of her. Sophie had wanted to give Allegra and Lyric a chance to find their own love matches.

They had—but it was one-sided in both instances.

She lay awake, her thoughts drifting, until Lyric stretched.

"Ready to face another bleak day?" she asked her twin.

"I think the bleak days are behind you," Lyric replied. "You are a very strong woman, Allegra. I see only good things in your future."

She slipped her hand around her sister's. "Whatever the future holds, we will face it together."

They rang for a maid, and both were soon dressed for the morning.

"What is the activity today again?" she asked Lyric.

"Aunt Dinah took our suggestion and has planned a picnic by the lake. We will be dining there and then taking rowboats out."

She swallowed the pain. "It will be a good way for some of the couples to have time alone. Have you written to Georgie yet about Miss Bancroft and Lord Tillings?"

"I have not had a free moment to do so, and you know it," Lyric said, laughing. "Besides, I will not write of their budding romance until Lord Tillings makes it official."

Lyric went on to tell Allegra about her conversation with both Miss Bancroft and Miss Markle in the sitting room yesterday. How furiously Miss Bancroft blushed when speaking of Lord Tillings and how Miss Markle was drawn to Lord Lamkin.

"They are both very nice ladies," Lyric finished. "Although Miss Markle frightened me a bit when she spoke of the Season."

"Why so?" Allegra asked.

"She said it was quite hard to form friendships with the others making their come-outs. That the Marriage Mart was more a competition."

"I can see that occurring," she agreed. Reaching for Lyric's hand, she squeezed it. "But we will have one another, won't we?"

"You have decided to partake in the Season next spring?"

"I believe it will be the best way to get over the heartache

Lord Carroll has brought to me. I doubt rakes such as himself attend many events of the Season. Even if they do, it would not be often. With so many people in a crowded ballroom, I think I could easily avoid him. I have told myself that I am not going to let this incident stain the rest of my life. Will I find love again? That is yet to be determined. But I am going to go to town next spring and dance and laugh and be open to the possibility."

Her sister's brow furrowed, and Allegra wondered if she had been too bold in speaking of her plans. She had to remember that Lyric's heart was broken, the same as hers, and her twin might not yet be at a point where she was ready to commit to a Season.

"It is a long way off. Next spring. You have plenty of time to decide if it is something you wish to do or not, Lyric."

"I am hungry this morning," her sister said brightly, changing the topic. "I did not think I would be, but I am."

"You do not wish to wait until later and try to avoid Lord Blankenship?"

Lyric linked her hand through Allegra's arm. "As you said, why let those two rogues color our actions, both at this house party and down the line? I have you by my side. That is all I need to face the world."

They headed downstairs to the dining room, and Allegra decided to adopt her twin's positive attitude. If she saw Lord Carroll or Lord Blankenship, she would take the high road and be gracious. After all, it was only for another few days, and then she would hopefully never see either of them again.

CHAPTER TWELVE

ALLEGRA AND LYRIC joined the other ladies who gathered in the foyer. They had all decided to walk down to the lake together for this afternoon's picnic.

"I saw servants carting tables and chairs to the lake from my window," Lady Lida said, her hand about that of Lady Viola's.

Allegra thought it significant that Lord Motley had asked if he could have his daughter at the picnic—and that Lady Lida was the one who had retrieved the girl from the nursery and would now hold her hand the entire way there.

"Tarts!" the young girl declared with glee.

Lady Lida knelt. "Yes, my little love. There will be plenty of tarts at the picnic. I already checked with Cook, and she has made certain that you will have some."

Allegra and Lyric exchanged glances, and her twin said, "That was most thoughtful of you to speak with Cook to ensure tarts would be baked, Lady Lida."

Rising, Lady Lida said, "It is the least I can do. Lady Viola has a bit of a sweet tooth. I wanted her to enjoy the picnic."

"Rowboat," the girl said brightly.

Lady Lida stroked the young girl's hair and gave her a fond smile. "Yes, your papa is going to take us out on the water in a rowboat." She turned to the others and explained, "We have been talking of the lake and boats when we have played in the nursery."

Allegra knew Lady Lida accepted Lord Motley's daughter fully and would be a good mother to her and the other children they would have together. She only wondered when the betrothal announcement would be made as she saw Lady Crowell smile at her only child.

Aunt Dinah and Sophie were the last of the women to arrive. James was with them.

Her aunt said, "We are going to walk to the lake now. Their Graces will be taking a cart part of the way."

"Would anyone wish to go with us?" James asked.

"I would," the elder Miss Bancroft said.

Though she did not think the woman infirm in the slightest, she had detected a pretentious air about Miss Bancroft, and thought she merely did so in order to later have a story to share about the time she rode to a picnic with a duke and duchess.

The trio left for the waiting cart, and the rest of the party set out for the lake. Allegra noted the colorful parasols on display and complimented Miss Bancroft on her violet one.

Miss Markle asked, "Do you use the lake very often? I have always enjoyed the peace of sitting by the water."

She said, "Our cousin Pippa is the one who is most fond of the lake. She has fished in it for many years, as well as walking and riding the entire circumference."

"Fishing?" Miss Bancroft asked. "I have never done any of that."

"I have asked for rods to be brought to the lake," Aunt Dinah informed them. "Why, you should give it a try, Miss Bancroft. Perhaps Lord Tillings might be willing to demonstrate to you how it is done."

Miss Bancroft turned a bright scarlet, and everyone laughed merrily. Allegra was glad to see the young woman knew the laughter was in fun. She feared the wallflower had had her share of cruel jokes during her Seasons.

"The viscount is well-versed in many things," Miss Bancroft said. "I will see if he might teach me how to fish."

"Pippa used to fish with Viscount Hopewell," Lyric told the group. "She and Lord Hopewell were great friends for many years. It was almost as if she were a ward to him. Then when he passed, his heir came to Hopewood." Her twin smiled. "And not soon after, Pippa became Lady Hopewell."

"Someone mentioned that they are touring the world for their honeymoon?" Lady Crowell asked.

"Yes," Allegra replied. "Viscount Hopewell was a sea captain before he inherited his title. Pippa always has longed for adventure. They will be gone close to two years."

Lady Crowell patted Aunt Dinah on the back. "That must be very hard for you, Mrs. Andrews, having your girl gone for so long. And your other daughter is honeymooning in Scotland, I take it."

Aunt Dinah nodded. "Yes, Georgina and Lord Edgethorne went to his country home, Edgefield, for a few days after the wedding. Then they made their way up to Scotland, to a property left to the marquess by his mother. Neither had been to Scotland before, but from what Georgina writes, the Scottish Lowlands are the most beautiful place on earth."

"When will they return?" Miss Bancroft asked.

"Soon, I hope," Aunt Dinah said. "I expect, from what she writes to the family, that they will be home within the next two weeks."

"Oh, I wish they would arrive before the house party ends," Miss Bancroft exclaimed. "Lady Georgina became a good friend to me during this last Season. I was so happy when she and Lord Edgethorne decided to wed."

They arrived at the lake, and Allegra saw that a canopy had been set up, protecting two long tables of food from the plentiful sunshine. She also saw several tables with accompanying chairs had been placed on the wide path, while several blankets were strewn about the grass close to the water. The gentlemen were huddled in two groups, and she noted Lord Carroll had actually deigned to make this event after skipping out on tea and charades yesterday. He spoke with Lord Blankenship and Lord Tillings.

She headed to the table where James was seating Sophie and asked, "Was the cart too bumpy for you?"

"A bit," Sophie admitted. "I was not going to miss this, however. I have never attended a picnic before, and I have been looking forward to it."

Captain Andrews joined them. "I have not been on a picnic myself, Your Grace. It was the only thing that got me out of bed this morning."

Allegra caught the innuendo in his tone and saw Aunt Dinah blush furiously. She wondered if the couple might try for a babe and hoped they would. She would love to have a little cousin to fuss over.

"Have a seat, love," the captain said, pulling out a chair for Aunt Dinah. "You two can keep one another company while His Grace and I fix plates for all of us."

She glanced about, seeing Lord Carroll still standing with the other gentlemen. She would keep her eye out for where he went. If he took a seat at a table, she would sit on a blanket. If he chose a blanket, then it would be a table for her. She had no plans to be in his vicinity, much less have to make small talk with him.

"I will go with you, Captain," Allegra said, slipping her hand through his arm.

They headed toward where the food was displayed, but he steered her away from it and the others.

"Dinah told me you've had a bit of trouble with Lord Carroll."

She bit her lip. "That is certainly one way of putting it."

"Do you want me to kick his arse for you?"

She burst out laughing. "Actually, if that is done, I think I would take the greatest pleasure in doing so myself."

"He's a fool," the captain said, shaking his head. "That Lord Blankenship, as well. You girls are incredible women. If these so-called gentlemen are too blind to see it, then they are not good enough for you."

"We are trying to tell ourselves that," Allegra said lightly.

"If you need anything of me, you know you only have to ask," he told her.

"I do know, and I thank you for it." She went up on tiptoes and kissed his cheek.

They returned to where the other guests were placing food on their plates. Allegra took a bit of the roasted chicken and a healthy portion of the salmagundy.

"What is that?" the captain asked.

"It is salmagundy, a very popular picnic item. It uses either the white meat of turkey or chicken. I see Cook has sliced chicken for us today. It also contains cucumbers, hard boiled eggs, pickled red cabbage, and beetroot. Oh, yes, I also see some cooked ham. It's been cut into strips."

"You will like it, Captain," Lyric said from his other side. "I planted and harvested the cucumbers myself."

"Then I simply must taste it," he said, piling salmagundy high on his plate and placing some on another plate for his wife.

Allegra also took a few pieces of sliced fruit and sprinkled nuts over them, as well as accepting bread with jam and butter already spread on it by a footman who was helping serve the guests. She finished filling her plate with salad, thinking she would come back for dessert.

Glancing over her shoulder, she saw Lord Carroll standing at the end, plate in hand. Since he hadn't taken a seat, she couldn't. That caused her to accompany Captain Andrews and James back to their table. She watched them seat themselves.

"Is there anything else I might get for the four of you?" she asked.

"No, thank you, Allegra," James replied. "Go and have some fun with your guests."

She swallowed, glad to know that James and Sophie were not aware of her falling out with Lord Carroll. Turning, she saw Lyric speaking to Lord Carroll, which caused her to go still.

Then her sister walked away. Allegra decided Lyric must have been telling the earl to keep clear of them. She thought she might do the same favor in return and went to the end of the line, where Lord Blankenship stood.

"Please refrain from coming near my sister," she said firmly. "Your attentions toward her are unwanted."

Before he could utter a sound, Allegra whirled and walked away. She saw Lord Carroll had taken his plate to a blanket. The other tables had filled up, so she joined Lord Motley, Lady Lida, and Lady Viola on another blanket. The child was sprawled so that no more room appeared available.

"I hope you do not mind if I sit with you," she said.

"Please join us," Lord Motley encouraged. "Viola, come and sit next to Papa. You need to eat."

"I want to sit next to Lida," she said, cozying up to the woman, who looked pleased.

Feeling eyes on her, Allegra glanced up and saw Lord Carroll watched her. She nodded curtly at him and turned to her companions.

"I am glad you thought to bring Lady Viola to the picnic. Children need their fair share of exercise."

"I agree," Lady Lida said. "In fact, we have been taking Viola for a walk each day."

Allegra noted she used the word *we* and couldn't help but smile.

Lord Motley cleared his throat. "I know this house party is being held in honor of you and Miss Lyric, Miss Allegra, but Lady Lida and I feel blessed that it has given us the chance to come together. This was the very atmosphere we needed in which to get to know one another better, especially with Viola present."

He paused, looking to Lady Lida, who nodded. Already, Allegra knew what was coming.

"We plan to wed as soon as possible," the earl informed her. "We would like to make the announcement of our betrothal at

Shadowcrest, however. Do you and Miss Lyric have a preference as to when we might do so?"

"First of all, let me express my congratulations to the both of you," she said sincerely. "It does my heart good to see the two of you have found one another. As for your announcement, why don't you speak with Her Grace and my aunt? I will do the same. I know you are eager to share your good news with the others, and I will convey that to Her Grace and Mrs. Andrews."

"I will do so, Miss Allegra," Lord Motley said, happiness oozing from him. "Thank you so much."

"We will raise Viola to know that she had another mother, but she is young. I am grateful that I will also be able to call her my own," Lady Lida revealed.

"You will make for a most wonderful mother," Allegra assured her. "I hope you fill your nursery with many children."

They enjoyed the food and sunshine, and then she excused herself so she might talk with Sophie and Aunt Dinah. Lord Motley and Lady Lida took Viola down to where the rowboats were stored, and they would then go out onto the lake.

Making her way to the table, she deliberately did not search for where Lord Carroll was. She was afraid to make eye contact with him. He tempted her far too much, and she could not give in to his kisses again.

"I have a request," she began when she reached her destination, explaining how Lord Motley and Lady Lida wished to announce their engagement during the house party.

"Traditionally, betrothal announcements are made the last night of such an event," Aunt Dinah said.

Captain Andrews took his wife's hand and kissed it. "But who cares for tradition?" he said, turning the hand over and kissing her palm. "If they want to share their happy news with others, they should do so." He grinned. "In fact, it might even inspire others to make their own announcements."

"I agree," Sophie said. "Would you or Lyric mind if Lord Motley did so this evening, Allegra?"

"I can ask Lyric, but she and I are always of the same mind. I agree with the Captain. Let the earl claim Lady Lida publicly, the sooner, the better."

"Go check with Lyric now, dearest," Aunt Dinah encouraged. "If she agrees, Lord Motley can do the honors tonight after dinner when we gather in the drawing room."

"I will do that, Aunt."

Allegra looked about, not spying her twin anywhere. She stopped by Miss Bancroft and Lord Tillings, who was in the middle of teaching Miss Bancroft to fish, and asked, "Have you seen Lyric? I need to ask her something."

"I believe she went down to the boathouse, Miss Allegra," the viscount said.

"Thank you."

She hurried that way, wondering who Lyric might wish to go out on the water with. When she arrived, she saw Lord Motley had already put a rowboat into the water's edge and was assisting his daughter into it. Lady Lida already sat in the boat, smiling happily at the pair.

Waving to them, she spied Lyric standing next to another boat.

Lord Carroll stood beside her.

Anger sizzled through her, and Allegra marched toward them, saying, "You do not have to keep him occupied, Lyric. He should know well enough to stay away from me."

The earl's gaze met hers, his so intense that she sucked in a loud breath.

"Miss Lyric thought you and she might go for a row on the lake," he said. "I assisted her and brought the boat down for her."

The two of them getting away from everyone and out on the water was a brilliant idea on Lyric's part. They wouldn't have to keep avoiding Lord Carroll and Lord Blankenship and could relax as they floated along in peace.

"Splendid idea," she declared, brushing past him and stepping into the boat, taking her seat. "Ready when you are, Lyric," she said to her twin.

Her sister wore the oddest expression on her face. Their eyes met, and suddenly, Allegra knew this was a trap. That Lyric had betrayed her.

Lord Carroll quickly pushed off, jumping into the boat and taking up the oars. She clenched her jaw tightly as he rowed away from the shore. Away from the Judas that stood watching them.

Lyric mouthed, "I'm sorry," but Allegra was having none of it.

She wouldn't shout. She refused to make a scene in front of their guests. But she'd be damned if she said a single word to him. Lord only knew how long it would take her to forgive her twin for such perfidy.

"I know you are angry at me. And at Lyric."

He was calling her sister by her Christian name?

"Yes, she was complicit in getting you to the boat. It is because of what she knows I wish to tell you."

So, Lyric had confronted him without telling her about the conversation. Her twin was not given to betrayal. In fact, Allegra could not think of a single instance throughout their lives when they had even been angry at one another.

"All I ask is that you hear me out," he pleaded. "If you do so, I will return to shore at once and never try and speak to you again. But we needed to be alone for this."

"For what?" she snapped.

He withdrew something from his coat's inner pocket. "Read this. It will explain all."

With trepidation, Allegra accepted the folded parchment from him. She opened it and began to read.

CHAPTER THIRTEEN

ALLEGRA SAW NO salutation and realized it wasn't a letter to her.

It was a poem.

Her heart slammed against her ribs, thinking he had taken the time to write a poem for her. This arrogant, self-assured lord had humbled himself and taken up a quill. All for her.

She dared not look at him. Instead, she focused on the page before her.

In your arms, I found my place
In all I do, I see your face
My heart does beat in perfect time
To show my love for you in rhyme.

In your voice, I hear a song
The music stays within me all day long
Its melody one which lingers on
A symphony that makes me strong.

In your kiss, I taste the fire
My body flames upon the pyre
My passion for you will never tire

The flames now burn with pure desire.

My one true love, my heart's desire
Without you near I fight the mire
I pray you might open your heart
From this day forth we ne'er part.

Allegra, my love, in your heat
I am lost but still complete
Forever yours, my pledge to you
Forevermore, I will be true.

Allegra read the poem a second time, and then a third. With each pass, her throat grew tighter, the yearning in her greater. Finally, she could bear it no more. She lowered the page to her lap—and met Sterling's gaze.

In it, she saw his love for her. Truly saw it. And believed it. It wasn't something he could fake. No, the look in his hazel eyes echoed what the poem had revealed.

The Earl of Carroll loved her.

He had rested the oars as she read, so his hands were free to capture hers.

"I wrote it for you," he said, his voice hoarse. "For you alone, Allegra. I love you."

He choked when he uttered the last word. No, it was a sob. He was crying.

Because he thought she would not believe him. Believe in them.

"You wrote it for me," she said solemnly, squeezing his fingers. "You wrote it for me. The Earl of Carroll, notorious rake of London, penned a poem. For me."

"For you," he agreed, his eyes watery. "From now on, everything I do will be for you. That is, if you will—"

Allegra jerked him to her, the boat rocking slightly. His mouth fell against hers, and her hands went to his nape. Locking her fingers behind it, she made certain Lord Carroll wasn't going anywhere.

The kiss ignited the passion which had built over the past few days of being apart. Hungrily, greedily, they drank in one another, both slightly bewildered how this moment had come about.

When he broke the kiss, he said, "I love you, Allegra. I hope you will believe me when I tell you this."

"Only if you tell me every day, Sterling," she said pertly, her smile widening. "If you forget even one day, I will have to rid myself of you. Unless," she added, "you write me another love poem."

"I will write you one every day. It might kill me, but I will do it."

"I did not know you could write poetry."

"There is much you have to discover about me, Allegra Strong. I have written poetry for years. You are the first to learn of it. No, actually, Lyric was the first."

"You conspired together."

"We did," he admitted.

She pulled him toward her and kissed him again. "Is that why you went missing?"

"Yes," he said sheepishly. "Though I have penned poetry for years, I had never written a love poem before. I have never *been* in love before." He sighed. "It took many tries before this came together."

"I will cherish it always. I will frame it and place it by my bed."

"Our bed," he corrected. "You are going to marry me. We will share a bed. Always."

"Isn't that a bit . . . scandalous?" she asked, though she knew James and Sophie did and assumed Aunt Dinah and her captain did, as well.

"Yes. Couples in Polite Society keep to their own rooms. A husband will visit his wife upon occasion, trying to get an heir or spare off her. We will be different. We will share rooms, and I will bed you each morning when we awake and each night before we fall asleep." He grinned. "And possibly sometime during the day, as well."

"During the day?" she asked in mock horror. "In the light of the day? Why, you sound like a rake, my lord."

"My days as a rakehell are far behind me," he swore. "I promise to be faithful to you, my beloved wife. It will only be you. I love you." He shook his head. "It is so easy to say now. I cannot explain why I could not voice those three simple words before. I did love you when I offered for you. When you told me you loved me."

Allegra stroked his cheek. "You weren't ready to say them. You had to test yourself. See what it was like when we were apart."

"I failed the test miserably," he admitted. "I thought of you every waking moment, and I dreamed of you at night." He kissed her, hard. "Promise me we will never be apart. Ever."

Smiling broadly, she replied, "Well, if you are to tell me you love me every day, I suppose we must remain together. In sickness and in health. Until death do us part."

"If you go before me, I will follow you into death,'" he said. "I would not wish to stay on this earth without you in my arms and by my side."

Sterling kissed her again, the most tender kiss of their acquaintance.

"Thank you for forgiving me," he said earnestly. "And please do not hold anything against Lyric. She read the poem. I told her I loved you. She pledged to help bring us together."

"My twin did her part. We will do ours by marrying."

"When?" he asked eagerly. "I do not wish to wait long."

"You will have to wait a couple of weeks," she told him. "Georgie and August are due back from Scotland, and the part of my family touring the Lake District should also be back by then. That is Aunt Matty and my cousins Mirella and Effie. Miss

Feathers, as well. She is Effie's governess and was once mine. They all must be at our wedding and share in our joy."

"Do you wish to wed at Shadowcrest?"

She nodded. "Strongs always wed in the chapel. It is not far from the house. Do you mind waiting for the others to arrive home?"

He kissed her. "I would marry you tomorrow if I could, but I understand how deep your family ties are. We will wait until your relatives are all home. Reading the banns takes three weeks, though. They could return sooner. Because of that, I plan to leave tomorrow and purchase a special license. That way, we can marry as soon as they arrive."

Allegra laughed, joy filling her at his eagerness to become her husband. "At least give them time to freshen up from their long travels," she teased. "Don't worry. Aunt Dinah will have everything prepared and ready to go. We will simply say the word, and she will make things happen."

"I like your aunt very much," Sterling said. "She is the one who had faith in me. Who saw something others didn't. If not for this invitation, I doubt we would have come together."

"It was fate," she said. "Shall we announce our betrothal this evening? There is already another one which will be made known."

"Tillings and Miss Bancroft?" he guessed.

"Actually, Lord Motley asked for Lady Lida's hand and wishes to inform the house party guests this evening of their plans."

"Then yes, by all means, let them go first. Then we can share our own happy news."

Her heart grew heavy a moment. Already, he could read her so well and asked, "What is it? Lyric, I assume."

"Yes. While I know she will be happy for us, her own heart has been trampled upon by Lord Blankenship."

"I think things will work out the way they are meant to be," he said cryptically.

Allegra thought Sterling knew something about Lord Blankenship's feelings regarding Lyric, but she supposed he had been sworn to secrecy by the viscount. She hoped it would be the last secret ever that lay between them, because she wanted them to always share everything with one another.

"Row us back to shore," she said. "I will need to tell Aunt Dinah there is to be more than one announcement tonight."

"I will need to thank your aunt personally. I should also speak with His Grace." Sterling frowned. "Or perhaps Mr. Strong?"

"You may give them advance warning of the betrothal announcement, but they both have let me know that this decision is mine alone to make. You do not need to seek their permission."

"Then I will tell them of our plans and let them know the wedding will take place as soon as everyone returns to Shadowcrest. Will Lyric stand with you?"

"Yes. It could only be her. But what of you?"

He frowned. "I would ask Blankenship, but I don't know how he would take being around Lyric during such a happy occasion. I would also not wish to make it uncomfortable for her in any way."

"We can speak of it later," Allegra said, pinning her hopes on Lord Blankenship gathering enough courage to admit to Lyric that he loved her.

They returned to the boathouse, having seen other couples out on the lake. Blankenship was missing, while Lyric sat with her aunt and the captain. Hand-in-hand, they went to the trio. She saw Lyric's sweet smile, and her twin flew from her seat, rushing to Allegra and throwing her arms about her.

"Oh, you said yes. I am so happy for you!" her twin exclaimed. She turned to Sterling and offered him a hug. "It will be nice having you in the family, my lord."

"Sterling. Please. After all, you are to be my new sister. I never had siblings, and now I have more than I can count."

They went to the table. Aunt Dinah beamed at them, and said, "It is another love match in the Strong family."

"It is, Mrs. Andrews," Sterling said. "I love your niece more than I thought possible. She will no doubt keep me in line."

Aunt Dinah laughed. "They say reformed rakes make the best husbands."

"They do?" Allegra and the captain asked in unison.

"They do," Sterling assured them. "Allegra told me that Lord Motley wishes to announce his betrothal this evening. Might we also make ours known after that?"

"Of course," Aunt Dinah said. "I will leave now and make certain champagne is chilled. We can share the news when we gather in the drawing room after dinner this evening." She looked to Lyric. "How are you?"

Lyric smiled ruefully. "I have been better. But I am ecstatic for Allegra and Sterling. I think they will be most happy together."

"If not for your interference, Lyric, this would not have happened," Sterling said. "Thank you." He took Lyric's hands and raised them to his lips, kissing them tenderly.

"Shall we return to the house, love?" the captain asked, helping Aunt Dinah to her feet.

"Do you wish to tell James and Sophie?" Aunt Dinah asked as they all fell into step.

"We will do so together," Sterling replied for them both. "And seek out Mr. Strong and let him know, as well."

When they reached the house, Aunt Dinah and the captain headed for the kitchens. Allegra turned to Lyric, hugging her tightly.

"Thank you again for your intervention. I would not be so happy now if not for what you did."

Lyric smiled. "What are twins for?"

EPILOGUE

Three weeks later—Shadowcrest's Chapel

STERLING PACED BEHIND the chapel, eager to get on with the ceremony. He looked to Silas, who stood looking out at the perfect September morning. His friend appeared so calm.

"How can you be standing there so patient?" he demanded. "I am champing at the bit. Ready to make Allegra mine."

His friend, a man with whom he had spent many a wild night over the years, smiled at him. "Patience, Sterling. I know it is not your strong suit."

The only place he had shown patience was in bed. With Allegra. After he had purchased the special license in Doctors' Commons and made a quick trip to Carrollwood to inform his staff that he would be bringing home his countess in a few weeks, he had returned to Shadowcrest. Allegra had come to him each night. They had not wanted to wait to consummate their marriage. If a babe appeared a couple of weeks before nine months, well, babes did that kind of thing. Came in their own time.

And every babe that Allegra birthed would be one who was utterly and completely loved.

Sterling showed the most incredible patience in bed, teasing and tormenting his sweet love until she was panting with desire. Lovemaking with Allegra had been a totally unique experience, unlike his couplings with any other woman. She was fire and light and love, all rolled into one.

"I am merely ready to be wed," he told Silas.

The two men had grown close over the past few weeks. Silas, too, had gone straight from London to Chase Oaks to take care of business matters and make certain preparations had begun to welcome his wife to her new home. Fortunately, Carrollwood was in East Sussex, slightly over fifty miles from Chase Oaks, located in Essex. While not close neighbors, the distance could be covered by two good teams of horses in three hours or so, with Shadowcrest situated between the two estates. Sterling believed the two men would be seeing one another often because their wives would require regular visits between their families and their loved ones in Kent.

He looked to Silas, whom he had gambled and wenched with many a night, content that their friendship had taken a new turn. Both men had found love, and their priorities had changed drastically. Sterling looked at Silas as the brother he had never had, just as he looked upon Lyric as a sister.

Of course, the Strongs had pulled both men into the loving arms of their family, something he would be eternally grateful for. He was able to see how a true family acted toward one another and was determined he would raise his in the same vein.

James appeared. It was still a little difficult for Sterling to call the duke anything but His Grace, but he was trying hard to do so.

"The family has all been seated. My cousins' carriage is almost here. Sophie and Dinah said you are to come inside."

He looked to Silas. "It looks as if we are doing this."

Silas grinned. "It appears that way. Shall we?"

While they stepped through the rear door of the chapel, James parted from them, heading around the chapel to the front. No doubt he wanted to greet his cousins before taking a seat with the rest of the family.

As they entered the building and moved to the front, he looked out at the large, extended family he would now be claiming as his own. Though he and Silas had yet to meet Pippa and Seth, who would not return to England for some time, they had become friendly with August and Georgie, who had arrived from Scotland less than ten minutes after all the betrothals had been announced. The marquess and marchioness were a delight, and when Sterling looked at August, he barely saw the scars the man bore from his time at war or gave August's eyepatch a second thought.

Aunt Matty had arrived a week later, bringing Mirella, Effie, and Miss Feathers, the governess, with her. The older woman mothered both Silas and him, while Mirella and Effie were friendly. Mirella, who planned to make her come-out next Season, would undoubtedly take the *ton* by storm with her beauty and poise. Effie, who was a tomboy and the most outspoken girl he had ever met, was a sheer delight. Sterling hoped his new sisters would find as satisfying a love as he and Allegra had.

The two men stood at the front of the chapel, the local clergyman from the village next to them.

Leaning close, he told Silas, "Lyric did an outstanding job decorating the chapel."

His friend grinned. "She did have help from her sisters, but it was all her vision. I cannot wait for her to get her hands on the gardens at Chase Oaks."

James appeared, striding down the aisle and taking a seat beside Sophie, who was enormous at this point. The babe was due to come sometime next week. Sterling prayed that Sophie would at least make it through the wedding without interruption.

James nodded to Mirella, who sat at the pianoforte, and she began to play. The doors opened, and Caleb Strong stepped through the arch, one of his sisters on each arm. Proudly, the Shadowcrest steward led the trio up the aisle.

His heart melted at the sight of Allegra. Her stable hair was piled high atop her head, and her wedding gown hugged her curves. Caleb kissed her cheek and handed her off to Sterling, who slipped his bride's hand through the crook of his arm. He basked in the warmth of her, still amazed that this lovely creature was all his. Or would be, as soon as they spoke their vows.

They did so, his voice strong, his heart committed to the woman by his side. When Sterling slid the wedding band onto Allegra's finger, a sense of calm enveloped him.

He looked on as Silas and Lyric repeated their own vows. Lyric's russet hair was brushed back from her face, swept into a simple chignon. She carried an arrangement of orange blossoms, a scent she often wore, while Allegra held a bouquet of celosia and asters. Both arrangements had been put together by Mrs. Andrews for her nieces.

Silas's face told the world how much he loved his bride. Sterling supposed his own reflected the great love he held for Allegra.

Then his friend slid Lyric's wedding band onto her hand, and both couples faced the clergyman. A final prayer was offered, and then the man announced they were husbands and wives.

He took his countess into his arms for a slow, lingering kiss. Their first as man and wife, with thousands more to come over the years.

Breaking the kiss, he gazed down at his bride. "I love you, darling Allegra."

"I love you more, you handsome devil," she teased.

They moved up the aisle to applause, which came from not only the Strong family but others who had come from the village to witness the double ceremony. Also present were the newly-wedded Lord and Lady Motley, along with Lady Viola. Seated beside them were the new Lord and Lady Lamkin, as well. Lord Tillings had sent his regrets, saying his and Miss Bancroft's wedding would be taking place the following day at her parish church in Somerset. The viscount had invited them to visit whenever they liked, however, and they all looked forward to attending next Season together.

Sterling assisted Allegra into the coach and climbed in beside her, stealing another kiss from her. Silas and Lyric joined them, and the coachman drove them the short distance to Shadowcrest. He would return for the duke and duchess. These days, the duchess only took a few steps at a time, saying she grew short of breath even crossing a room.

Soon, everyone was gathered at the wedding breakfast. Toasts were made and food was eaten. Mrs. Andrews had hired some local musicians, and even dancing occurred during the celebration.

Captain Andrews pulled Sterling and Silas aside, telling them, "You have wed true jewels, gentlemen. Treat them kindly and love them well. Dinah looks upon those girls as hers because she raised them. That means I am their father now—and you will have to answer to me," he joked.

"We are happy to be related to you, Captain," he said. "But it is time we said our goodbyes."

"I agree," Silas said.

Both men were taking their brides to their country estates. Trunks had already been packed and loaded, and Sterling went to find Allegra.

"It is time," he said. "We will be back in a week or so," he promised.

Both twins had insisted upon returning to Shadowcrest once Sophie had given birth. He readily agreed, knowing he would have his wife to himself for a week or more. Besides, he did not mind returning to Kent to celebrate the birth of the duke and duchess' first child.

They made a quick trip about the room, thanking their guests for coming. Then all the Strongs went outside where the carriages were waiting. Allegra and Lyric hugged all their relatives and then each other, whispering in one another's ears and giggling.

He handed Allegra into his coach and waved goodbye to everyone. "We will see you soon."

Once inside, the door closed behind him, he scooped up his

bride and placed her in his lap as the carriage traveled down the lane.

"What did you and Lyric find so humorous?" he asked.

She blushed. "Just twin talk," she said.

"Might it have to do with comparing wedding nights?" he said knowingly.

"Oh, you are impossible," his countess declared before wrapping her arms about his neck and kissing him thoroughly.

After a long time, she broke the kiss. "How long did you say it is until we reach Carrollwood?" she asked, mischief written across her heart-shaped face.

"If you are asking if we have time to make love in a moving carriage, we most certainly do."

"It is bouncing along the road, almost as riding a horse is," she noted. "I think I would like to be on top, Lord Carroll. I rather like that position because I feel in control when I ride you."

He kissed her. "And I like you there, Lady Carroll."

As their carriage bumped merrily along to East Sussex, they made love not once—but twice.

And both times were the best couplings of his life.

Sterling held Allegra close, her face buried in his neck as she snuggled against him.

"I love you, Sterling," she murmured.

"I love you, Allegra. Forever and ever."

THE VISCOUNT'S HEART

Part 2 of
Courtship at Shadowcrest

Alexa Aston

PROLOGUE

Chase Oaks—Essex—February 1810

S ILAS CHASE, VISCOUNT Blankenship, grinned at his uncle. Raising his glass, he said, "Happy Birthday, Uncle Oscar."

"Same to you, my boy," his uncle replied, tapping Silas' snifter against his own and then taking a deep drink of the whisky.

They sat in the study at Chase Oaks, his country estate. Although Silas held the viscountcy, it was his uncle who ran the estate for him. Uncle Oscar, who had never wed, had been steward at another lord's estate when his brother dropped dead from a sudden heart attack. Silas had only been eight and ten, about to leave for university, bewildered by what he should do.

Uncle Oscar had smoothed everything over, handling matters with the solicitor, promising his nephew that he would come to Chase Oaks and manage the property for him, along with anything else that came up. He had told Silas university was a time of exploration. To learn about himself and the world. That Chase Oaks would be safe while he matured.

His uncle was the only one who ever made Silas feel loved. His parents ignored him, as did most adults of Polite Society when they produced children. They eagerly awaited an heir and when they got one, promptly abandoned them to the nursery. It was a familiar story he had heard, over and over, both at Eton and Cambridge. Everyone talked about how you were supposed to value family, but Silas had never felt a connection to his, other than with Uncle Oscar.

Because he had never felt loved by his parents, he had sought it elsewhere, from the classroom to the playing fields. He was bright and charming, which took him a long way. Other boys wanted to be his friend, and his good looks allowed him to get his way in school—and with women. Through his education, Silas had hated rules and broke all he could, often in the company of his friend, August Holt. August had left for the war, though, after they had finished their careers at Cambridge. He had lost track of the man he had called brother, thinking of August often and hoping his friend wasn't dead at the hands of some French bastard.

"Now that you are an entire quarter-century old, what plans do you have for your life?" Uncle Oscar asked.

Silas was almost ashamed, knowing he had none. Ever since he had left Cambridge, he spent quite a bit of his time in town. The *ton* looked upon him as one of its most charming rogues. He drank and gambled and ran with a fast crowd in London, but he did come home to Chase Oaks upon occasion. Those weeks had grown special to him. Uncle Oscar had made considerable improvements on the estate, and it ran like a fine Swiss clock. In a way, he almost wished he would remain in the country for greater lengths of time, especially since his life as a rake was growing old.

"Are you thinking me long in the tooth?" he teased. "If anyone is, it is you. I might be five and twenty today, but you are celebrating five and fifty today, Uncle."

For a moment, his uncle's countenance turned sad. "I have little to show for my years on this earth, Silas. I never wed. Never had children. Never owned a house—or anything else."

"You are like a father to me," he insisted. "Much more one than my blood one ever was. Papa and Mama ignored me for the most part."

Uncle Oscar shrugged. "It is the nature of Polite Society, my boy. Our father did the same to us. The cycle merely repeats itself." He paused, meeting Silas' gaze. "But I do believe family is very important. I hope you will be a different man—and a much different father—than the one you had. I pray every night that you will find a woman to love and that you will be a father present in your children's lives."

He snorted. "I have no plans to wed anytime soon, Uncle Oscar, and you know it."

His uncle grew serious. "I have said nothing to you, Silas, but this is a milestone birthday, so I will loosen my tongue for a bit. You are a man now. A viscount. You have an estate full of tenants who depend upon you. I know I encouraged you to find yourself. Sow your wild oats. But the time has come to grow up."

Frowning, he said, "You mean settle down. You want me to wed."

Nodding, Uncle Oscar said, "Yes, I do, Silas. I believe you can break out of the mold of rogue and become happy with what you have in life. I wish for you to become more actively involved in the managing of Chase Oaks. I hope you will find the love of a good woman and produce several children."

"Where is this coming from?" he demanded. "While I do enjoy my visits with you when I come to Chase Oaks, I have a life in town, Uncle. Yes, I will wed at some point and produce the necessary heir apparent. As far as love is concerned? Frankly, I doubt it exists. I have never witnessed it between a man and woman, certainly not any of the couples I see during the Season."

Uncle Oscar smiled ruefully at him. "Your parents gave you no love, and you have sought it in the arms of others. I know. I hear things, Silas."

He flushed, uncomfortable at the turn of their conversation. It was true. He had desperately thought to find love. Instead, only emptiness abounded everywhere. It was why he remained a rogue, a man who refused to commit to one woman. Silas assumed eventually, he would make the typical *ton* marriage, coupling with his wife to get an heir and spare off her, but leading a separate life from her, with a mistress and spending time with his friends.

"It is hard for me to listen to you preach about the value of family when you had none yourself," he said, a bit too harshly, causing his uncle to flinch.

Tempering his tone, Silas said, "If you need me to spend more time at Chase Oaks, I will commit to doing so. You already have me interested in crops and gardening, in particular, something my friends in town tease me about unmercifully. As far as taking a wife, though? That is nothing I am concerned about anytime soon."

Uncle Oscar drained his snifter and set it down. "I want so much for you, my boy."

He frowned. "What has caused you to become so contemplative, Uncle? Is it this birthday you had today? Do you feel you are in the twilight of your life? Are you having any regrets?"

"I do not have long to live, Silas," Uncle Oscar revealed.

He sucked in a quick breath. "What?"

"I have been short of breath lately. It is harder for me to get around. The doctor says it is my heart. That something is wrong with it."

Concern filled him. "How long has he given you?" he asked carefully, tamping down the emotions surging within him.

"Not long. He thinks a few months. Perhaps longer if I behave myself. Take my medicine and get plenty of rest." His uncle smiled. "So, this is, most likely, the final birthday I celebrate. I just want you to be happy, Silas. Truly happy. You think you are, gadding about town, wearing the latest fashions, throwing money at women and upon gaming tables. But I tell you now—happiness is here."

His uncle tapped his chest. "It is within you. And if you can find a woman to love and partner with, it will flourish."

"You should not have kept this from me," he chided, a feeling of panic beginning to descend upon him. His uncle was the one true, good thing in his life. He could not imagine a world without Uncle Oscar in it.

"Well, now you know. Promise me that you will go into this upcoming Season and instead of playing the rake, you will have an eye to finding a wife."

Silas shook his head. "I cannot promise that, Uncle."

Uncle Oscar laughed. "Then I hope love smites you hard, my boy. That you fall hopelessly in love with a woman and find that you cannot live without her."

He stiffened. "The most I will do is look more closely at the ladies paraded about on the Marriage Mart, Uncle. I may take a wife sooner than I anticipated, but love will not be a part of this complicated equation that is marriage."

His uncle sighed. "At least you will look. That was more than I expected from you. I know it will be difficult to pull away from the friends you make merry with. Leaving your roguish ways behind might be the hardest obstacle you have faced in life."

"Let me help you to bed," Silas offered, his mind spinning. "You need your rest. You said so yourself."

Worry filled him. He had come to depend upon Uncle Oscar more than he realized.

Taking his uncle's elbow, he helped him rise from the chair. Why hadn't he noticed his uncle's hair had grayed more over recent visits? Or that he moved more slowly and wore a pained expression? Silas had been so caught up in himself that he had not thought to think of the only person who had ever shown him a sliver of love.

He guided Uncle Oscar to his bedchamber. The Chase Oaks steward had always been given a cottage upon the estate, but Silas had insisted that his uncle live in the main house and dine in it. Uncle Oscar had drawn the line at having a servant assigned to be his valet, though, preferring to take care of himself.

"Do you need any help?"

A loud snort sounded. "I am not that feeble, Silas."

"Then I bid you a good night."

Returning to his own rooms, Silas rang for his valet and readied for bed. He lay awake a good while, thinking on everything he had discussed with his uncle.

In the morning, he went down to the breakfast room, fretting when he saw his uncle had yet to arrive.

"I think I will go check on Mr. Chase," he told the butler.

When he tapped on Uncle Oscar's door, he received no response. Pushing open the door, Silas entered the bedchamber, which was still dark, with its curtains drawn.

He found his uncle still in bed, his lips turned up in a smile, as if he were content.

His uncle was also gone. Silas touched his cheek, finding it cold. Uncle Oscar had passed sometime during the night. He wondered if in telling his nephew of his condition, it allowed Uncle Oscar to finally let go.

One thing Silas did know. It *was* time he grew up. No more playing the rascal, merely seeking a good time. He now bore the full brunt of his responsibilities on his own shoulders, ones which Uncle Oscar had taken on for Silas when he was too young to do so himself.

The death of his beloved uncle had him completely rethinking his life. He would go into this Season with purpose, finding a wife and planning for his future. For all he knew, the heart problems which had troubled his father and uncle might have been passed down to him, as well. He needed to secure an heir—and the future of Chase Oaks.

Bending, he pressed his lips against Uncle Oscar's brow.

"I love you, Uncle. And I will become the man you thought I could be. That, I promise."

CHAPTER ONE

Shadowcrest—Kent—August 1810

Lyric Strong eagerly joined her twin and aunt as they made their way outside to wait for the guests in the first carriage rolling up the lane now. She was excited about the house party James and Sophie were giving in her and Allegra's honor. They had not made their come-outs as planned this past spring, mainly due to Allegra being so incensed by their father not contributing a farthing to the process.

She did not like to think about her father or brother Theodore. Her father had abandoned all responsibilities to his motherless twin daughters, placing them into the hands of Aunt Dinah, who had been the Duchess of Seaton. Aunt Dinah raised her own twins alongside Allegra and Lyric, and eventually added two more daughters to the nursery. Mirella and Effie had left yesterday with Aunt Matty on a tour of the Lake District while the house party would be going on. Mirella preferred to make her own come-out next spring and did not want to harm her cousins' chances of finding a husband during the party.

She and her twin had asked Aunt Dinah who had been invited to Shadowcrest, and they had learned about the three women and their chaperones. Her aunt had been vague in regard to the gentlemen invited to the house party, saying she did not wish to unduly influence her nieces' opinions by speaking too much about the gentlemen who had been invited. Lyric trusted her aunt's good judgment, knowing those men would be not only suitable but also honorable ones.

More than anything, Lyric hoped that Lord Blankenship would be among those five.

The viscount had come to the wedding held in June in the Shadowcrest chapel. Her cousin Georgie had wed August, and the couple was now on their honeymoon at Dalmara in Scotland. Sophie had thought to invite Lord Blankenship to the ceremony, and he stood with August during it. Apparently, they had been the closest of friends while at Eton and Cambridge, only parting when August left for war.

Something had struck Lyric about Lord Blankenship. She had studied him during the wedding ceremony and found him pleasing to her eye. Knowing he was dear to August, a man Lyric already thought the world of, she decided the viscount was someone worth knowing.

Unfortunately, they had never even exchanged a single word. After the ceremony ended, they all returned to Shadowcrest for the wedding breakfast in the dining room. Lord Blankenship was placed at the far end of the table, seated between her Aunt Matty and Allegra. Lyric glanced at him surreptitiously throughout the breakfast but was too far away to make any conversation with him.

When Georgie and August left immediately after the breakfast, Lord Blankenship did, as well. He spoke of business in town and thanked Sophie for inviting him to witness the marriage of his good friend.

As the viscount mounted the steps to his carriage, he had turned and waved farewell to all the Strongs. His gaze had come to rest upon Lyric for a moment, sending a chill up her spine. Not one of fear, but a delicious tingling which she wished to explore.

That was why she hoped Aunt Dinah had thought to include

Lord Blankenship on the guest list.

The grand carriage pulled up to the house, followed by a more modest one which would contain servants and luggage. Soon, she was meeting Lord and Lady Crowell and their daughter. Lady Lida was friendly and talkative, as was her cousin Miss Markle, another guest. While Allegra showed Lord and Lady Crowell to their bedchamber, Lyric guided the cousins to their shared one. She even stayed while a maid helped them to unpack, learning that Miss Markle enjoyed dancing and doing needlework, while Lady Lida was interested in riding and dancing.

Allegra arrived and told the ladies that hot water was being sent up and they should rest from their journey, asking them to meet in the drawing room at four o'clock for tea.

Within a quarter-hour, another carriage appeared, and they went out to greet the new arrivals. James and Sophie would not meet any of their guests until tea this afternoon. Sophie was increasing and had a little over a month before she delivered their first child. The duchess was trying to rest as much as possible, as well as getting some work done for her shipping company.

A gentleman emerged from the carriage, and immediately, Lyric noted the air of sadness which clung to him, guessing he was the widower Aunt Dinah had mentioned to her and Allegra. He assisted a woman who held a small girl with golden curls in her arms. The girl reached for the gentleman, and he took her from the nursery governess' arms.

Turning, he greeted them. "Good afternoon, Your Grace."

Aunt Dinah smiled indulgently. "It is good of you to accept our invitation, Lord Motley."

"I would not have come unless you had allowed me to bring Viola. Not many hostesses would have found that acceptable, and I thank you from the bottom of my heart, Your Grace."

"I have wed recently, my lord. I am Mrs. Andrews now. May I introduce to you my nieces?"

Aunt Dinah did the honors, and Lyric and Allegra said hello both to Lord Motley and his daughter.

Her aunt asked, "Might I hold her? It has been many years since I have been around a little one."

"She is a bit shy. I will see if she will come to you, Mrs. Andrews." The earl looked at his daughter. "Viola, we have come to visit Mrs. Andrews and her nieces. Would you like to go and see her?"

The little girl's mouth trembled slightly.

"I would be happy to show you the nursery, Lady Viola," Aunt Dinah said to the girl. "I raised my girls in it, and they have left some toys behind that you might wish to play with. Dolls. Blocks."

The girl's eyes lit up. "Dolls? Dolls," she repeated.

Aunt Dinah held out her arms, and the child came to her willingly.

"Lady Viola and I will go to the nursery now."

"I will go with you, Aunt Dinah," Allegra volunteered. "I can show Lady Viola some of our dolls and tell her their names."

The group left the nursery governess following, and Lyric turned to Lord Motley. "Might I show you to your bedchamber, my lord?"

"Thank you, Miss Strong."

As they entered the house, she told him, "Please call me Miss Lyric. Aunt Dinah believes it would be too complicated to have two Misses Strong at the house party this week, so I am to be Miss Lyric, and my sister is to be Miss Allegra."

"I can do so, Miss Lyric." The earl, with golden curls just like his daughter's, smiled at her, and she felt they were off to a good start.

Half an hour later, another carriage arrived, this time bearing two gentlemen coming from town. Aunt Dinah introduced her and Allegra to Viscount Tillings first. He was quite good-looking but appeared completely tongue-tied in the presence of women. His companion was the Earl of Lamkin, and he was jovial and outgoing, smoothing over his friend's shyness.

Allegra, being the more talkative of the two of them, suggested that she escort Lord Lamkin to his bedchamber. Her twin nodded at her, and Lyric knew she had done so on purpose. Of the two of them, Lyric was the more reserved. She hoped she might be able to draw out Lord Tillings.

Smiling at the viscount, she said, "Allow me to take you to your bedchamber, my lord."

He smiled shyly. "Thank you, Miss Lyric."

She allowed Allegra and Lord Lamkin to get far ahead of them before she took Lord Tillings inside the house.

"Your friend seems quite gregarious," she commented.

He shrugged. "Lamkin is better than I am in social situations, Miss Lyric."

"My sister and I are twins. I am certain you noticed that we favor one another in the face, but we are very different people. Allegra has never met a stranger and converses easily with all she meets. I can be a bit withdrawn at times and have a tendency to study others before approaching them and sharing anything of myself."

She smiled brightly at him. "I believe we will enjoy getting know one another during this house party, my lord. Aunt Dinah created the guest list, and I know it will be a good mix of individuals."

They reached his bedchamber, and the viscount said, "Thank you for opening up a bit to me, Miss Lyric. I have just come off the Season, and I found it overwhelming. I prefer to retreat to the country and recover from having listened to so much talk going on about me." He paused, sincerity in his tone as he added, "But I believe this house party might give me a chance to know others better. I look forward to spending more time with you and the other guests."

She let him know that tea would be served at four, and he promised to be in the drawing room at that time.

The next to arrive were the Misses Bancroft. The elder was aunt to the younger and quite domineering. Lyric felt sorry for how she ordered her niece about and offered to take the younger

Miss Bancroft up to her bedchamber.

As they ascended the stairs, she said, "I hear that you are good friends with my cousin Georgie."

Miss Bancroft, whose face was quite plain, suddenly changed before Lyric's eyes. Her smile transformed her features into a pleasant countenance.

"Oh, I quite admire Lady Georgina," Miss Bancroft shared. "I will admit to you, Miss Lyric, that I am a wallflower through and through. My aunt demanded I do a Season. Then another and another. I am not popular with the gentlemen of the *ton*. As you can see, my face is plain."

"Everything is not about your appearance," Lyric insisted. "Georgie would be first and foremost to say that."

Miss Bancroft nodded sagely. "Your sister was quite brave, going against the *ton* and following her heart."

Lyric understood what this young lady meant. August had been terribly scarred in the war, even losing an eye in battle. While Polite Society had most likely judged him harshly for even making an appearance during the Season, her cousin had seen beyond the scars and to the man August truly was. Theirs was a great love story, and when Lyric looked at August, she—like Georgie—did not even notice his scars.

"The *ton* can be most judgmental," Lyric said, "but people who are sincere will never judge you strictly on your looks, Miss Bancroft. I am certain the guests my aunt has invited to this house party will be more than willing to get to know you better."

The woman smiled wistfully. "I do not hold any expectations of a betrothal for myself by the end of this house party, Miss Lyric, but I do hope I will make a few friends." She smiled shyly. "Including you."

"You are friends with Georgie, which means you must become friends with Allegra and me."

Lyric let Miss Bancroft know about tea being served at four and told her she looked forward to speaking further with her then.

As she started down the stairs, their butler was coming up them.

"Miss Lyric, another carriage is about to arrive. Mrs. Andrews asked that you come outside to greet these guests."

"Thank you, Forrester," she said, hurrying down the stairs and out the door.

She went to stand beside her aunt, Allegra on Aunt Dinah's other side, and watched the carriage pull up. She could see two men within, and her heart began racing.

One of them was Lord Blankenship.

Her heart continued to pound rapidly as they exited the vehicle. Aunt Dinah welcomed Lord Blankenship first, and he greeted the three of them. The other gentleman was Lord Carroll. He, too, was nice-looking, but she found her attention wandering back to Lord Blankenship and offered to take him to his room.

The viscount turned his gaze upon her. "I am sorry we did not get a chance to speak at the wedding breakfast, Miss Lyric," he told her. "I cannot tell you how impressed I was when I entered the chapel at Shadowcrest the day of the wedding. August told me you had been the one to decorate it, and I was amazed by your creativity."

She felt the blush heating her cheeks. "Thank you, my lord. I have always been interested in gardening and have spent many hours on my knees, digging in the dirt. Aunt Dinah taught me all I know about arranging flowers, and it is something I enjoy doing. We have had three weddings at Shadowcrest this past year. The duke wed the duchess. My cousin Pippa married Viscount Hopewell. And then you were present when my cousin Georgie married your friend. I decorated the chapel for each of those weddings. I also arranged flowers for Aunt Dinah's ceremony. It was held in town recently."

"Yes, I saw the announcement in the newspapers. I think it wonderful that Her Grace seems so happy in her new marriage. She is glowing."

They reached the bedchamber which had been assigned to

him, and Lyric paused.

"Aunt Dinah was made to wed the Duke of Seaton when she was quite young. She was most unhappy over the years, saying the only joy in her life came from her girls. Because of that, she is adamant that we all be free to choose the man we wish to wed and not be forced into matrimony."

His gaze bore into her, and Lyric shivered involuntarily.

"Then I will make my intentions known, Miss Lyric. I wish to get to know you much better during my stay at Shadowcrest. I hope a friendship will spring up between us—and that it blossoms into something more."

CHAPTER TWO

SILAS READIED HIMSELF for dinner with the help of his valet. He had enjoyed the first gathering of the guests at tea and made certain that he joined the small group seated with Miss Lyric when the teacarts arrived. Lord Lamkin and Lord Tillings had joined him, as had Miss Markle and Miss Bancroft. Lamkin was cheerful as always, and he and Miss Markle seemed to be drawn to one another. Silas had danced with Miss Markle twice during the Season and found her a bit too talkative for him.

As for Tillings and Miss Bancroft, they were both very quiet when tea began. He and Miss Lyric had spent teatime trying to draw each out of their shells. He had known of Tillings at Eton, but the future viscount had chosen to attend Oxford, while Silas had gone to Cambridge. The past few years, the crowd Silas had run with was far too boisterous for the likes of Tilling. Yet Silas now enjoyed the conversation he had with the viscount, as well as Miss Bancroft.

He had never seen her before. Or rather, he had never noticed her before. She mentioned that she had been out for three Seasons now. He assumed because of her looks that she had gathered with the other wallflowers at the far end of ballrooms, a group he had always avoided. Yet, Miss Bancroft surprised him. She was quite witty and well-read. Silas regretted having been so shallow as to judge women strictly on their attractiveness.

At least she and Tillings opened up some, and he hoped they might find common ground. Miss Markle began telling the pair of a carriage ride gone awry in Hyde Park.

Which allowed him time to speak with Miss Lyric.

He had boldly declared his interest in her when she escorted him to his bedchamber and was glad he had, especially seeing the gentlemen the Duke and Duchess of Seaton had invited to the house party honoring the duke's cousins. All the men were intelligent and handsome. Silas knew, despite his reserved nature, Tillings would be on the hunt for a wife. He assumed the same of Motley, who had been widowed when his wife died in childbirth.

As far as Lamkin was concerned, the earl was always popular at gatherings and may well have been invited merely for his outgoing nature and sense of humor, though Silas had heard rumors that Lamkin's mother wanted her son to wed. The guest who surprised him most was his former close friend, Lord Carroll, who was known for seducing women and his abilities to tell a story better than most. Carroll was the last man Silas would have expected at a house party, simply because they had the reputation of being a hotbed for betrothals. The last thing the Earl of Carroll searched for was a wife.

While Carroll might not be interested in settling down anytime soon, it was a strong possibility with the other three gentlemen. All had good qualities and would make for respectable husbands. If they vied for Miss Lyric's hand, he would have stiff competition. It made him doubly glad to have let her know of his interest in her.

Silas did not expect to make a love match with Lyric Strong, but he was definitely attracted to her. He thought they could make a solid marriage and be respectful of one another. She had a large family who obviously supported her, and he—being an only child—was curious to witness the dynamic between her and those family members present. Miss Lyric had spoken of her aunt's desire for her niece to wed her choice of gentleman.

Silas wanted to be the man she selected.

He tied his own cravat now, something he preferred to do, and then dismissed his valet. At tea, he had learned tonight would be a typical evening, dinner followed by the ladies entertaining them in the drawing room with their musical prowess. He hoped if he were not seated next to Miss Lyric at dinner, that he could sit with her later in the evening.

Tomorrow, they were to go riding and see a bit of the area. Tea would take place that afternoon on the terrace, and then Her Grace had mentioned they would break into pairs for an evening of card play.

Silas intended to be by Miss Lyric's side every step of the way.

He wouldn't make a pest of himself, but he wanted to take every opportunity he could in order to get to know the serene beauty, as well as allow her to learn about him.

In the corridor, he came across Lord Motley and Lord Tillings, both leaving their bedchambers. The three of them went to the drawing room together, where they were to gather for a drink before going into dinner each night.

Motley explained, "I just came from seeing my daughter put to bed."

"You brought your child to a house party?" he asked, surprised by the admission.

"Viola and I are very close," the earl explained. "I have been both mother and father to her since I lost my wife. I think it was generous of the Seatons to allow me to use their nursery while I attend the house party."

"Are you looking for another wife?" Tillings asked quietly.

"I have made no secret of it," the earl said. "I am afraid I found too many of the women in town to be blinded by wealth and titles. While I do have both, I did not come across one whom I believed would accept Viola as her own."

"You must admit, Motley, that would be hard for a young woman," Silas pointed out. "Naturally, a woman would favor a child she birthed over a stepchild."

Motley's mouth set stubbornly. "If a woman cannot accept Viola completely, then she has no business being my wife."

Silas turned to Tillings. "Are you hoping to make a match at Shadowcrest, Lord Tillings?"

The viscount nodded nervously. "I am hoping to do so, my lord. I will confess that I do not care for the Season at all. Too many people. Too much noise. Too many judging others too quickly. My greatest hope is that in this type of environment, I might truly get to know a few ladies and see if one values privacy and family as much as I do."

Silas already knew Miss Lyric cherished family. She would look after Tillings and make certain he participated fully in the events planned during the house party. He seemed a decent sort, even if he were a bit too reserved. As for Motley, he was kind and intelligent. The fact he thought enough of his daughter to want to bring her with him spoke of how he, too, valued family. That would appeal to Miss Lyric, as well.

He realized the competition for her hand would be greater than he realized. He only hoped she wouldn't be drawn to the cheerful Lamkin, who made everyone feel special. Silas also felt the need to warn her about Carroll's wicked reputation, despite the fact they had once been close. It was because he knew Carroll so well that he wished to keep the earl away from Miss Lyric. How his former friend had been invited to such a party still seemed odd to him.

In the drawing room, he made a point to speak to the duke and duchess, who were talking with Mrs. Andrews and another fellow Silas recognized from the wedding.

"Good evening, Your Graces. Mrs. Andrews. And it is good to see you present, Mr. Strong."

"Likewise, Lord Blankenship," said Caleb Strong, cousin to His Grace and the steward at Shadowcrest. He had spoken briefly to Strong before he departed the wedding and liked the man a great deal.

Even though he wanted to focus on Miss Lyric, he said, "I

was hoping I might spend an hour or two with you, Mr. Strong. My uncle, who served as my steward at Chase Oaks, passed away in early February. I have hired a new fellow, but he is a bit green. Might I ask you a few questions about how you manage things here at Shadowcrest over the course of the house party?"

Strong smiled. "While I would be happy to answer whatever you might ask, my lord, I do not want you to miss out on any of the festivities."

"I don't plan to," he said. "But there is always time before breakfast or even during breakfast itself. Do you take it at the house?"

"I do. Why don't we plan to meet in the breakfast room tomorrow morning. Is seven-thirty too early for you?"

Mrs. Andrews had told the guests that breakfast would be served buffet style in the drawing room each morning between nine and eleven. Meeting Caleb Strong even earlier and away from the others would be even better.

And still allow him to keep company with Miss Lyric during the meal.

"Not at all," he assured the steward. "I will see you at seven-thirty. Be prepared to be peppered with questions," he joked.

"It is wise to take an interest in your affairs in the country," the duke said. "Fortunately, I have my cousin to watch over things for me. It allows me to spend more of my time dealing with matters at Strong Shipping Lines."

He turned to the duchess. "I hear Your Grace has continued to run your own shipping line, even after marriage to His Grace."

The duchess smiled. "I have." She patted her belly. "But as you see, Lord Blankenship, I will soon have a little one who will keep me occupied a great deal. Thank goodness Her Grace here recently wed Captain Andrews. I have placed him in charge of Neptune Shipping and have begun teaching him everything Mr. Grant, my first husband, helped me to learn. I am passing along all my knowledge, and the captain is like a sponge, soaking it up. Soon, he will take on the brunt of the decisions and run Neptune for me."

"My husband will arrive at the end of the week," Mrs. Andrews said, love for him shining in her eyes. "He will meet with Her Grace about business, and he has promised to stay several days. Then we will return to town together once the guests depart."

"Will you spend most of your time in town now that you have wed?" he asked.

She nodded. "A good deal of it. Of course, we will always visit at Shadowcrest and retreat to my country estate, which is but ten miles from here. Thank goodness my twins wed men who live fairly near Shadowcrest. Hopewood is the next estate over, and the two properties share the lake we will be visiting later this week. Edgefield is in Surrey and only about an hour away."

"That is convenient for you, Mrs. Andrews," Silas said.

She laughed. "I only hope the rest of my four girls will make love matches with men who are a day's carriage ride away. Or less."

He couldn't help but wonder if that had been part of the criteria for being invited to this exclusive house party. If so, it was the only reason to explain Lord Carroll's presence, with Carrollwood being located in East Sussex.

"I do thank you, Your Graces, for including me as a guest this week."

The duchess smiled fondly at him. "You are August's friend, so you are almost like family to us, my lord. We are happy you could visit with us during this time, but please, go and converse with some of the other young people."

Silas excused himself and headed directly to Miss Lyric, who stood with her twin, Lord Carroll, Lady Lida, and Miss Markle. He slipped in next to her, listening to the conversation. A footman circulated, distributing flutes of champagne. When everyone had one, the Duke of Seaton claimed their attention.

"Thank you all for coming to our house party honoring my cousins, Allegra and Lyric Strong. They were raised in this very household, alongside my four sisters, and they are looked upon more as siblings than cousins. If you have need of anything at all during your stay at Shadowcrest, please let Her Grace or Mrs. Andrews know."

The duke raised his glass. "To family—and my beloved cousins, Lyric and Allegra."

Silas downed his champagne, understanding more and more how family was at the center of the Strongs. He had been ignored by his own mother and father and never felt they loved him. He had seemed more of an inconvenience to them. Yet this family he now visited treasured their family connections and seemed to pull in others to their orbit, as they had August when he wed Lady Georgina.

Could he be comfortable in such a situation? Would Miss Lyric even consider him marriage material with his lack of family?

The butler announced it was time to go into dinner. Without hesitating, he offered his arms.

"Miss Allegra? Miss Lyric? Might I escort both of you to dinner?"

The twins placed their hands lightly on his forearms. When Miss Allegra touched him, it was as always when he politely guided a woman to a room, a buffet line, or the dance floor.

He felt nothing.

Yet when Miss Lyric's fingers grazed his sleeve, Silas came alive, an electricity filling his body. Heat surged through him, and the need to kiss her completely filled him.

He only hoped she felt a smidgeon of what he did. If so, he was bound to find success in his pursuit of her.

CHAPTER THREE

LYRIC HAD ENJOYED dinner and the musical evening last night. Though the house party was being held in her and Allegra's honor, they had spoken with Aunt Dinah and decided the first evening they would ask their guests to play. Both Miss Bancroft and Miss Markle played a few pieces at the pianoforte and possessed a decent if unremarkable talent. Lady Lida had played and sung. Her pianoforte skills were sorely lacking, but she made up for it with her lilting soprano.

The group had turned in shortly after that, many tired from their journeys to Shadowcrest, and knowing there were plenty of activities occurring tomorrow. While Lyric and Allegra had discussed their female guests at length while they readied themselves for bed, Allegra had grown uncharacteristically quiet when it came to talking about the gentlemen and had left their bedchamber, saying she wished to claim a book from the library.

Lyric had an idea why her twin had avoided the topic—and she was determined to find out this morning.

She dismissed the maid and went to stand by Allegra, who sat at the dressing table, resecuring an errant curl with a pin.

"What are thinking about?" she asked her twin.

Allegra shrugged.

"It is not like you to go quiet on me," she admonished. "I

want to truly hear what you think about our guests, especially the gentlemen. I am curious if you are drawn to any of them. Perhaps Lord Carroll?"

Her sister's blush at the mention of the earl told Lyric she was right in suspecting Allegra had feelings for the dashing earl.

Instead of talking about Lord Carroll, however, Allegra said, "Lord Tillings is quite nice, even if he is a bit reticent. It is hard to believe that he is such good friends with Lord Lamkin, who is as gregarious as they come."

"I thought Lord Motley was interesting," Lyric interjected, deciding to ease into their discussion. "I think it speaks quite highly of him, that he wished to bring Viola to the house party."

Allegra nodded enthusiastically. "Yes, he is one gentleman who knows family is important. He told me that he often visits the nursery and his daughter would have been brokenhearted if he were gone for an extended period. He said if he tried to explain to her where he went, she would not understand at her tender age. Lord Motley said that he had a close relationship with both his parents growing up, and he wants the same between him and his own children."

"What did you think of Lord Blankenship?" Lyric asked, curious to see if Allegra had any interest in the viscount.

Allegra smiled. "He is one of the better-looking men present and most amiable. I rather enjoyed talking with him at Georgie's wedding. But do I feel any attraction to him? Not a bit."

Relief flooded her. "I see. And what of Lord Carroll? We have not spoken of him yet."

Allegra blushed again at the mention of Carroll. "I am not certain why Aunt Dinah invited him. He is much too handsome for his own good and knows it. When he flashes that smile . . ." Her voice trailed off.

"Your heart flutters when he does so?" prodded Lyric.

Her twin sighed. "I am ashamed to admit that it does. Oh, he is a charming rogue. Too arrogant for my tastes." She paused, tears suddenly swimming in her eyes.

Lyric took her sister's hands in hers. "Go on," she encouraged. "You know you can tell me anything."

"He . . . kissed me last night," Allegra confessed.

"He *what?*"

Allegra nodded guiltily. "Worse, I liked it. More than I should have."

She knew her twin had never kissed anyone and said, "What was it like?"

A faraway look came into Allegra's eyes. "Quite dreamy, if I am to be honest. I experienced a rush of emotions, and my insides turned into jelly."

"You yourself have said he is a rogue, which means he has a good deal of experience in kissing."

Her twin nodded sadly. "I told him that I did not want to be one of his conquests. That he needed to keep his lips and hands to himself in the future."

Lyric's jaw dropped. "You *said* that to him?"

"I most certainly did. And yet, I did not mean it, Lyric. I want to kiss him again. Very badly. So much that I ache in a way I never have."

"You have always had a good head on your shoulders, Allegra," she told her twin. "If you have feelings for this gentleman, this house party will give you the opportunity to explore them. If you feel he is insincere, move on and get to know the other guests. In fact, that would be my advice to you now. Spend time with each of the other gentlemen first."

"I think that will only make Lord Carroll try to pursue me more," Allegra admitted, her lips trembling.

She squeezed her twin's hands. "Remember, Aunt Dinah invited all these men for a reason. Hopefully, we will want to make a match with one of them, and it might surprise us which one. I say stick to my advice and have conversations with all the men present. Your heart will tell you what you need to know. That is what Pippa and Georgie have told us."

"You are right," Allegra agreed, taking a handkerchief and

dabbing her eyes. "Shall we go to breakfast?"

They went downstairs to the dining room since the breakfast room would not hold everyone. Aunt Dinah had informed their guests that breakfast would be served buffet style between nine and eleven each morning. They entered the room at half-past nine, finding it already three-quarters full.

Immediately, Lyric's eyes swept the room, finding Lord Blankenship chatting with Miss Markle, who sat across from him.

She and Allegra went to the buffet, selecting dishes for their morning meal. When she moved toward the table, a footman carrying her plate, her gaze locked with Lord Blankenship's.

"I have a seat next to me, Miss Lyric," he said.

Knowing she could not let her eagerness show, she calmly indicated for the footman to place her plate at the open spot on the viscount's left side. Blankenship himself stood and seated her.

"I was disappointed you and your sister did not play for us last night," he said. "I was looking forward to that."

"We wanted to give our guests a chance to shine."

"Then I hope one of you will play for Lady Lida the next time she sings," he said softly as he leaned toward her. "While she has an excellent voice, her playing is atrocious."

Lyric couldn't help but laugh. "We will definitely play sometime during the party," she assured her companion. "Will you be going riding this morning with the group?"

"I am happiest when I am in the saddle," he told her. "Riding has always been my favorite activity. What of you? I assume it would be gardening."

She nodded. "There is something about pushing my hands into the dirt that brings me such joy. I love to spend time with our gardeners. I have learned so much from them over the years. What plants are annuals and which are perennials. Which varieties are hardy and which are fragile. I know what season to plant which types of flower. Most of all, I enjoy walking through the gardens and seeing how they spring to life in different ways through the various seasons."

"I am only beginning to learn about gardening," he shared. "It was a passion for my uncle Oscar. I hope to follow in his footsteps and learn all I can about gardening, as well as crops."

"You lost him recently, didn't you?" she asked.

Lyric saw the shadow cross his face, and he said, "I did. Back in early February." He hesitated and then asked, "Would you care to show me the Shadowcrest gardens this morning before the group goes riding? We could do so once you finish your meal. I have heard we are not to ride until noon, so it would give us plenty of time for you to show them off and then change into your riding habit."

She wanted to be alone with him desperately, and yet she was afraid he might kiss her since he had already declared his interest in her. It was something she yearned for, but it terrified her at the same time. Lyric decided she must at least try a kiss with him, though, especially since she had never been kissed. She wanted to feel what Allegra had, and she most likely would discuss the kiss with her twin since they shared everything.

"I would be happy to show you our gardens, my lord." Her heart beat rapidly at the thought of them surrounded by the sweet-smelling blossoms, alone, no one present.

She turned to her left and asked Miss Bancroft a few questions, trying to get her emotions under control. She liked this friend of Georgie's, who was intelligent and kind.

"Are you enjoying the house party so far, Miss Bancroft?"

"Surprisingly, yes," the woman admitted. "For one, my aunt has not pestered me the entire time. Your aunt, Her Grace, and Lady Crowell have kept her occupied, so much that she has not berated me once since shortly after we arrived. That, in and of itself, is like a breath of fresh air. As for the company, I am finding it stimulating and enjoyable. Thank you for asking, Miss Lyric."

"I noticed you speaking with Lord Tillings at length after you played the pianoforte for us last night."

Color rose in Miss Bancroft's cheeks. "Yes, his lordship and I did have a rather pleasant conversation." She paused. "I have told you I am chief amongst the wallflowers at *ton* events, but I have felt so accepted here at Shadowcrest by all your guests."

"I am delighted to hear that, Miss Bancroft. Will you be riding today?"

"I most certainly will," her new friend replied, enthusiasm in her voice. "I ride often when I am in the country, but I have no one to do so with in town. I am eager to see the land around Shadowcrest. Kent is so beautiful. It is my first time here."

"I am looking forward to our ride, as well as tea on the terrace this afternoon," she said. "There is nothing like dining al fresco on a pleasant day."

Lyric finished her meal and saw that Lord Blankenship had done likewise. They excused themselves, and she led him to her aunt's sitting room, where they exited through the French doors.

"This is the quickest way to the gardens," she said.

"I must thank you for making the time to show them to me, Miss Lyric. You Strongs are generous with your time."

His comment puzzled her. "How so, my lord?"

"I was with your cousin Mr. Strong almost two hours this morning."

"What did you and Caleb talk about so long?" she asked, puzzled by his admission.

"As I mentioned before, I lost my uncle several months ago. Uncle Oscar was more like a father to me than uncle these past few years. My own parents were quite distant. To be honest, they completely ignored me my entire life. They spent the majority of their year in town, leaving me alone at Chase Oaks a good deal of the time."

The concept was so foreign to her because Aunt Dinah had always taken all the girls to town when the Season began. "I cannot imagine parents who would leave a child in such a manner."

"Yes, your upbringing was quite different than mine. You have a close, loving group of relatives here at Shadowcrest."

They entered the gardens and she said, "We have more in

common than you might believe, my lord. My own father ignored Allegra and me from our birth. My mother died giving birth to us, and Papa saw no value in females. He finally handed us off to Aunt Dinah for good. She was both mother and father to us, and has always treated us more as daughters than her nieces. I suppose that is why I hold family so dear. Because Allegra and I could easily have been in your circumstances. Raised by servants and governesses. Instead, we were enfolded into a family and always felt we belonged and were loved."

"I will admit I am a bit jealous of your upbringing, Miss Lyric. When my parents died, I know it sounds coldhearted, but I felt nothing. Absolutely nothing. I'd had no relationship with them. They were, in effect, strangers to me."

She slipped her arm through his crook and said, "You do not have a heart of stone, Lord Blankenship. You seem to be a most kind, generous man."

"You are right about being raised by servants. My tutor. The few times I did run across my parents in the household, they looked startled by my presence. I am afraid since they never emphasized family, I never did myself."

He halted and turned, clasping her elbows, filling Lyric with a rush of warmth.

"It is no secret to anyone in Polite Society. I have sown quite a few wild oats, Miss Lyric. I think I have always been searching for something I never had. Something just outside my grasp. When my parents died, Uncle Oscar, who was a steward at another estate, came and took on that role at Chase Oaks since I was about to leave for my first year at university. I let him. I cared nothing for the estate I had inherited, nor thought about the responsibilities involved. I was all about seeking thrills, having a good time, gambling and drinking with my friends. I continued that life even after I left Cambridge, never giving a thought about tomorrow."

His grip tightened slightly. "Then I lost Uncle Oscar suddenly. It was the saddest time of my life, and yet it helped fill me with new resolve. I determined to be a better earl—and a better man."

The feelings rushing through her were new and exciting.

"I want to build a life with my viscountess. I wish to enjoy a friendship with her."

His gaze bore into her, and Lyric felt as if he saw her soul laid bare before him.

"I searched this past Season for a bride on the Marriage Mart and found no one to my liking. You interest me a great deal, Miss Lyric. I would not be so foolish as to offer for you right now because I believe we must get to know one another better." He smiled. "I would like to do that now by asking if I might kiss you?"

Lyric's breath hitched. She gazed into his eyes, dark as melted chocolate, knowing her reply might change the course of her life.

"Yes, Lord Blankenship. I think we should kiss."

CHAPTER FOUR

LYRIC HAD NO idea what to expect from a kiss. Only this morning had she heard from her twin how wonderful one could be. She did not know much about Lord Blankenship, other than he was an incredibly attractive man and seemed to be a good one, as well, despite his admission to previously being a rogue.

His fingers gently caressed her cheek, causing a spark to shoot through her. He gazed at her with those deep brown eyes, and she seemed to be swallowed whole by them.

His palm now cradled her cheek as his mouth moved toward hers. Though they were surrounded by the sweet smell of the blooms in the garden, she caught a hint of the sandalwood from his cologne. It caused her heart to flutter.

Then his lips were on hers, gently caressing them. They were soft and yet somehow firm at the same time, a dichotomy she couldn't explain.

The kiss was sweet, bringing a deep yearning within her. Lyric's arms raised, her hands settling on his shoulders. They were broad and solid, and the feel of them made her feel safe.

He made her feel safe.

He broke the kiss and immediately kissed her again. His lips grew more familiar to her now, and her fingers tightened on his shoulders. Breaking the kiss again, he feathered soft, quick kisses along her brow. Her eyelids. Her cheeks. Then he returned to her mouth for one final kiss, their lips pressed together for a very long time.

When he lifted his head and smiled down at her, mixed feelings ran through Lyric. While she had liked the kisses very much, they did not seem to be the same kisses of Allegra's experience with Lord Carroll. She remembered the dreamy expression that had filled her twin's face when talking about it, and Lyric wondered if what had occurred between Lord Blankenship and her was merely a pleasant experience and not the soul-shattering one of Allegra's encounter with Lord Carroll.

Realizing she still clung to him, Lyric released her grasp upon him, her hands dropping in front of her. She laced her fingers together and looked up at him.

"Thank you for the kiss, my lord. It was my first."

"I expected it would be, Miss Lyric. Thank you for allowing me to kiss you."

Instinct told her that Lord Carroll had not asked permission to kiss Allegra. She shouldn't keep comparing Lord Blankenship to Lord Carroll. She had no attraction to the earl, while she did feel a strong pull toward this man.

"Would you like to continue strolling through the gardens?" he asked. "We still have time."

"Yes, I would like that," she told the viscount, accepting the arm he offered and sliding her hand into the crook of his arm. She liked being near him. She did like him. She had enjoyed their kisses.

Yet something was missing.

While Lyric did not believe necessarily that love came at first sight, she had thought when she kissed Lord Blankenship, it would let her know if she did love him or not. Then again, they did not know one another well. Perhaps love did—like a flower— need time to grow. Today, they had planted the first seed, which must now be watered and tended to. Even encouraged. She hoped over the duration of the house party that a friendship would spring up between them, and possibly that friendship might blossom into love.

As they strolled, he said, "Tell me about the layout of your gardens and what is blooming now that you are most fond of. I am only beginning to be interested in such things. I hope I will come to love plants as much as my uncle did."

Over the next half-hour, Lyric guided them through the Shadowcrest gardens, pointing out her favorites.

"The peachleaf bellflowers bloom most of the summer. I like their long stems because they make for an unusual choice in a flower arrangement."

Bending, she smelled some blooms and indicated for him to do the same.

"Oh, these are wonderfully spicy," he declared.

"They are cottage pinks, a type of dianthus. Because they are so short, you see how we have planted them toward the front, so that they are not lost."

They continued on, and he pointed. "What are these? They have such an unusual shape."

"Delphiniums." Lyric chuckled. "They can be a bit temperamental, but I believe they are worth your time. Because of their height, the wind and rain can knock them down, so you see how they have been placed in a more sheltered spot."

"Are they summer blooms?"

"Actually, delphiniums can withstand cold winters. They do not like heat, though, and they require a lot of moisture. Fortunately, both English soil and weather are perfect for them."

She continued on, pointing out hollyhock, geraniums, and lavender, sharing with him a bit about each. He asked several questions, good ones, about how the soil was prepared and when the planting of various flowers took place. His interest seemed genuine, and she eagerly shared with him, enjoying being with him.

By now, they had toured the entire gardens and had circled to the entrance.

"Thank you for spending this time with me, Miss Lyric. I appreciate you tutoring me about various flowers and the seasons in which they grow. I might have questions for you in the future, though."

"I would be happy to answer them for you, my lord. I usually spend time in the gardens every day. This house party is an exception to my usual routine. Aunt Dinah has various activities planned in order for our small group to get to know one another better. I would prefer spending my time with our guests because I can always return to gardening once the party has ended."

He smiled at her, and it was as if the sun warmed her from within.

"Perhaps we might sneak away early some morning, before the activities of the day," he suggested. "You could show me a bit about what you do to maintain such lovely blooms."

"I would like that," she said sincerely, happy he wanted to spend further time in her company. If he were willing to dirty his hands in order to be with her, the raw, tender feelings she was beginning to feel toward him might build further.

Other gentlemen were present at this house party, however, and she needed to spend time with all of them. Except for Lord Carroll. Lyric had already ruled him out since he was a rogue. She would have nothing to do with him. It was up to her to make an effort to get to know the other three gentlemen. She owed that much to Aunt Dinah—and herself.

They returned to the house, and she excused herself, saying she needed to change into her riding habit. When she arrived in the bedchamber she shared with Allegra, she saw her sister was already wearing hers. Since they shared everything, Lyric wanted Allegra's opinion on what had just occurred.

She dismissed the maid, saying that her twin could help her change clothes. The servant didn't find that odd in the least since the twins often did that for one another, especially when they wished to speak privately.

"What has happened?" Allegra asked eagerly as she helped

remove Lyric's day gown.

"You are not the only one who has been kissed," she revealed.

"Lyric! Well, that was certainly fast work. Tell me about it. Tell me everything. Start with the gentleman's name."

Suddenly, she wanted to keep the experience to herself, but she did not want to disappoint her sister, especially after Allegra had been so open about Lord Carroll and their kiss.

"Lord Blankenship asked if I would guide him through our gardens. He knows that is a particular interest of mine and said he, too, has recently become interested in flowers."

Allegra gave her a knowing look. "I wonder if the good viscount's interest is because of you. So, he kissed you in the gardens. Go on," she encouraged.

"He admitted that he is looking for his viscountess and that he did not find a suitable bride on the Marriage Mart this Season."

"That was quite frank," Allegra pointed out.

"He expressed his interest in me. Then he asked if he might kiss me."

"He *asked?*" Allegra frowned. "Lord Carroll certainly did not ask me."

Lyric clucked her tongue. "You yourself have declared the man a rake. I do not suppose they go about asking permission. Lord Blankenship did so because he is a gentleman."

Her twin's frown depend. "You do not seem affected by his kiss, Lyric. I suppose that is telling in itself. That he is not meant for you."

"I am struggling with it," she admitted. "I enjoyed his kiss quite a bit. It wasn't merely one. He would brush his lips across mine and break it. Then go back and do it all again. He even kissed all over my face. His kisses were tender and very sweet, Allegra. They moved me. But . . . I cannot explain it. I liked the feel of him. The nearness of us. The warmth and security he seemed to represent."

"But there was no passion," her twin said sadly.

"Yes, I suppose that was missing. Did Lord Carroll stir that within you?"

Allegra nodded. "I am reluctant to admit it, but he did. He kissed me . . . in a different . . . manner than Lord Blankenship kissed you."

Confusion filled her. "How else would you kiss, other than putting your lips together?"

"That is what I thought it was all about," Allegra said. "And I will say that Lord Carroll started out the same way as Lord Blankenship did." She hesitated. "But Lyric, he used his . . . tongue."

"I do not understand at all what you mean, Allegra."

"I had no idea kissing involved tongues, but it does," her sister said brightly. "Somehow, he persuaded me to open my mouth to him, and he placed his tongue against mine."

Shock filled Lyric. Then she nodded, saying, "Perhaps that is what I wished for Lord Blankenship to do. He was so sweet and gentle with me. Something did stir inside me. Something telling me I wanted—no, needed—more from him."

"Well, I would not make a final judgement just yet about the viscount," her sister advised. "If you say you liked the kind of kiss he gave you, I would think it is only a start. It would make sense for a gentleman to kiss a little more properly the first time than a rogue would. But I believe that Lord Blankenship does know how to kiss like that. All men must know how. I believe he was merely being gentle with you because it was your first kiss."

She had not thought of it that way. "You may be right," she agreed. "He is very kind and has lovely manners. I do not know when I have met a nicer gentleman. Perhaps kissing like that is something he believes a couple should lead up to, when they know one another better."

"I highly recommend trying it. While I realize that Lord Carroll has no interest in becoming betrothed during this house party, my experience with him has let me understand what is out there. What I want for myself with the man I love."

"So, you do plan to kiss another gentleman during this house party?" Lyric asked, anxious that Allegra might want to do so with Lord Blankenship.

"Oh, don't be a ninny," her sister chided. "I can tell you have feelings for the viscount. I have already told you I like him, but more in a brotherly fashion. I will not go about kissing your viscount."

"He is not *my* viscount," she said defensively.

Allegra's eyes gleamed with mischief. "But he could be. Especially if you kiss him with your tongue. In fact, that is what I suggest. Kiss him again—and do that very thing."

"I do not know how to do that!" she protested. "I do not even know how to begin to ask him to kiss me again, much less me take the lead in a kiss."

Allegra thought a moment. "If he has feelings for you, he will want to see if you are compatible. That will mean kissing you in the way I just told you about. If you hint at it, he might take the hint."

She snorted. "And I am to say what, Allegra? My dear Lord Blankenship, would you please allow me to place my tongue in your mouth, or perhaps you wish to thrust yours inside mine?"

Her twin burst into laughter. "No, that is something Lord Carroll might appreciate." She thought a moment. "Perhaps you should kiss Lord Carroll that way. As you said, he is an experienced rogue. He might teach you something you could try with the viscount."

"I could never do something like that!" Lyric said, stomping her foot to emphasize the point. "I cannot imagine kissing anyone *but* Lord Blankenship"

A knowing look entered her twin's eyes. "Oh, so now it comes out. You do not truly wish to kiss any other man at this house party. You have already made up your mind that Lord Blankenship is for you."

Lyric collapsed on the bed, sighing in exasperation. "I do not know what I want. I have never been this confused in my entire life."

Allegra sat next to her. "I feel the same," she admitted. "The feelings Lord Carroll stirred within me overwhelmed me. For the first time in my life, I believe I felt desire. But desiring a rake is the last thing I should want. No, I am going to take the lesson the earl taught me and test it with another guest at this party. Perhaps Lord Lamkin. He is so exuberant and friendly. I think having a husband such as Lamkin would make for a merry marriage indeed."

She slipped her hand around her twin's. "Promise we will keep talking honestly to one another about these confusing feelings, no matter how awkward they are."

"You know we always share everything with one another. I will let you know if there is another gentleman I grow fond of and if I kiss him." Allegra grinned. "And *how* I kiss him."

Lyric hugged her twin tightly. "Thank you for letting me share this with you."

Her sister helped her finish doing her riding habit, and they left their bedchamber.

She said, "I will admit I do have feelings for Lord Blankenship. I wish to explore them further, and that will mean I must kiss him in the way Lord Carroll kissed you. Only then will I discover if passion lies between us. Passion which could lead to love."

"I wish you the best, Lyric. Now, let's go and enjoy our ride with our guests."

They had agreed to assemble at the stables, and Lyric took her usual mount. Caleb was taking time from his day to lead the riding party so that he might point out various things in the area. Not only were they going to see Shadowcrest, but they would ride the surrounding area, even stopping in the village for a cup of cider.

Lord Tillings helped her to mount her horse and climbed upon his own. She watched as Viscount Blankenship assisted Miss Bancroft and then mounted himself. He looked as if he had been born in the saddle, so comfortable did he appear.

Their gazes met, and he nodded to her, the corners of his mouth turning up in a smile.

Lyric turned her horse and followed Caleb as her brother led them cantering across the meadow.

She would need to be alone with Lord Blankenship soon.

Perhaps even sometime during this ride.

CHAPTER FIVE

S ILAS HAD ENJOYED riding ever since his nursery governess had allowed him to be placed in a saddle. From what he understood, he had been a rambunctious child, always into mischief and being chased about. He supposed the poor servant was frantic, trying to keep up with him, and thought riding lessons might distract him from the frequent mischief he got into. Whatever the reason, he had begun riding from the age of three and continued to do so to this day. He had no idea if either of his parents ever rode. The conversations which had taken place between him and them probably were no more than the fingers on his two hands.

Again, he couldn't help but be grateful for Uncle Oscar coming to take over at Chase Oaks upon his brother's and sister-in-law's deaths. It allowed Silas to go away to university as planned. Regret still filled him for not coming to his country estate more often. When he did, his uncle had been happy for them to ride about the property, keeping Silas informed of all the improvements which had occurred, as well as telling him about the lives of his tenants. He had listened, not because he was particularly interested, but because he enjoyed being with his uncle.

The death of his last living relative had sobered Silas, though. He berated himself for neglecting Chase Oaks as much as he had, even though Uncle Oscar had it running smoothly and efficiently. Silas also regretted not having siblings to depend upon and share things with. That was why he was determined to take a wife. The sooner, the better. He also craved the closeness he witnessed between the Strongs. They seemed so comfortable in one another's company, talking and teasing with ease. He knew it was no act they put on for their guests. These were people who genuinely liked and cared about each other.

He wanted that for himself. Perhaps that was part of the attraction he felt toward Miss Lyric, though he didn't feel any pull at all toward Miss Allegra. As they rode, Silas reflected upon kissing her in the gardens. He had wanted to do so much more but was conscious of the fact she had never been kissed. It was obvious from the first moment their lips touched. She was slightly hesitant but did respond to his kiss. Because of that, he hoped to kiss her again. A better kiss. One which might show her his growing feelings.

They'd had an interesting time in the gardens. She was so knowledgeable and spoke with ease about various flowers and plants. It was obvious how much gardening meant to her. He hadn't been trying to flatter her by claiming his own interest in it. Silas did like the peace to be found within a garden. Now that he fully was in charge of Chase Oaks, it was important to him to learn about every aspect of his estate, which included its gardens. He only wondered what Miss Lyric would do if he turned her loose in them.

As his wife.

He had no doubts about her now. She was beautiful and from a good family. He assumed she would have a dowry, but he was not in need of it. She was interesting and patient and seemed quite nurturing. Overall, Silas believed she would make for a perfect countess. He believed they would be a good match—just not the love match his uncle had predicted for him.

To him, love was merely a word that others used as an excuse to do as they wished. A man might proclaim his love for a woman in order to secure her hand in marriage, when all he truly wanted was his hands on her dowry to pay off his gambling debts. Or it was used to justify an affair between lovers in the *ton*, saying they loved one another and that was the reason they broke their vows to their mates.

Silas believed in fidelity. When he wed, it would be a woman whom he would be faithful to. He would only make love to her, hoping it resulted in numerous children. More than anything, he wanted to fill Chase Oaks with children, happy children, and bask in their happiness. But love for his wife would never be a part of his world. Respect, yes. Honesty, certainly. He only hoped he could convince Lyric Strong to marry him.

It was early, though. She would want to learn more about the other bachelors who had been invited to the house party. Suddenly, the thought of losing her hit him hard. He needed to let her know that he was more than a candidate for her hand. That he was the one she should choose.

And that meant kissing her in a way so that she could not forget him.

He decided the sooner he could make that happen, the better his chances were with her. During this ride might prove difficult. Tea this afternoon would be al fresco, served on the terrace. Tonight, they would play cards. Silas thought this evening might be the best time. He would conjure an opportunity to be alone with her—and make the most of it.

LYRIC HAD ENJOYED the exercise she had gotten during the group's ride. At the nearby village, they had stopped at the inn for cider and peach tarts. Caleb had let the innkeeper and his wife know they were coming beforehand, and they had been shown to an upper room.

She had talked with Lord Lamkin for much of that time,

finding him to be a delight. He was so open and positive during their conversation, she decided he would be the next gentleman she would kiss.

Then at tea on the terrace this afternoon, she had been seated at a table with Viscount Tillings and Lord Motley. She and the viscount both had a love of reading, and he recommended two books to her which she was eager to begin. Since James' country library had neither volume, Lord Tillings assured Lyric he would purchase copies in town and have them sent to her. She thought that quite refreshing and thought she better try a kiss with Tillings.

Then the nursery governess had brought Viola down to tea for a few minutes. When Lyric witnessed the pure joy on the faces of father and daughter at their reunion, she determined the earl was the best of fathers. Unlike her own father, who had barely acknowledged her or Allegra, Lord Motley truly enjoyed being with his child. He proudly had Viola show off, having her count to ten, and then had her recite her alphabet. When she skipped over a few of the letters, her father still praised her efforts. The widower impressed Lyric greatly, and she decided he would be worth kissing, as well.

Now that dinner had finished, the men were having cigars and a brandy before they rejoined the women in the drawing room, where they would be playing cards very soon. Aunt Dinah already had various tables and chairs set up around the room and told them they would be drawing for partners once the men joined them.

Lyric decided to go to her room to freshen up a bit before the gentlemen arrived. Miss Markle was playing the pianoforte, and it was easy to slip out. She started down the corridor. Surprise filled her when she spied Lord Blankenship coming her way. He was alone.

He paused in front of her, and she asked, "You did not want to stay and finish your brandy and cheroot, my lord?"

"I had other things on my mind and decided a quiet walk

might do me some good. Would you care to join me?"

Her pulse jumped. "I suppose I could for a few minutes, but card play will start shortly."

"We won't be long," he promised.

The viscount guided her outdoors, and she thought he might wish to stroll through the gardens again. Instead, he took her hand and slipped it through his arm, walking along the terrace. As before, she caught the scent of sandalwood and felt her heart beating erratically, simply because he was so near. Lyric found she couldn't say a word as nerves flitted through her.

Lord Blankenship did not seem to mind the lack of conversation, though. He led her to the end of the terrace and stopped, gazing out at Shadowcrest.

"The duke has a lovely estate," he remarked.

"Yes, it was so nice to grow up here," she replied. "Allegra and I have had a full life at Shadowcrest and always felt loved."

She caught the fleeting anguish in his eyes, and it passed quickly, so quickly that others might not have noticed.

"I have told you how my parents absolved themselves of any obligation to me. They were completely unaware of me my entire life."

Sympathy filled her. "That must have been very lonely," she said, one hand stroking his arm in comfort.

"It made me self-reliant. I knew I could only depend upon myself. I will admit I broke a lot of rules, testing the servants and later the adults at school. I was charming enough that I could always talk my way out of situations I had gotten myself into, though."

He paused, sighing deeply. "But it taught me that I want the exact opposite. Where my parents were strangers to their child, I want to be close to my own children. They lived in town. I wish to be there for part of the year, but since my uncle's death, I have a greater appreciation for the country and Chase Oaks. I plan to teach my own children to hunt and fish and ride. I admire Motley. Seeing him with little Viola at teatime today let me know I can be the type of father I want to be and not repeat the mistakes my own father made."

Suddenly, his hands encompassed her waist, startling Lyric.

"I asked to kiss you before, Miss Lyric, and I am asking to do so again. I fear I did not make quite the impression I wished to make on you with our first kiss."

She swallowed, her heart pounding against her ribs. "I told you that I enjoyed it, my lord."

He grinned. "Then you will enjoy this even more."

Pulling her to him suddenly, she took in a quick breath before his mouth came down hard on hers. This kiss was not like the gentle caress from before. No, it had a boldness to it, a fire, which excited her. The viscount's lips were insistent, his kisses rough and demanding.

And thrilling.

Lyric knew what she needed to do, and that was invite him in. Praying she was doing so the right way, she opened to him, feeling his surprise. All the same, he accepted her unspoken invitation, his tongue plunging into her mouth. He drank greedily from her, his hands anchoring her to him.

For her part, she felt compelled to touch more of him. Her fingers pushed into his hair, fisting, holding him so that his mouth could continue to ravage hers. Need pooled in her belly, and a strong throb began between her legs, making her aware of him even more. His tongue stroked hers and then warred with hers as she answered the call of his kiss. The blood rushed to her ears, the sound a loud whoosh which blocked everything out except the beating of her heart. She tasted brandy on him and inhaled deeply, wanting the scent of sandalwood to fill her nostrils.

Her breasts grew heavy with need, and she wished he would touch them, a thought which shocked her. He tugged on her, causing her head to tilt back, and deepened the kiss. Desire flooded her now.

This was the kiss Allegra had spoken of. This was exactly what a kiss was meant to be.

Lord Blankenship finally broke the kiss, his brow resting against hers, both of them breathing quick, short breaths. His thumbs stroked her ribcage, moving dangerously close to her breasts, and she thought about twisting slightly so that they would touch.

Then he released his grasp on her, tucking her hand through his arm again, strolling once more along the terrace. Her thoughts swirled, and she was not capable of speaking.

When they reached the doors to enter the house again, he stopped. His lips touched hers again, the kiss achingly tender.

"I hope you will remember our kiss, Miss Lyric, and that you will look favorably upon me."

He led her inside, and she excused herself, racing to her bedchamber. She fell into the seat before the dressing table, seeing the color flooding her cheeks. Quickly, she repinned a few stray locks and then touched her fingertips to her lips.

She had been kissed. Properly kissed.

And Lyric suspected she had fallen in love with Viscount Blankenship.

CHAPTER SIX

L YRIC ENTERED THE drawing room with Allegra, having just told her twin about the marvelous kisses she had exchanged with Lord Blankenship. Allegra had been supportive, but seemed a bit down herself. Because of Lord Carroll. She didn't understand her sister being drawn to the earl. Oh, he certainly was quite handsome. And he had kissed Allegra the way Lord Blankenship had kissed Lyric. Those two things alone would be enough to make Allegra's head swim.

But Lyric was concerned about her twin's attraction to such a rogue. In the end, she feared Allegra's heart would be broken by the man. It was difficult because she herself was on top of the world regarding her budding feelings for Lord Blankenship and had high hopes that, by the time this house party concluded, they might be betrothed. If Allegra were miserable, though, Lyric didn't know if she could be happy herself. She and her sister were so entwined with one another.

Should she speak to Lord Carroll? Would that be too brazen a thing to do? She would have to consider doing so, especially if he continued to toy with Allegra. Lyric determined to keep a watchful eye on the pair and intervene if she needed to.

The evening of card play went well. Everyone seemed to be enjoying themselves, though she and Lord Tillings did not win a single game. Usually, Lyric was quite good at whist, but she was distracted by watching Allegra and Lord Carroll. Though they were not partners, she couldn't help but keep an eye on them.

Lord Tillings proved to be a disaster as a player. For such an intelligent man, his card play was terribly unfocused. Then she began studying her partner and quickly understood his lack of concentration.

The viscount only had eyes for Miss Bancroft.

It became almost comical, watching Lord Tillings watch Miss Bancroft, who partnered with Lord Carroll. They definitely were the team to beat tonight. The more they won, the more Miss Bancroft laughed and smiled, which made her almost attractive. That distracted Lord Tillings even more. Lyric continued to play her best, but with a partner who couldn't concentrate on his cards, they rarely took a trick, much less scored any points.

She was happy for Miss Bancroft, though. The woman was a delight to be around. Lyric had noticed Aunt Dinah and Sophie distracting the elder Miss Bancroft often, so the woman would not harp at her niece. Yes, this house party was allowing the younger Miss Bancroft to shine. She hoped Lord Tillings would make the most of this opportunity and offer for her.

The last round of play began, with the two teams who had scored the most points going head-to-head. That meant Miss Bancroft and Lord Carroll faced Allegra and Lord Lamkin. Play at the other two tables quickly ended, with everyone gathering around Allegra's table to watch the two teams in action. Both pairs were skilled players. It did not surprise Lyric that Allegra was a part of this group. Her sister had always had a good memory for which cards had been played and regularly beat all the other Strongs at whist.

Lord Tillings, who stood next to her, seemed enraptured by Miss Bancroft. Surprisingly, Lady Lida and Lord Motley stood together, whispering. She had not thought them a match, but they seemed to be getting along well. Lyric only hoped that Lady Lida might accept Viola. That would be the key to winning Lord

Motley's heart.

It came down to who would take these last two tricks. The team who did would be the victors and claim the crystal bowl. Suddenly, a feeling came over Lyric, one of those twin moments when she could seemingly read her sister's mind.

Allegra was going to lose. Deliberately.

And Lyric understood why.

Her eyes locked with her twin's a moment, as if Allegra sought Lyric's approval. She nodded almost imperceptibly, and then Allegra played her card. Lord Carroll and Miss Bancroft took that trick—and the next.

Everyone congratulated the winning pair. Lord Tillings quickly helped Miss Bancroft from her chair, and Aunt Dinah presented the crystal bowl to Miss Bancroft, who graciously thanked Lord Carroll for helping them to victory.

Several people decided to return to the library for a drink, while a few others made their way to bed. Lyric vacillated and decided to go to the library, hoping Lord Blankenship might follow. She walked there with Miss Markle and Lord Lamkin, who retrieved punch for both ladies.

Lyric excused herself, feeling the two wished to speak alone, and went to the window, looking out on the lawn.

"Checking on your gardens?" a familiar voice asked.

"I enjoy viewing them," she told Lord Blankenship.

"Are we going to work in them anytime soon? I would suggest tomorrow morning."

She knew some of the vegetables needed to be harvested, and said, "I do have a task you could help me with if you are interested."

His eyes seemed to caress her, causing her breath to catch.

"I am interested in you, Miss Lyric," he said, his voice drawing her in. "And that means I am interested in anything you do."

"Don't wear anything you favor then," she warned. "It most certainly will get dirty. Meet me at half-past seven in the foyer."

His blinding smile made her toes curl. "I will see you then."

Lyric finished her punch and went to her bedchamber. Allegra was already there, undressing with a maid's help. They both climbed into bed and for the first time in a long time, neither said anything as they waited for sleep to come.

⇶✕⇷

LYRIC DRESSED IN a worn gown, placing a large apron over it, moving as quietly as possible so as to not awaken Allegra. She donned her work gloves and left her hair in a single braid, placing a bonnet upon her head and tying the ribbon under her chin. She did not have the knack of tying ribbons her twin possessed, but it would have to do. She hurried down the stairs, anticipation building within her, ready to spend time in Lord Blankenship's company.

He was waiting for her in the foyer, wearing dark breeches, a white shirt, and a waistcoat.

"I am glad you left your coat behind," she told him. "You would grow too warm wearing it."

He chuckled. "It sounds as if you are truly putting me to work."

"I am," she said saucily. "Follow me."

Leading him to the kitchens, she greeted Cook and said, "We are off to harvest more vegetables for you, Cook."

Cook eyed the viscount with interest. "Do you have time for that, Miss Lyric? I was going to send a couple of scullery maids to do so."

"No, you know I enjoy my time in nature. I have recruited Lord Blankenship to assist me."

Cook laughed. "Be careful, my lord. She's a bossy one when it comes to the gardens."

"I plan to follow Miss Lyric's orders to the letter, Cook," he said easily. "I am a foot soldier today in the army of General Strong."

His words caused Cook to burst into laughter. Wiping her eyes with her apron, the old woman said, "The baskets are waiting for you, Miss Lyric."

"Thank you, Cook."

She collected four from the table and indicated for Lord Blankenship to pick up the rest. They went out the back door, and Lyric took him to the large vegetable garden, which took up a large space.

"Spread the baskets out. I will find you some gardening gloves and claim a few tools for us in the shed."

When she returned, he had done as she asked, and he was walking around, inspecting things. Lyric handed him gloves, which he put on, and a small spade.

"You want to harvest fruits and vegetables when they are at their peak size and flavor," she explained.

She walked him through the vegetable garden, pointing out what the different plantings were.

"It is a good thing we have not had any rain for two days. Tomatoes should never be picked when wet because they absorb water. For a deep, intense flavor, you should always pick them when they are a bit dry. The same holds true for beans. If the plant is wet from any type of moisture—even dew—the moisture could spread disease. You could lose the entire plant."

"Fascinating," he said, and she saw he truly was interested and not just placating her.

Lyric taught him a pinching technique to harvest the beans and how to shear off lettuce so that the bottom of the plant remained, so that it would regrow.

"I know Cook needed more garlic. It is always planted in the fall and harvested the next summer. It is too late for scapes, which is the flower head of garlic. We have already collected those. But you can help gather some of the cloves."

She also had them pull onions from the soil, explaining how they were not to be washed and must be stored in a cool, dry place. They finished by gathering carrots and tomatoes, filling every basket they had brought with them. Lyric couldn't help but stare at the viscount's muscular forearms. He had rolled up his sleeves when they had begun to work. She had never witnessed a gentleman doing something of that nature and was fascinated by the tautness of them. The need to touch his bare skin overwhelmed her, and she fought the urge to reach out and stroke them.

Laughter coming from a child distracted her, and Lyric saw Lady Viola and her nursery governess heading their way. The little girl ran toward them and stopped, peering into one of the baskets.

Lord Blankenship, who was still on his knees, said, "Good morning, Lady Viola. Have you come to help us harvest some vegetables?"

The child looked from the basket to the man and then toddled toward him.

"Let me show you how it is done," he said, demonstrating to her how to remove a carrot from the soil and then having her do so.

Lyric watched them working together, Blankenship speaking gently and then teasing the girl, holding the carrot up and then hiding it behind his back, only to bring it into view again, causing her to giggle. Her heart melted at the sight of him playing with Viola. Instinctively, she knew that, despite his being an only child, he would make for a good father.

"Why don't you put the carrot in the basket with the other carrots?" he suggested, taking Viola's hand and leading her toward where the baskets were lined up. "Let's see—which one has carrots in it?" he mused.

"This one!" the girl cried, clearly delighted as she placed the carrot in the basket.

Lord Blankenship led her from basket to basket, telling the small girl what each held, even sharing some of the things Lyric had told him about harvesting. Viola listened carefully, repeating what each basket held several times as she led the viscount down the line.

"He's good with children, that one," the nursery governess observed to Lyric.

"Yes, he is," she agreed, her heart warming. She had always wanted children of her own.

And now she wanted them with this man.

"I think we are done," Lord Blankenship said. "Thank you for your help, Lady Viola. Now, when you see carrots or tomatoes on your plate, you will know where they came from."

She giggled and ran back to her nursemaid, burying her face in the woman's skirts.

"Thank you for assisting us, Lady Viola," Lyric told the child. "We appreciate your help."

Lord Blankenship joined her as the pair moved away, Viola dashing off as fast as her chubby little legs could carry her.

"You were quite good with her," Lyric told him.

"I was, wasn't I?" he said, looking a bit surprised. "I have never been around children, but Lady Viola certainly makes me think I would enjoy them."

He gazed at her longingly, and she hoped he might offer for her, here and now. Unfortunately, they were interrupted by one of the assistant gardeners, coming to help with the harvesting.

"It looks as if you have everything Cook needs, Miss Lyric," he said. "Don't worry, I'll take these baskets to her."

She thanked him and removed her gloves, seeing Lord Blankenship did the same. He rolled down his sleeves, covering those beautiful forearms.

"I have certainly worked up an appetite," he declared.

"I have, as well," she agreed, thinking how happy she had been in his company this morning.

They returned their gardening tools to the nearby shed and returned to the house.

"I certainly need to wash up," he told her. "Will you be at breakfast afterward?"

She nodded. "I will see you there."

"Are you going to participate in the archery contest at noon today?"

"I may watch it. I have never held a bow and arrow," she admitted. "Allegra has, though, and she's quite good at it."

"Perhaps you would allow me to teach you how to do so," he suggested.

The thought of him standing behind her, guiding her, touching her, caused a shiver to run along her spine.

"If you do not mind tutoring a novice, my lord, I would be happy to allow you to teach me some of the finer points of archery."

He smiled, causing the blood to rush to her ears. "Then I look forward to doing so, Miss Lyric."

CHAPTER SEVEN

S ILAS WENT TO the lawn in front of the house, a vast area where they would be participating in various games over the next few days, including lawn tennis and lawn bowling. Today, however, would be archery. He possessed a lean, athletic build and had always done well in sports from the time he went away to school. Archery and he were old friends. When teams had been created at school, he either captained them or was the first choice made.

He couldn't wait to teach Lyric the finer points of the sport. Not because he was an archery enthusiast, but because he would be able to touch her in an acceptable manner while demonstrating how she should hold her equipment. It would be necessary to guide her, pulling back the bow in order to release the arrow. Being physically close to her would hopefully feed the attraction between them. He had kissed her twice now, and he knew they were compatible. She had picked things up quickly, and he knew she would please him in bed. He had much to teach her and looked forward to the day she could be his.

Still, he was moving slowly. He feared, because of the love matches made in her family, she would have stars in her eyes and want the same for herself. While her appearance greatly appealed to him, from her heart-shaped face to her tiny waist and small, high breasts, he did not love her. Silas knew eventually she might fancy herself in love with him, but he wanted no part of that. Knowing they liked one another and would get along was enough for him. He would use the power of his kisses and persuasion to get her agree to marry him.

"Ready to lose gracefully?" Lord Carroll asked, striding toward him.

"I would ask the same of you, my lord. You are looking at an expert archer. I would have been quite successful five hundred years ago. Lords throughout England would have clamored for my services with a bow and arrow," he teased.

He liked Carroll. He always had. But he had placed distance between him and the earl this past Season, not wanting to be caught up in old, familiar patterns while he was on the hunt for a bride. Things seemed to be better between them now, and he was grateful for that.

"Is there any particular lady you wish to impress today?" Carroll asked. "Perhaps Miss Lyric? I have stayed away from her, you know, simply to honor what we once had between us."

"I appreciate your consideration," he replied. "Yes, I am interested in Miss Lyric. Has any lady claimed your eye?"

The earl's hazel eyes went green. "Stay away from Miss Allegra," he ordered.

He was interested in Allegra Strong?

"I do not think that is a good idea, Carroll," he voiced.

"Do you think I am not good enough for her?"

"I think His Grace would serve your head on a platter if he knew you dallied with his cousin." Silas paused. "Think hard, Carroll. You do not wish to make an enemy of Seaton. These Strongs are protective of one another. If he has an inkling a rake such as you is sniffing about Miss Allegra, there might not be much of you left."

"Then why the bloody hell was I invited to this house party?" the earl growled. He took a deep breath, obviously trying to calm himself. "Her Grace—Mrs. Andrews, that is—seems to think there is more to me," he said, raw pain painted on his face.

Silas asked, "Do *you* think there is more to you than the rake you play?"

"Yes. No one truly knows me. Not you. Not anyone. Not even myself," Carroll admitted. "But Mrs. Andrews seems to think I am redeemable. Somehow, I want to prove to her—to myself—that I am. That I am more than what the gossips believe me to be."

"You have a genuine interest in Miss Allegra?"

The earl nodded. "I do. I am going to prove to her—to everyone at this house party—that I can be someone to be proud of."

He placed his hand on his old friend's shoulder. "Then I wish you the best in doing so, Sterling." He hoped using Carroll's given name might soothe him somewhat.

"I know you have changed, Silas."

"I am trying to. I think I could better reach my potential with Miss Lyric as my wife."

Carroll flashed his famous smile at Silas. "Just think—we might soon be related if all goes well for us."

Warmth filled him. "I hope that will be the case."

Glancing up, he saw others approaching and said, "If you would, please do not make known my plans with Miss Lyric. I am making progress with her, but I don't want others talking prematurely."

His friend snorted. "At least you are making progress. I haven't a clue where I stand with Miss Allegra."

"We have more than a week left of this house party, Carroll," he said, slapping the earl on the back. "Let us make the most of it."

Servants began placing archery equipment on the lawn, setting up several targets a good distance from each other in order for practice to commence. Chairs also had been brought, and the Duchess of Seaton waddled over to one of them with the help of her husband. Silas couldn't help but see how the duke's love for his wife was written across his face and how the duchess glowed as she neared the end of her term. It troubled him that Lyric saw this on a daily basis.

Would she truly wish to wed him without love between them?

All he had to offer was the strong connection he felt between them. Passion lay there, but they were also forming a foundation based on friendship. Those coupled together should be more than enough for a successful marriage. At least, that was what Silas told himself.

He saw Miss Allegra sort through several bows and pick up one, aiming at a target and firing her arrow at it. The arrow struck close to the very heart of her mark. Obviously, she would need no lessons from Lord Carroll or anyone else.

Going to Miss Lyric, he said, "Are you ready to allow me to instruct you in the finer points of archery?"

"Only if you will not become discouraged by any lack of progress on my part, my lord," she said, laughing.

He took her elbow, leading her to several bows which had been placed upon the lawn.

"First and foremost, you must find a bow for your size. If you choose one too small, it will break because you will pull back too far."

She giggled. "Look at me, my lord. I am but two inches over five feet. I do not think they make a bow too small for me." She glanced about the ground. "Besides, most of these look so large, I doubt I would be able to pull it back all the way."

He sorted through them and brought one up. "I think this one will do."

"Shall I find us some arrows?" she asked.

"Not yet. We will perfect how you hold the bow first and talk about aiming before we test arrows."

Silas led her away from the group. "Even though you have no arrows now, it is always best to behave as if you do. Safety is important where archery is concerned. Never aim and shoot when anyone is in front of you. When shooting with others, stand in a line, side-by-side. And for goodness' sake, wait until all arrows have been fired before you try to retrieve your own."

Lyric sniffed. "That is merely common sense, of which I have plenty, Lord Blankenship."

"Did you claim any guards, Lord Blankenship?" called the duke. "We have several."

"No. Thank you, Your Grace. We will find some now."

"What are guards?" she asked, following him to where her cousin pointed.

"There are two types of guards. I am glad to see both here. An arm guard prevents string burn, while finger guards protect your fingers from being scraped when you pull back the bowstring."

He showed her how to don both, and they returned to her bow. Bending, he retrieved it and held it in his hand.

"Your stance is critical. You want your side facing the target, with your feet shoulder-length apart, though one foot will rest in front of the other."

She situated herself, and he nodded approvingly. Now came the part he had been looking forward to.

Bringing the bow to her, Silas handed it over, asking, "Which is your dominant hand?"

"I am right-handed," she replied.

"This will seem odd, but you will hold the bow with your left hand then," explaining how her right would draw the bow back. "Your dominant hand is stronger."

"That makes sense," she agreed.

"But, we must check for your dominant eye, as well."

Lyric frowned. "How do you know which one that is?"

He stood behind her, covering her left eye with his palm, catching the scent of orange blossom which always seemed to cling to her.

"Look at the target in front of you," he instructed.

"I am," she said, her voice shaking.

He dropped his hand and covered her right eye. "Look again.

Do you see any difference?"

"No," she said thoughtfully. "Am I supposed to?"

"Some see better out of one eye than they do the other," he explained. "Can you see the target clearly?"

"Yes. I have no need for spectacles. At least not at my age."

"Then we can continue."

He remained standing behind her. Close. The intoxicating scent of her surrounded him as he told her to lift the bow. He placed his hands over hers. Her back was pressed closely to his front, his heart thumping against his ribs. He sensed she trembled and was afraid he did, as well.

"Look at the target," he said into her ear, his lips brushing the lobe. "Focus on the center. That is where you aim to send your arrow, as close to the center as possible."

They practiced together, pulling the bow back and releasing it several times.

"It stings," she complained. "I am thankful for the protection of the guard."

"You will be quite sore in the morning, Miss Lyric," he warned. "Today, you will use muscles you are not used to using often. Even a little bit of practice, and your muscles will be strained."

"Are you telling me I will not be able to leave my bed, my lord?" she asked.

The thought of her, naked and in bed, almost did him in. He swallowed. "You might need assistance from your maid," he said tonelessly, hoping his cock would not swell. "Are you ready to try it with an arrow?"

"Yes, please," she said eagerly.

He stepped back from her and collected several arrows. Picking one up, he said, "You must nock your arrow." He touched the end. "Since this end does not have a point, this is your nock. You must insert it near the middle of your bowstring."

Silas paused, reaching out and running his thumb and index finger over the bowstring. "Yes, it is here."

Taking her hand, he had her run her fingers along the bowstring, asking, "Do you feel that tiny metal piece?"

"Yes."

"This helps you when you aim. Place the arrow end with the tip on the end of your bow. Never rest the arrow on your hand. I promise you, it stings when you let go, and you don't wish to injure your hand.

"I understand."

Stepping behind her again, he moved to where their bodies were touching once more, his hands over hers.

"Draw the string back. That's right. Let your hand rest against your face. Good girl. Now, look down the shaft and—"

"What is that?"

"The shaft? It is the long stick of the arrow."

"I am looking," she said, her body tense, shaking from holding the bow back that long.

"Then point the arrow at your target. And fire."

Lyric released, the arrow sailing through the air. "I hit it! I hit the target! On my first try."

"You did. Not bad. It is halfway between the center and the edge."

She glanced over her shoulder, their lips close. "Only because you were helping me to aim."

"Try again," he said, bending and claiming another arrow, allowing her to nock it. He still remained close, feeling her body heat, his hands atop hers. The first time, he had aided her in drawing back the string. This time, he had her rely entirely on her own strength, though his hands still touched hers.

"This is most difficult," she complained.

"I told you that you would be using muscles."

She sniffed. "Well, I do not have the muscles you do, my lord. They are everywhere. Even when you rolled up your sleeves this morning. Your forearms are even muscular."

So, she had noticed his build. He liked that.

"Quit talking and aim," he ordered.

Lyric did so, pausing a moment, and then she let the arrow fly through the air. This time, it struck hallway between the arrow protruding from the target and the center.

"Better," he praised. Reluctantly, he released his hold on her, stepping away. "Let us see how you fare now, all on your own."

She missed the target entirely.

But she laughed, a good sport about it, and accepted the next arrow he handed to her. She continued practicing and improved with each shot.

"I am becoming accustomed to all I need to do," she told him. Lowering the bow, she added, "You are a patient tutor."

"Thank you, Miss Lyric. I am certain you will make me proud in the competition."

"I know I will never beat Allegra, but second place would feel like victory to me."

In the end, she did take the second spot behind her twin, who outshone all the competition. Miss Bancroft and Miss Markle made a decent showing, however, while Lady Lida never hit the target once in any of the five rounds. It didn't seem to matter, though, because Lord Motley consoled her. Silas had not seen that pairing coming, and he hoped it might last.

The gentlemen were to compete next. Even His Grace joined in the fun. While the ladies had each aimed five times at their targets, the men went head-to-head in pairs, with the winners advancing over double the rounds. It did not surprise Silas when he and Lord Carroll were the last two standing in the competition.

"I hope I did you proud, Allegra," the duke said, adding, "My cousin gave me a few archery lessons before today, just as my sister Effie has been teaching me to ride. I suppose between the two of them, I might make for a country gentleman, after all."

Servants removed the arrows from the targets and set things up for the final match. Silas and Carroll were close in their skill level, but it was his friend who snatched the victory on the final shot.

"That took longer than I expected," Mrs. Andrews said, once the competition ended. "Why don't we save lawn bowling for another day? Everyone must want to go in and freshen up since tea will be served in the drawing room in half an hour."

He shook hands with the earl. "A good match."

"Indeed," Carroll said, his eyes roaming.

"She is behind you," Silas said quietly. "Coming this way."

Turning, he took a few steps, being met by Lyric. He loved how her russet hair gleamed brightly in the sunlight.

"No one in your family possesses your hair color," he noted.

"All the Strongs have cornflower blue eyes, and most of them, like Allegra, were born with dark hair. My cousin Mirella got her auburn hair from her paternal grandmother, while Cousin Effie's golden hair comes from her maternal grandmother. My hair, which looks more brown than red indoors, changes color when I am in the sun. Much more of the red is visible." She paused and quietly added, "Aunt Dinah told me my mother had hair the same shade of russet."

Then she brightened. "You shot quite well, my lord."

"Not well enough to win," he said ruefully.

"Your skill with a bow and arrow is obvious."

"I believe Lord Carroll had added incentive, wanting to impress your sister."

She frowned. "I do not think he should pursue her. He is a rake. Allegra deserves much better than that. Even if she has kissed him."

"They have kissed?" Silas asked, intrigued by that.

"Oh, I should not have said so. Please do not mention that I did to Allegra."

"Your secret is safe with me, Miss Lyric."

"I feel safe when I am with you, Lord Blankenship," she said, her words intriguing him even more than the kiss her twin and Lord Carroll had shared.

She glanced around. He did, too, seeing they were alone. All others had retreated to the house, and servants had claimed the archery equipment and were walking away. No one had eyes on them.

Boldly, he took her waist, tugging her toward him. "I may not be eligible for a victor's kiss, but I would like to kiss you all the same."

She didn't speak, but her eyes gave him permission. Silas hungered for her, but they were still in the open. He did not want to force them into a betrothal. He wanted her to say yes on her own.

Because of that, he slowly brushed his lips against hers a moment and then released her, pleased when he saw disappointment reflected in her eyes.

"Thank you for the kiss, Lyric."

"Don't . . . don't you want . . . a better one?" she pleaded.

"Not in the open when anyone might catch us at it," he said. "But if we found an alcove later tonight, I would be up for a much different kind of kiss."

She smiled—and he almost gobbled her whole.

"Aunt Dinah has asked Allegra and me to play for our guests this evening. Perhaps afterward we might go for a stroll in the gardens."

"As long as you do not make me pick weeds," he countered, causing her to laugh. "No, a stroll would be lovely. And anything that happened on that stroll."

Lyric's gaze met his. "Until tonight, my lord."

She left him, and he felt as he always did when she was gone. Silas knew for certain that he must have her. That no one else would ever do.

Tonight, he would offer for her.

CHAPTER EIGHT

LYRIC AND ALLEGRA got ready for the evening, a maid helping them to change their gowns. Lyric sat before the dressing table's mirror and asked for the maid to dress her hair simply. The maid suggested an elegant chignon, and she agreed to the style.

When it came time to dress Allegra's hair, she sat, looking out of sorts. Lyric felt she must say something.

"What is wrong?" she asked her sister. "You have been so quiet. Is it Lord Carroll who has you feeling so morose?"

Her twin's chin moved up a notch in defiance. "We do not need to discuss Lord Carroll," she said dismissively.

Lyric picked up the brush, signaling to the maid to leave them. She began brushing her twin's long, dark hair. She had a talent for arranging hair, and she often played with Allegra's, testing new styles.

"I do not think he is good for you," she said quietly, pinning her sister's hair into place.

"He might not be—but he is the one I want," Allegra admitted.

She stepped back and sat on the bed. Allegra spun to face her.

"If you are in love with him, you should be happy, Allegra. You aren't. You are miserable. And just because you love him, it does not mean that he loves you in return," she pointed out.

"Well, thank you for being so frank," snapped her twin. Immediately, Allegra burst into tears, and apologized. "I am sorry, Lyric. I do not want Lord Carroll—or any other man—to ever come between us."

She patted the bed, and her twin came to sit beside her. Lyric put an arm about her, hoping to comfort her.

"I am glad that you have found someone yourself," Allegra said, sniffing. "I told you before how much I like Lord Blankenship. I hope by the time this house party ends, the two of you will be betrothed."

Lyric hoped the same. It was mad how quickly she had fallen in love with him. She did not even know where his country residence stood, much less his favorite food. Yet she knew from what Georgie had said about the Season that a girl making her come-out might dance with a man a handful of times and suddenly find herself betrothed to him without knowing much about him at all.

It did not matter. She knew the essence of Lord Blankenship. That he was a kind, caring man who would make for an excellent husband and father. She only hoped he loved her as much as she loved him.

"I hope the same," she said, responding to her sister's comment. "I worry about you though. I am noticing how couples have begun to form attachments. Miss Markle and Lord Lamkin seem quite attracted to one another. Lord Tillings and Miss Bancroft are smitten. And surprisingly, Lady Lida is spending quite a bit of time with Lord Motley. In fact, I found her coming down from the nursery earlier today. She told me she had been playing with Lady Viola."

Lyric took Allegra's hand in hers. "That means you have been left out. The only man available is Lord Carroll. Please, Allegra, promise me you will not do anything rash. That you will not fall for his seductive airs. I know he is a handsome devil, but you have always had good sense about you."

"What if he has changed?" Allegra asked. "Aunt Dinah believes there is more substance to him than he reveals to others. He did make a poor first impression upon me, but he has tried to amend that impression ever since. I know he and Lord Blankenship were friends at one time, Lyric. Perhaps the viscount's influence on Lord Carroll has helped bring about a change within him."

She squeezed Allegra's hand. "I do not want to see you hurt. Please, be careful."

"I will," her twin promised.

But Lyric knew Allegra better than anyone. Allegra was already in love with Lord Carroll, and it would most likely prove to be disastrous. Men such as the earl did not make for good husbands even if they did decide to wed. She did not want her sister imprisoned in a marriage which would make her miserable for the rest of her life. Allegra might love Lord Carroll, but he would never love anyone but himself.

"If no betrothal from Lord Carroll comes by the end of this house party, would you participate in the Season next spring?"

Allegra was silent but finally said, "I cannot think that far ahead. Let us get through this house party and see what happens."

They went downstairs and met the other guests in the drawing room, going into dinner after that. Allegra was seated between Lord Tillings and Lord Carroll, but Lyric noted all her twin's time was devoted to the earl. She watched them carefully throughout the entire meal. They spoke continuously. She shook her head, thinking this would end badly.

As the ladies withdrew to the drawing room, Aunt Dinah reminded Lyric that she and Allegra were to entertain their guests this evening. She suggested they go to the music room to collect their sheet music, hoping her twin might reveal something about her dinner conversation with Lord Carroll. Allegra never mentioned the earl's name, however, and Lyric thought her twin already prickly enough, causing her to refrain from mentioning him herself.

They decided the pieces they would play, and Allegra suggested they sing a duet together for their final number. Their voices had always blended well together, and Lyric readily agreed, thinking their guests would enjoy it.

She and Allegra went to the music room after the meal to retrieve their music and even played a song apiece to warm up their fingers. They returned to the drawing room as the men came in from their after-dinner brandy and cigars. Aunt Dinah nodded to her. Lyric made her way to the pianoforte to play her two songs.

Much to her surprise, Lord Blankenship joined her.

"I will turn the pages of your music, Miss Lyric," he volunteered. "You have no need to worry. I do read music, you know. I will not cause your fingers to stumble as you play."

She performed her two selections and retreated to a nearby settee, the viscount joining her on it. Just sitting next to him, their shoulders brushing against each other's, caused her belly to feel as if a thousand butterflies swarmed within in it. She hoped during their stroll in the gardens later that he would make known his feelings to her because she was dying to tell him how much she loved him.

Once Allegra had played her songs, Lyric rejoined her twin at the pianoforte. Allegra played while the two of them sang. A sadness tinged their performance, however, with Lyric thinking the day was coming when she would not see her twin every day. They woke up together each morning and spent much of their time during the day together, sleeping in the same bed at night and sharing confidences before they fell asleep.

Aunt Dinah suggested that the group sing a few songs, so Allegra remained seated and played several folk songs they all knew. Their guests gathered around, enjoying singing in a group. Even with so many voices, two stood above the others. Lady Lida's sweet soprano floated above the women's, while Lord Blankenship's rich tenor reverberated among the men.

As they finished singing *The British Grenadiers*, everyone else silenced their voices, allowing the viscount to sing the last verse solo. Lyric could imagine nights after they supped, with her playing and her husband singing to her—and eventually, one day—their children. It filled her with a tremendous warmth, and love for this man poured from her.

Their chaperones, along with James and Sophie, talked about heading to bed. The younger people, however, were not ready to do so. She watched as those they had spoken about paired off, and Lyric joined the viscount after commenting to Lady Lida that she thought they might stroll through the gardens to cool down.

He offered his arm to her, and she slipped her hand into his crook, enjoying the feel of her fingers against his strong arm.

They reached the gardens and leisurely strolled through them, speaking of the various guests and how budding romances seemed to be forming.

"I am worried about my sister, "she confided. "With couples forming attachments, Allegra has been left out. The only bachelor available to her is Lord Carroll."

"Would that be such a bad thing?" he asked. "Yes, Carroll has been a wild one up to this point, but he and I have shared a couple of conversations in recent days. I believe the earl is quite taken with your sister."

"So much that he could change his rakehell ways overnight?" she demanded.

Lord Blankenship shrugged. "That, I could never guarantee. It is up to Miss Allegra to decide if she wants a life with him, and it is up to Carroll to decide if he can be the man your twin needs him to be."

By now, they had reached the gazebo, an octagonal structure which had benches lining all but one of its sides. They ascended the stairs up to it and moved to the center, the sweet smells of the garden's blooms floating about them.

He placed his hands on her shoulders. His touch alone had Lyric's pulse leaping and her nipples tightening.

"Thank you for agreeing to be alone with me this evening, Lyric. I wanted to spend time with just us so I might demonstrate the depth of my feelings for you."

His words told her this was the man for her.

"Kiss me, Silas," she insisted. "Kiss me. Now."

He smiled down at her. "It is what I want to do most in life, my dearest. Something I wish to do every day from now on."

That told her he would be offering for her. They would create a life together as man and wife. She had never been so certain about anything as she was about Silas Chase.

His lips grazed hers. He did not rush. Lyric knew they had all the time in the world. His arms went about her, pulling her against him, and she reveled in the feel of his hard body. His kisses became more demanding, and she gave over to them. To him.

To her future husband . . .

She raised her arms, locking her fingers behind his nape. As they continued to kiss, his tongue swept along her bottom lip, causing her breasts to swell and her core to tighten. Need pooled low in her belly, and Lyric opened to him. The heady kisses caused her to lose all track of time. She wanted to live in this moment forever. Her tongue teased his playfully, and he growled, his hands sliding down her back, gripping her buttocks, kneading them. Flames burst within her at this touch. She wanted so much of him. No, all of him.

He broke the kiss, his lips trailing down the column of her throat. He nipped at it, causing a new rush of desire to rage through her.

Breaking the kiss, he took her hand and led her to a bench. Silas sat, pulling Lyric down, not next to him, but into his lap. She brought her arms around him and bent, kissing him. She liked taking some initiative with him, this man she would vow to love always.

They kissed for a long time, the kisses growing more heated. His hand ran back and forth along her thigh, its heat easily felt through her clothes. Her core now throbbed unmercifully, and Lyric wanted more from him.

She broke the kiss. "I feel so funny all over," she revealed. "I . . . want your hands on me. Everywhere. Does that make me a wanton?"

He smiled lazily at her. "If it does, then you are *my* wanton." Gazing intently at her, he said, "We can do something to help alleviate the need within you. Do you trust me?"

"I will always trust you, Silas," the comment laying her soul bare to him as she used his given name for the first time.

He kissed her hard, and broke the kiss. "Then if you trust me, know that when I say you will feel as you never have before, I mean it. You will do this with me—and no other."

His hand slipped under her skirts, stroking her calf, sending wonderful tingles throughout her. His fingers danced up to her thigh, brushing the inner side of it, causing her core to throb with renewed need.

Her breath hitched when he touched her intimately, caressing the seam of her sex. She watched as his eyes darkened.

"You are wet for me, Lyric."

"What does that even mean?" she asked, knowing how naïve she must sound to him.

"It means you will truly enjoy what we do next. Close your eyes and give over to the new sensations you feel."

She did as he asked, and his fingers went to work on her. He stroked her, causing her breasts to grow heavy. He continued kissing her as he did this, and suddenly, he pushed a finger inside her, mimicking with it what he did with his tongue.

Lyric's hips raised instinctively, and he chuckled against her mouth.

"That's it. Feel. Move. Accept the pleasure."

He dipped a second finger into her, caressing her deeply. She gave over to the impulse and began rocking against his fingers. Something began building inside her, something forbidden and wonderful. She realized she was on the cusp of some new, wonderful adventure.

And then she tumbled over the edge, crying out, rocking violently against him, a warmth like sunshine spreading through her that flowed to her fingertips and toes. The incredible sensations filled her, and then finally trickled away. Lyric went limp, her head falling against his chest.

"What was that?" she murmured, hearing the low rumble of laughter within him.

"That, my darling girl, was an orgasm. It is but one of the ways a man can pleasure a woman."

Suddenly, she came to her senses, her head snapping up. "Did we just make a babe?" she worried.

He smiled indulgently at her. "No, my sweet innocent Lyric. No babe will result with something such as that. Has your aunt not explained such things to you?"

She shook her head. "Aunt Dinah said once we are betrothed, she would tell us what happens between a man and woman."

"Well, you have had a glimpse of what is to come. Suffice it to say, there are many more things we will do together to make you come alive as you just did."

Shyly, she asked, "Are there things I can do for you to make you feel that wonderful?"

He seized her mouth, kissing her passionately.

"Yes, there are things you, too, can do to make me feel the same way."

Silas cupped her cheek. "You know this moment between us has been coming Lyric. I want to make it official between us. Will you marry me?"

"Yes!" she cried enthusiastically, throwing her arms about him and covering his face in kisses.

When her lips touched his, more heated kisses began. Lyric knew the happiness that other Strongs had known. She loved and was loved.

She broke the kiss this time and smiled at him. "We are going to be so happy together, Silas. I love you so very much."

He stiffened at her words, and she frowned. "What? Did I say something wrong? Oh, I know. *You* are supposed to tell me first that you love me."

Lyric waited. He said nothing. Her heart thumped against her ribs.

"Silas? Talk to me."

He took her hands in his. "You know how much I wish to be with you, don't you?"

"Yes," she said slowly, searching his face.

"And that we are suited for one another."

"Yes," she agreed again, panic starting to rise within her. "But?"

"I enjoy being with you Lyric. You are unlike any woman I have ever known. I know when we kiss that we are meant to be man and wife."

Understanding struck her. "But . . . you do not love me."

He raked his hands through his hair. "I simply do not believe in it, Lyric. I know you say you have seen it in your own family, but I believe it is the flush of passion your cousins have with their mates."

Silas grabbed her hands and kissed them. "We, too, have that passion between us. I promise I will always be faithful to you. You are the only woman I wish to be with, the only one I wish to make love to. We will have a good life together and make babes."

Dully, she said, "But you will never love me."

"I *like* you, Lyric. A great deal. That is what is important. Passion can fade, but we always remain husband and wife. I will always care for you and respect you."

"Yet love will not play a part in our marriage."

He kissed her hands again. "We do not need love. We have passion and each other. We can build a good life together, different from most couples of the *ton*."

Lyric jerked her hands from his. "*I* need love, Silas. Your love. I love you so much it hurts. I will love you until the end of time and beyond."

She rose. "What I refuse to do is speak vows with you which you do not believe. If you cannot love and cherish me, then there will be no marriage."

He shot to his feet, his hands fastening on her shoulders. "Do not be ridiculous, Lyric."

"I am being ridiculous?" She stepped back, breaking the contact between them. "What I am being is true to myself. Strongs marry for love. I will settle for nothing less."

He looked at her sadly, and she knew she had lost him. "Then you are a fool. We could have had a good life together. You are the only one preventing that now."

Rage filled her. "That's it. Go and pout. Or run away." Lyric shook her head. "You are afraid, Silas Chase. I never thought you a coward, but that is exactly what you are. I have no intention of wedding a man who is a coward, much less a man who cannot love me in return. I wish I had never met you!"

Lyric hiked her skirts and took off, dashing from the gazebo and through the gardens. She ran, leaving them behind. Leaving him behind. She ran until she could not run anymore, collapsing on the ground, gut wrenching sobs gripping her. As the tears flowed, she regretted ever meeting him. Kissing him. Doing such intimate things with him.

Finally, her tears subsided. She picked herself up and trudged back to Shadowcrest, entering through the front door. The footman on duty leaped to his feet, shock filling his face when he saw her.

"What is wrong, Miss Lyric?" he asked, causing tears to fall again.

"Nothing," she said softly. "Nothing at all."

Going up the staircase, Lyric did not regret telling the servant a lie. It would be one she would tell others for the rest of her life. That she was fine. That nothing was wrong.

What would never change was that Lord Blankenship had trampled upon her heart—and she was ruined to ever love any man.

Except the one who could never love her in return.

CHAPTER NINE

A s Lyric climbed the stairs, a sudden rush of emotions ran through her.

Something was wrong with Allegra . . .

Growing in the womb together had formed an unbreakable bond between the twins, and they often finished one another's sentences. They could communicate with a look between them, no spoken words necessary. Instinct now told Lyric that something terrible had happened to her twin. She rushed the remaining way to their shared bedchamber and flung open the door.

Allegra sat on the bed, staring into space. Her eyes were red and swollen from crying.

She moved to the bed and sat upon it, her arm going about her sister. Allegra rested her head against Lyric's shoulder, and they sat in silence for many minutes.

Allegra finally lifted her head and looked into Lyric's eyes. "Sterling does not love me," she said dully.

If she thought she had hurt before, Lyric ached even more now, seeing her twin suffering so.

Taking Allegra's hands in her own, she said, "Can you tell me about it?"

"I can—simply because it is you. I can never tell anyone else what passed between us."

Allegra burst into tears, which caused her to do the same. They wrapped their arms about one another and cried for several minutes. Finally, Allegra pulled away, wiping her tears with the backs of her hands.

"We did things we should not have done," her sister began. "Intimate things."

Guilt rushed through her, and Lyric knew her cheeks heated at that comment. She hoped that Allegra would not notice. She wasn't certain just how much she was willing to share with her twin.

"You warned me about him. I should have listened to you," Allegra said bitterly.

"Tell me what you can," she encouraged.

"Everyone went their separate ways. We remained in the drawing room. When I think now that anyone might have come in and seen us in such a compromising position . . ." Her voice trailed off. Then Allegra sighed. "Thank goodness no one did. Because I would not want to be chained to such an unfeeling rake for a lifetime of misery."

They sat again in silence for some minutes before Allegra spoke up again.

"He kissed me the way he has before. The way that makes me throw all caution to the wind. I lose myself in him, Lyric. Sterling's kisses take me to a different place, where time does not exist."

Her twin paused, swallowing visibly. "I do not wish to talk of the rest. Only that he . . . touched me . . . intimately. Where only a husband touches his wife. Thank goodness, we did not do more than we did. If we had coupled—if I had become with child— frankly, I do not know if he would have done the right thing and wed me. And I don't know if I had become with child if I would agree to wed him after what he said to me."

Sympathy filled Lyric. "What did he say?"

"It wasn't what he said. It is what he could not say." Tears swam in Allegra's eyes. "He does not love me. He told me it was my choice to do the things we did together tonight. I did them willingly, only because I love him." She corrected herself. "Loved him. I cannot love a man who only loves himself."

"Did he offer for you?" she asked, think how Allegra's experience echoed that of her own.

Her twin nodded. "I do think in his own way, Sterling believes he has changed. Enough so that he was willing to marry me. But when talk turned to love? It was as if I were speaking a foreign tongue to him, one which he could never learn, much less understand."

Lyric could believe how similar tonight had gone for the both of them. The same thing had occurred at the exact time. The men they had loved with all their hearts had dashed the Strong sisters' hearts. She doubted either of them would ever be the same.

"I broke all ties with him," Allegra continued. "Before Pippa and Georgie wed for love, I would have been happy with the arrangement Sterling offered. It would have been physically satisfying to the both of us. But after seeing our cousins—even James and now Aunt Dinah—be so completely happy, I knew that I could not settle for anything less."

Allegra touched her fingers to Lyric's cheek, concern suddenly filling her face. "I have prattled on and on, but your eyes are too swollen for them to be simply from tears you have shed with me now, Lyric. What happened to you and Lord Blankenship?"

"I will repeat what you have shared with me," she said sadly. "We walked in the gardens, and I suspected he would offer for me." She blushed. "We also exchanged . . . intimate touches. Ones I am sure you are familiar with now because of Lord Carroll."

Lyric swallowed painfully. "Silas did ask me to marry him, and in my enthusiasm, I blurted out how much I loved him. He looked as if I had slapped him. It was the same song—only a different verse. He told me we had passion, and that would be enough for a solid marriage. We could build something special that other couples of the *ton* do not have. But he let me know he could never love me."

Her voice broke on that last word, and she began sobbing. Her twin wrapped her arms about Lyric, and the two of the wept for the loves they had lost tonight.

When their tears were finally spent, Allegra looked at Lyric determinedly.

"We cannot let these two rogues ruin our lives."

"Silas already has ruined mine," she said quietly. "I love him more than I ever thought possible, Allegra. I do not see myself ever feeling the same about another man."

"I feel the same way about Sterling," her sister confessed. "That does not mean we cannot find love in the future, though. We are raw and bruised at this point. What we must do now is hold our heads high. Continue with the house party."

"How?" she cried. "How can we see the two of them? I would hope the pair would be off to town in the morning and not even show their faces."

"Sterling will try and win me back," Allegra said matter-of-factly. "I can tell he is a man who does not ever like to lose. Leaving Shadowcrest will be the last thing on his mind. However, I plan to stand strong. I will refuse to be alone with him again. you and I must put on a brave face for the sake of our guests, Lyric."

"Why?" she asked, doubting Silas would remain. She had made it perfectly clear she wished to have nothing to do with him ever again. If he had any sense or decency, he would leave first thing tomorrow.

"Although this house party is in our honor, it has brought other couples together," Allegra explained. "Look at how Lord Tillings lights up whenever Miss Bancroft enters the room. And despite her plain features, Miss Bancroft transforms when she smiles at the viscount. I doubt they ever would have discovered one another during the Season, but Aunt Dinah's house party has brought them together."

She nodded. "I agree. I do see Lady Lida and Miss Markle possibly forming attachments with Lord Motley and Lord Lamkin. You are right. We cannot mope about. Nor can we ask our guests to leave. We must give a chance for these other romances to play out. I assume Lord Tillings will announce his betrothal to Miss Bancroft by the party's conclusion. It is a strong possibility another engagement might also be forthcoming."

Lyric drew in a long breath and expelled it slowly. "It is going to take every ounce of courage the two of us possess in order to keep going, however. I will make certain to keep Lord Carroll away from you."

"And if Lord Blankenship decides to stay, I will do the same for you," Allegra promised.

"We must make Aunt Dinah aware of what has happened," she insisted. "Hopefully, she might structure the remaining activities so that we will not have to partner with either of them."

"I will speak to her after breakfast tomorrow morning."

"We should try and get some sleep," Lyric said. "It is late. I would prefer not to ring for a maid."

They assisted one another in getting ready for bed. They climbed into the bed they had shared for so many years, both lying on their backs, linking their fingers together. Lyric lay awake for a long time, finally drifting off to sleep.

THE NEXT MORNING, they dressed in silence. Lyric noted both of their eyes were no longer swollen. If they had been, she would have insisted they breakfast in their bedchamber.

They waited until ten o'clock to go down to the dining room, both hoping they would avoid the earl and viscount. Fortunately, neither was present at the table. Only a handful remained, the others having breakfasted earlier.

She engaged Miss Bancroft's aunt in conversation. The querulous woman had a bevy of complaints regarding her health, and Lyric listened with only half an ear, nodding sympathetically and murmuring every now and then. She saw her twin sitting with Lord Motley and Lord and Lady Crowell.

Aunt Dinah entered the room and informed them, "The gentlemen will be hunting in the forest this afternoon. Caleb will be taking them out at noon. In the meantime, easels will be set up with blank canvases, giving the ladies an opportunity to paint this afternoon."

"Where will this take place, Aunt Dinah?" Lyric asked.

"Down by the lake," her aunt replied. "That way, if you wish to paint the water, you may. Or you can turn your easel and paint the surrounding landscape and flowers. I know Miss Markle and Miss Bancroft have gone to my sitting room to write letters this morning. You might wish to join them there."

"I will do so know," she said, knowing Allegra would be sharing with their aunt what had transpired last night. Her twin would not give any details regarding the intimacies they had both exchanged with these selfish lords, only that an irreparable break had occurred between both couples, and they would wish to avoid the two gentlemen as much as possible.

"Shall we go to Aunt Dinah's sitting room?" she asked Miss Bancroft.

"No, I feel a headache coming on," the older woman proclaimed. "Both talk and the smell of paints will only exacerbate it. I plan to remain in my room today."

"I am sorry to hear that. I hope your headache will pass quickly."

Lyric thought that best. The younger Miss Bancroft became reticent anytime her aunt was nearby. Having the chaperone gone would allow her new friend to shine around others. She excused herself and went to Aunt Dinah's sitting room, where she found Miss Bancroft and Miss Markle working on their letters.

"Ah, Miss Lyric, I am so glad you could join us," Miss Bancroft said. "Did you hear that we are to paint today?"

Lyric couldn't help but chuckle. "Attempt to paint is more like it in my case," she revealed. "My cousin Mirella is quite good at painting and pursues it weekly. She can paint both still lifes and landscapes, and she has just begun trying to paint portraits, as well."

"She sounds most talented," Miss Markle said. "I am sorry your cousin did not stay for the house party."

"Mirella was to have made her come-out this past Season."

Lyric explained how Mirella had slipped in Hyde Park and broken her arm in two places.

"Why, that must have been so painful!" Miss Markle exclaimed.

"It was. Mirella had to wear a plaster on her arm from the spring into the summer in order to allow her bones to heal properly. More than anything, my cousin enjoys dancing. The doctor forbade her from doing any during the Season because of the heaviness of the plaster. She preferred to make her debut next spring. Because she was not out yet, she did not feel it right to be present at the house party."

"I believe someone mentioned that she went with your aunt to tour the Lake District?"

"Yes, along with my youngest cousin Effie and her governess. They are visiting friends of Aunt Matty's and also touring several houses in the area."

"I think that would be a lovely trip," Miss Bancroft said. "I have never had the opportunity to do much traveling."

"Where are you from, Miss Bancroft?" Miss Markle asked. "It has never come up."

"My father's country estate is in Somerset. While it is quite beautiful there, the only place I have been is there and to town for the Season. I was happy to receive the duke and duchess' invitation to this house party in order to be able to visit Kent, as well as hopefully make new friends."

Miss Bancroft smiled shyly at both of them, and Miss Markle said, "Well, I for one, am delighted to have made your acquaintance, Miss Bancroft. I hope that our friendship will continue beyond this house party. I was raised with Lida because my parents died when I was quite young. Lida is my closest friend. While I had hoped to form other friendships during my come-out this past Season, I found it to be more of a . . . . competition."

Miss Markle frowned. "No one seemed to wish to be friends. All they wanted was to land a husband. And I didn't find any of the men there appealing."

"But you are enjoying the company of the gentlemen invited to this house party, aren't you?" Lyric asked.

Miss Markle's cheeks pinkened. "It is no secret that I have been drawn to Lord Lamkin. While it is still early, I am appreciative that we have more time left to get to know one another."

She looked to Miss Bancroft. "And what of you, Miss Bancroft? Are you finding the company at Shadowcrest pleasant?"

Miss Bancroft's face flamed. "I do believe you are teasing me, Miss Lyric. I am certain it is obvious that I have enjoyed time spent with Viscount Tillings. Why, he is so intelligent and extremely kind. For some reason, he enjoys my company, as well."

"Do not underestimate yourself, Miss Bancroft. I believe you have quite a bit to offer a gentleman. Why, I suspect you will leave Shadowcrest betrothed to Lord Tillings."

Lyric did not think the young woman's face could get any redder, but it did.

The door opened, and Aunt Dinah and Allegra entered, along with Lady Lida and her mother.

Aunt Dinah's gaze fixed upon Lyric as the three other women took a seat. "May I speak with you, Lyric?" she asked.

Rising, she excused herself and retreated from the room with her aunt. Allegra stayed behind in order to entertain their guests.

Her aunt led them to the library, which was empty. Closing the door, Aunt Dinah enveloped Lyric in an embrace. She could feel the love and concern pouring from her aunt into her, bolstering her.

Aunt Dinah withdrew. "Allegra has shared with me the outcome of last evening. I am very sorry, Lyric. I had thought you and Lord Blankenship would be an excellent match. I also had high hopes for Allegra and Lord Carroll. Allegra told me that both men offered for each of you."

"Yes, Aunt Dinah, they did. Perhaps we are being foolish, throwing away the opportunity to wed titled gentlemen. I know Lord Blankenship and Lord Carroll believe we are. In our hearts, though, a physical attraction—great as it is—is not a good enough reason to wed."

"But you do have other things in common with the viscount, don't you?" her aunt pressed.

"We are perfectly suited in every way, other than the fact I love him will all my heart—and he does not possess one."

Aunt Dinah slipped a hand around Lyric's and squeezed it. "You love him, Lyric. Do you think he could grow to love you?"

She shook her head vigorously. "No, he made his feelings on that topic perfectly clear. He explained it would be a good marriage, but he would never give way to love."

Aunt Dinah squeezed her hand again and released it. "I understand. I respect the decision you and Allegra have made. I will do my best to keep you apart from these gentlemen for the remainder of the house party. Hopefully, one or both will find it necessary to leave Shadowcrest. Will you try to come and paint with the other ladies this afternoon?"

"I will come, Aunt, and put on a happy face. I do like all the ladies you have invited to Shadowcrest and am forming friendships with them all."

"Very well," her aunt said. "I will see you by the lake at noon then."

Lyric remained in the library, wondering how long she would be able to avoid Silas.

CHAPTER TEN

SILAS HAD BEEN grateful the men and women had been scheduled for separate activities today. He couldn't bear to see Lyric. Just glimpsing her on her way to the ladies' painting session at the lake had almost done him in. He had wanted to run after her, begging her to want him.

Even love him.

It amazed him after all these years how much his parents and their marriage still influenced him. They hadn't wanted to be bothered raising a child, and he had been handed off to servants. In all the time before their deaths, Silas had never learned how to please them or make them like him. As for love, that had never entered the conversation. If he truly analyzed what had gone on during his childhood, he could now see just how much the lack of attention he received from his parents shaped his life. He had become a person wanting to please others. He became charming, learning to get his way with his tutors at school and various classmates. When he got older, he learned to use his good looks and beguiling smile to seduce women of all ages.

Yet throughout his life, he had been a loner. Those on the outside would have thought he had numerous, close friends and not a care in the world. The truth was that he had countless acquaintances.

And no one to confide in. No one to lean on. Not a soul who truly understood him. He was, in truth, the outsider who had wormed his way into the core of everything, but he had remained rootless. Friendless. Except for Uncle Oscar.

What would his uncle think of this predicament Silas found himself in?

All his life, he had searched for acceptance from his parents and anyone else he encountered. He was the golden boy, with an abundance of intelligence, looks, and charm. But his life had been devoid of any close connections.

Until Lyric.

It didn't matter. It was over between them. What seeds had been planted had been unceremoniously uprooted, the garden of the growing relationship and the life they might one day share obliterated.

He had never hurt as much as he did in this moment.

Foolishly, he thought he could go on the hunt with the other guests this afternoon. He was distracted, though, and almost lost his seat from the horse more than once. For a skilled horseman such as himself, that alone was shocking. When Lord Carroll had left the hunt, Silas had followed him on a whim, deciding to seek advice from his one-time friend. He had poured out his heart to the earl, only to learn they were in identical situations. Both men had offered for a Strong. Both had been accepted.

And both had been unwilling—or unable—to speak the words of love their intended needed to hear.

Should he remain at the house party? He had berated Carroll for even thinking of leaving, telling his old friend his attempt to leave with nothing but his pride was mad. The earl had admitted he loved Allegra Strong, just as Silas loved Lyric. What was wrong with the two of them, that they could not express their feelings?

For his part, he still blamed his absent parents. Not only had they spent next to no time in the same household as him for over two decades, but they were also haunting him from the grave with their coldness and lack of feelings for their only son. Their behavior had shaped him, so much that he could not even utter the words in his heart. Words of love that Lyric needed—even deserved—to hear from him. Because of it, he had lost her. He had racked his brain, trying to come up with ways to convey the depths of his feelings for her, fearing any words he spoke to her, she would brush off as a poor attempt to persuade her to change her mind and marry him.

A knock at his door sounded, and Silas knew it was his valet, here to get him ready for tea. He admitted the servant to the bedchamber and said nothing, stripping off his clothes and changing into the new ones laid out for him.

Tea was held in the drawing room. He made certain to join a group with neither Lyric nor her twin. Instead, he sat with Lord Crowell, the old Miss Bancroft, Her Grace, and Mrs. Andrews. Mrs. Andrews kept trying to catch his eye, but Silas was in no mood for conversation with the former duchess. He merely drank his tea and tried to get down a scone while he ignored the laughter coming from Lyric's group.

"Are you quite all right, my lord?" Mrs. Andrews finally asked, her gaze pinning his.

He glanced and saw the others in their circle in conversation. Knowing there was no escape from her scrutiny, he shrugged.

"I would expect you to reply, Lord Blankenship," she chided. "It is not like you to brood."

"I am not brooding," he snapped, immediately regretting the words. "I am not, Mrs. Andrews," he added, softening his tone considerably.

"Then what has you so glum? You have been downcast ever since you entered the drawing room. Caleb told me you and Lord Carroll left the hunt early." She glanced about. "I see that Lord Carroll has not shown up for tea. Do you know where he might be?"

Carroll might have gone through with his plans and left Shadowcrest, but even Silas didn't think the earl would be so rude as to leave the house party without informing his hosts.

"I have not seen him," he said, taking a sip of his tea.

"Have you and Lyric quarreled, my lord? I thought you were getting along splendidly."

So, she had not yet spoken to her aunt of the events of last evening. He swallowed. "I would not term it a quarrel, Mrs. Andrews. Merely a parting of the ways."

"You are no longer interested in keeping company with her?" she asked, clearly concerned.

He needed to end this conversation right away. "It is a private matter," he said coolly. "One which I do not feel comfortable sharing with you. Perhaps your niece may wish to enlighten you at a later time."

Her gaze now bore into him. "Some things are worth fighting for, my lord. It takes a discerning gentleman to know when to let go—and when to take a stand."

Something told him that Lyric *had* spoken to her aunt. That Mrs. Andrews knew much more than she let on.

"Let it go. Please," he pleaded. "My heart is already heavy enough as it is."

She nodded sagely. "I will. For now. But if you have need of someone to listen to your problems, know that I am available."

Silas only wished he could speak openly to her about what had occurred, but she was Lyric's aunt. She would be on her niece's side. Not that there were sides to be had. Blast! He was so confused and upset, he no longer made sense.

"If you will excuse me, Mrs. Andrews, I think I will go and check on Lord Carroll and find out why he is absent from tea."

Without waiting to see if she protested, he quickly left the drawing room, having no intention of looking for Carroll. Instead, Silas retreated to the library. A maid was dusting the room, so he returned to his bedchamber and lay on the bed. He hadn't slept much last night, and he now fell into a fitful sleep.

What awakened him was his valet knocking again, ready to help Silas change for dinner. His eyes still felt gritty, and his sprits remained glum. He would make an appearance at dinner, though. Perhaps Lyric might be seated next to him, and he could try again. Of course, what she wanted to hear from him were words he felt in his heart but ones he could never express to her.

Because, in the end, he wasn't good enough for her. He never would be.

Lyric needed a man who came from a family such as hers. She needed someone who understood familial love, as well as the love a man felt for a woman.

He was not—and never would be—that man.

She would always remain in his heart, but he needed a wife who came from the same background as his. The marriage he eventually made would be the typical business arrangement of most marriages. He would return to town next Season and find a bride, thinking to look among the wallflowers. Any of them would be grateful to be plucked from obscurity and made a viscountess. They could wed and bed. Get him his heir. Life could then go on. He would spend most of it at Chase Oaks, caring for the estate and his tenants and enjoying time with his children. When in town, he would accompany his wife to *ton* events, but he simply couldn't have much to do with her.

Not when he would always want another woman in the role of his wife.

Dressed for dinner, Silas returned to the drawing room, where others were assembling in small groups. He joined Lord Lamkin, Lady Lida, and Their Graces, walking past Lyric without a glance in her direction. Accepting a drink from a footman, he forced himself to sip at it instead of draining it in one gulp. There would be plenty of time to get properly drunk after this house party concluded.

Then the atmosphere in the drawing room seemed to change. Silas watched a man in his late thirties stride across the room. He was about six feet in height, lean but appearing strong. He had thick, dark hair, and his face was bronzed by what had to be many hours spent in the sun.

The stranger went straight for Mrs. Andrews. He turned her and caught her in his arms, kissing her right in front of everyone gathered in the drawing room. It wasn't merely a quick kiss of greeting. It was a kiss which spoke of the connection between them.

He surmised this must be Captain Andrews, the seaman she had recently wed. He had learned that Andrews had given up his seafaring ways upon the marriage and was now heading up Neptune Shipping, the company owned by the Duchess of Seaton.

Spellbound, he could not pull his gaze away as the captain continued kissing the former duchess. The other guests seemed equally entranced. Silas dared a glimpse at Lyric and saw the wistful smile on her face.

Andrews broke the kiss. "I have missed you, love," he said, his voice raw with emotion. He looked about the room. "Forgive me for my brazen behavior. We are still newlyweds and have been separated for almost a week."

"No apologies are necessary," His Grace said. "We are happy to have you back at Shadowcrest, Captain Andrews. I know my duchess will be itching to talk business with you."

"Business will have to wait until tomorrow," Andrews said. "I am going to require time with my wife tonight."

Mrs. Andrews beamed at her husband. "You must meet our guests, Drake, and at least sup with them."

He smiled at her, and Silas saw the power in that smile—and the love this man had for his woman. "If you insist, love."

As they waited to be summoned to dinner, Mrs. Andrews took her husband about the room, introducing him to everyone. Once the captain had met the newcomers, he began to tell a few stories of his days at sea. The man was compelling, and the guests were easily drawn to him.

When he finished a story, Andrews said, "Enough from me. I must visit with my girls a bit before we go in to dinner."

Immediately, Lyric and Allegra flew to his side, and Silas

could see how close the three seemed. He found it interesting that the former sea captain had referred to the twins as his girls. Again, he wondered what it was about this family that drew them to one another, the bonds so strong, seemingly unbreakable.

The butler announced dinner, and the only lady near Silas was the elder Miss Bancroft. He escorted her to the dining room, where a place had been added for Captain Andrews. Silas found himself seated between the younger Miss Bancroft and Miss Markle, but neither lady was interested in conversing with him. Instead they—and the entire table—continued to be spellbound by Captain Andrews and the stories he and the duke told.

Silas quickly figured out that the two men had been at sea together for many years. At one point, Andrews even referred to His Grace as Captain, arousing everyone's curiosity as to what had occurred during the years James Strong had been absent from London.

Dinner ended, with Her Grace saying the men could forgo their brandy and cigars one night, asking they all withdraw to the terrace instead.

"Wine and cakes will be served once we arrive," Her Grace told the guests. "Then we will return to the drawing room for charades."

He looked to Carroll. The earl had worn a distracted look ever since he had appeared in the drawing room. Carroll shrugged.

"As for my wife and I, we will see you tomorrow. Or the next day." Captain Andrews grinned shamelessly, and Mrs. Andrews blushed, swatting him playfully.

The group left the dining room, and he watched Lord Carroll slip away, heading up the stairs without a word. He only wished he could have done the same. But with a man down, it would be rude to not follow the others outside and then partake in the party game.

Once they had their wine and sweets, Her Grace suggested that they break into teams of males and females to play.

"We must show the gentlemen how swiftly we think, ladies," the duchess teased.

Silas was grateful they hadn't been paired up and thought it possible that Lyric and her twin had something to do with the arrangements this evening. Neither of them had looked at him once this evening. When his turn arrived, the twins had not made a single guess.

Two hours after dinner, the group broke for the evening. Her Grace reminded them they would be picnicking at the lake tomorrow afternoon. He returned to his bedchamber, up for hours, trying to think of excuses to leave the house party. None seemed good enough. Telling a duke and duchess he was leaving their event early was unthinkable.

He supposed he would have to make the best of the situation and continue to avoid Lyric as much as possible.

CHAPTER ELEVEN

SILAS SKIPPED BREAKFAST. He had no appetite for food or conversation. He lazed about in bed, not wanting to get up.

A knock at the door forced him to rise. He climbed from the bed and opened the door, seeing his valet on the other side.

"I was worried, my lord," the anxious servant said. "When you didn't summon me to dress you this morning, I thought . . ." His voice trailed off.

"You thought what?" he asked.

The valet looked at him sheepishly. "I hope I am not speaking out of turn, my lord. I know you are one for the ladies."

"You thought I had some chit in my bed—or that I was in another bed?" he demanded, the thought of being with anyone but Lyric making him queasy.

"I did," the servant admitted. "Then you missed breakfast, and I thought you might be catching up on your sleep. But it is almost time for the picnic to start at the lake, Lord Blankenship. You must go to it," the valet insisted.

"You are right. Set out clothes for me at once."

"Right away, my lord."

The valet hummed to himself as he went about preparing Silas for the day. He had brought hot water along and shaved Silas before helping him to dress. As always, he looked just right for the occasion. Today, he wore a bottle green coat, fawn breeches, white shirt, a white and gold brocaded waistcoat, and a cravat tied to perfection.

"Your hat, my lord," the servant said, handing it over to Silas. "I hope you enjoy the picnic, my lord. The kitchens have been busy for hours preparing the food."

"Take the rest of the day off," he said generously. "I will not need your help to dress this evening."

"What . . . what do you mean, my lord?" the servant sputtered.

"What I said. I am a grown man. I can change my shirt without your assistance. Flirt with one of the maids. Go on a picnic of your own."

"Why . . . . thank you, Lord Blankenship. That is most generous of you."

Silas watched his valet leave and then went downstairs, where he ran into Carroll.

"I assume you are headed to the picnic," the earl said. "Would you care to go together?"

They set out for the lake, with Silas saying, "I am surprised you are attending the picnic. You have certainly made yourself scarce lately. I thought you had decided to return to town."

"I had wanted to," Carroll admitted. "But then some man I used to call friend scolded me like a schoolboy, telling me it was the wrong thing to do if I wanted to try and win back the woman I love."

"Have you a plan?" he asked. "To convince Miss Allegra you are the man for her?"

Silas wasn't above stealing any idea which might give him another chance with Lyric. Then he chastised himself, telling himself he would never be the man for her and reminding himself to keep his distance from her for the remainder of the house party. He already had formulated his plan, and that was to pluck a wallflower and have a meaningless *ton* marriage.

"I do," his old friend said with confidence. "I think you, too, should come up with your own measure to persuade Miss Lyric that you are meant to be together."

"I will not be doing so," Silas said stiffly. "I will choose a bride from those on the Marriage Mart next Season."

Carroll halted. "You are a gutless dolt, Blankenship."

"I suppose I am," he agreed tonelessly, continuing to walk.

The earl caught up with him. "You cannot mean what you say, Silas."

"I am not the man Lyric needs," he said frankly. "She is the most heavenly creature ever placed upon this earth. I am not worthy of her."

"So, you will wed and bed to get your heir—and spend the rest of your life pining for her," Carroll said flatly.

"Yes," he said, his throat feeling as if someone had rammed their fist down it.

"I have written a love poem for Allegra," the earl suddenly announced. "It's bloody good. I only hope it is good enough to convey the depth of my love for her."

His words startled Silas. "You wrote a poem. You."

"Yes. Me. I write poetry. It is something I have always kept to myself. Now, you know."

He stopped and placed his hand on Carroll's shoulder. "I think the effort alone will convince Miss Allegra to take you back. That—and you saying the words she longs to hear."

"I can say them," Carroll said stubbornly. "I even practiced before the mirror." He paused. "And if I say them, you can, too, Silas."

"But I won't," he said stubbornly. "I told you. I am unworthy of Lyric and her love. She needs to meet a man who can—"

"Who can what?" the earl demanded. "You are plenty good enough for her, and you bloody well know it. If I can be good enough for Allegra, you most certainly can be for Lyric. You are a better man than I am, Silas. You always have been. You simply need to believe in yourself more. Believe in you and Lyric together."

He dropped his hand. "I will not ruin her life."

"But you will ruin your own—and the woman you take to wife?"

He shrugged. "She will not care. She will become a viscountess and lack for nothing. She will have her friends and do the things she chooses to do. I will get my heir."

"And you will be miserable."

"Very much so," he agreed. "But it gives Lyric the chance to find someone else. Yes, she is hurt now, but she will recover. She has all those Strongs surrounding her, bolstering her. When the rest of her family returns to Shadowcrest, she will have even more support. Now, leave me be, Carroll. Go read your love poetry to Miss Allegra. Truly, I wish you the best. I hope she will forgive you."

Silas strode off, the ache inside him so intense, he almost doubled over in pain. He did want what was best for his old friend and Allegra Strong. If Carroll had summoned the courage to write a love poem, of all things, he could also say those words to Miss Allegra.

The picnic showed him just how out of place he was. Six of the guests had obviously formed strong attachments. Envy filled him as he saw Lady Lida with Lord Motley and his young daughter, already looking like a family. They ate their meal spread on a blanket, Miss Allegra with them. Miss Markle and Lord Lamkin paired off, sitting on a blanket by themselves. Miss Bancroft and Lord Tillings sat at a table with Lord and Lady Crowell and the elder Miss Bancroft and Lyric. The remaining table held the Duke and Duchess of Seaton and Captain and Mrs. Andrews.

He had no place to sit and no reason to be here.

He decided to walk around the lake instead. No one would miss him. Silas set off, finding the scenery beautiful despite his misery. He sat on a large rock, feeling sorry for himself, staying away a good two hours before he started back. When he did, he saw a couple of rowboats on the lake. Motley had taken out Lady

Lida and Lady Viola, while Lord Carroll and Miss Allegra sat in another. He saw them kissing and knew the earl's love poem must have worked its magic.

Deep down, Sterling Ayles was a good man. He wore a mask in Polite Society, much as Silas had his entire life. No one knew the true men behind those masks. He gathered Allegra Strong would get to know all of Sterling and love him even more. Silas would never begrudge or resent his friend for turning over a new leaf. It only made him sorrowful to know he would never be close to Sterling again. No more working their way through the female population of London. Sterling would be faithful to the Strong he wed. Of that, Silas had no doubt.

He watched as Lord Tillings helped Miss Bancroft to maneuver a fishing rod. Lord Lamkin did the same with Miss Markle. Even across the lake, their laughter carried.

Never had he been more miserable. Silas plopped on the ground, determined to wait out the happy couples. It was another two hours before everyone left the area, leaving a bevy of servants to retrieve the tables and chairs and cart them and the blankets and remaining food back to Shadowcrest. Following at a distance, he decided he would speak to the Seatons tonight and leave Kent in the morning.

Slowly, he walked toward Shadowcrest. He would carry many memories of this place with him. He would certainly use what he had learned from Lyric about gardening and spend time with his own gardeners at Chase Oaks. Every time he worked in the dirt, he would remember the woman who held his heart.

He had no doubt that she would attend next Season. Because of that, he rethought going himself. Instead, he would take time to get to know his neighbors in the country. Surely one of them would have a daughter of marriageable age. He could wed her quietly and remain in the country, never having to set eyes on Lyric again. Yes, that would be best. Marry a country girl and tell her he had no taste for city life.

Silas returned to the house and his bedchamber, peeling off

his clothes and slipping into his banyan. He rang for hot water, and a servant brought it to him so he could wash the heat of the day from him. He had heard Mrs. Andrews say since they would be at the lake so long today, they would forego tea and simply meet in the drawing room this evening before dinner as usual.

He washed and dressed, sitting quietly in a chair, knowing this would be his last night with the Strongs. Maybe he could forget Lyric. Try to make a go of a marriage. He knew he wanted children and that he planned to spend time with them, teaching the boys to ride and fish. He supposed he could also teach any girls the same things. Resolve filled him. He would have a quiet life and do the best he could to make his children feel wanted and loved.

When the time came, he made his way down to the drawing room, joining Lord Motley and Lady Lida and her parents. By the way Lady Lida glowed, Silas would not be surprised if a betrothal announcement was forthcoming.

"Viola was certainly tired," Lord Motley said. "It was quite an adventurous day for her. I took her to the nursery when we returned from the lake, and she could barely hold her head up to eat her milk and bread. By the time I left, she was already fast asleep."

"She told me that she wants a cat," Lady Lida shared. "That she had seen one in the barn. A mother cat with kittens. Perhaps you might ask His Grace if you could claim one for her when it is weaned from its mother."

Lord Motley smiled. "I can never say no to Viola—or you." The look in his eyes made Silas turn away so that no one could see how much he hurt.

The butler announced dinner, and he found himself sitting with Mrs. Andrews and her husband. Though Silas had always thought he had a talent for telling a tale, he appeared as an amateur compared to this man.

They were finished with the fish course when the captain said, "My wife tells me you were interested in Lyric."

It startled him to have it spoken of so openly. "Unfortunately, it was not meant to be."

"You offered for her," Captain Andrews said boldly. "You must have seen a future with our girl."

"I did—at one time," he admitted. "But Miss Lyric and I had differing opinions on exactly what a marriage should be, Captain. Because of it, she is free to pursue a different kind of man."

The former sea captain scratched his chin in thought. "You don't believe love has a place in marriage?"

"No," he said coolly, his gaze daring Andrews to continue the conversation.

"You're a hard-headed fool," the captain said dismissively, turning to his left to speak with the elder Miss Bancroft.

"He means well," Mrs. Andrews said. "He is very concerned about Lyric. So am I." She searched his face. "I am also concerned about you, Lord Blankenship."

"Do not be, Mrs. Andrews. I am fine," he assured her.

When fine was the last thing he was.

Dinner finally ended, and the men partook in their usual cigars and brandy. Silas put his out after only a few puffs, finding it tasteless. He did down the brandy, however, needing the courage it would provide to tell His Grace that he would be leaving the house party early. He hoped to get both Their Graces alone for a moment in the drawing room so he could so.

"Shall we join our ladies?" the duke asked, and the men rose from the table.

Silas found himself bringing up the rear of the group, the last to enter the drawing room. He glanced over his shoulder and noticed a few footmen following him into the room, seeing they carried trays with champagne flutes. He had been right. Lord Motley would announce his betrothal to Lady Lida this evening.

Glancing to Lord Carroll, he saw the earl stood beside Miss Allegra, his hand on the small of her back. The pair looked quite cozy. Perhaps there might even be two engagements announced tonight. When he spied Caleb Strong in the room, he knew he must be right. The Shadowcrest steward had not made a habit of joining them for dinner. His presence indicted that his sister's betrothal announcement would now occur.

"May I have your attention?" His Grace asked, and the room fell quiet. The duke slipped an arm around his duchess' waist. "We have some very good news to share this evening with our guests."

Silas took a deep breath, letting it out slowly. He braced himself, knowing his practiced smile would come in handy during the next few minutes.

"I wish to wed Miss Bancroft," Lord Tillings blurted out suddenly.

Chapter Twelve

Lyric smiled indulgently at Lord Tillings. He was a fine-looking gentleman, but more than a bit socially awkward. She had watched him come into his own, however, this week in the company of good men and was thrilled that the blossoming relationship the viscount had formed with Miss Bancroft would now come to fruition in marriage.

She glanced to the young woman, one who had been overlooked by so many in the *ton*. Yet now, Miss Bancroft grew quite pretty as she smiled radiantly at her intended.

Lord Tillings moved to stand before her, saying, "I should have offered for you privately, Miss Bancroft, but I got carried away. You are all that I can think about, and I am already richer for having known you. Might I accompany you to Somerset at the conclusion of this house party so that I may speak with your father and ask for your hand in marriage?"

"That will not be necessary," declared the elder Miss Bancroft. "She is of age. Her father and I hoped something would come of this house party. Go ahead, girl. Speak up. Let Lord Tillings know where you stand."

Miss Bancroft looked up adoringly at the viscount. "I would be honored to become your wife, my lord."

He took her hands and raised them to his lips, kissing her

fingers fervently. "You have made me the happiest of men, Miss Bancroft. I do wish to travel with you and your aunt home, however. I need to meet your father, and I assume you would like to be wed in your home parish."

Lord Tillings looked out at the room, zeroing in on his host. "Forgive me, Your Grace, for interrupting your announcement. I was caught up in the moment and my feelings for Miss Bancroft."

James smiled broadly at the viscount. "No apology is necessary, my lord. My duchess and I wish you the very best in your marriage to Miss Bancroft." He paused. "Back to my original announcement."

Laughter filled the room, and Lyric braced herself for the two betrothal announcements to come.

"First, I would like to share the good news that Lord Motley has asked Lady Lida to be his wife. Lord and Lady Crowell have given their full blessing to the match."

"Congratulations!" several people said enthusiastically, and Lord Motley took Lady Lida's hand, saying, "I have known the high of highs and the low of lows in my life. It is no secret about the tragedy I suffered in losing my wife all too soon. I have found someone special, though, in Lady Lida. She has accepted not only me—but Viola. Already, my daughter loves Lady Lida. I look forward to the life we will share together."

"Do you have a wedding date in mind?" Aunt Dinah asked the pair.

"We are eager to start our lives together," Lady Lida replied. "We have decided to wed in town with the use of a special license once the house party comes to its conclusion."

Lord Lamkin cleared his throat, and Lyric knew what was coming.

"I did not know I would be doing so this evening, but Lord Tillings' sudden proposal to Miss Bancroft has inspired me," the earl began. "Especially with Lord and Lady Crowell being present and having acted as Miss Markle's guardians all these years, I would like to ask their permission to wed their niece."

The earl and countess looked mightily pleased, and Lord Crowell said, "It would be wonderful to welcome you into our family, Lord Lamkin, along with Lord Motley and Lady Viola."

All eyes turned to Miss Markle, who beamed at the earl. "I would be delighted to become your wife, my lord."

"My mother will be pleased that I am finally settling down," Lord Lamkin said. "I cannot wait for Mama to meet you, Miss Markle. She will know with one look at my face how happy you have made me."

She swallowed painfully, all the betrothal announcements happy and yet distressing to her. Steeling herself for the final one of the evening, she concentrated on being excited for her twin after the rocky road Allegra and Sterling had traveled.

"This evening is full of surprises," James said. "We do, however, have one last bit of good news to share with everyone. Lord Carroll has proposed to my cousin Allegra, and we could not be happier to welcome him into our family."

Several gasps echoed throughout the room, and Lyric knew it was a surprise to many that such a known rogue was finally entering into marriage.

"I came to this house party a cynical rake," Sterling began. "In fact, I even questioned Mrs. Andrews here as to why she had invited me to Shadowcrest. My blackened reputation did not make me the ideal house party guest."

Sterling turned to Allegra and captured her hands in his, raising them slowly to his lips and brushing them across his fingers.

"I had yet to know what would hit me. A force of nature so great that she shook my world. Changed it permanently, in fact. There is no one I would rather wish to wed and spend a lifetime together than my feisty, beautiful Allegra. She has redeemed me in ways unimaginable. I suddenly find myself marrying into a loving family, looking forward to the many children we will add to the nursery at Carrollwood."

Several of the women sighed at the earl's words, Lyric among them. She had never seen her sister happier than in this moment, and she looked forward to being a doting aunt to the children the pair would produce.

"Shall we celebrate with champagne?" called James.

Immediately, the footmen distributed flutes about the room to each guest. Lyric accepted one, gripping the stem, her throat so tight she worried she would not be able to get the liquid down.

Her gaze met Allegra's, and she saw tears of joy in her twin's eyes. Despite the emotional upheaval Allegra had endured, Lyric was certain everything had been worth it to arrive at this moment. Her sister loved—and was loved, in return.

James raised his glass high. "We toast these four couples who have made the decision to go on life's most incredible journey together. May they find love and lasting joy throughout the years. To the happy couples!"

"To the happy couples!" the room echoed, the guests' glasses held high.

Lyric brought the flute to her lips, wetting them. Swallowing proved to be impossible because her throat was now almost swollen shut with unshed tears. Still, she must put on a brave front for the sake of Allegra and the other three brides-to-be.

She knew a heart could not literally break, but hers lay heavy within her chest. She had thought she would be one of the women being toasted by the end of this house party, which still had days to go. Now, all she wished was for the guests to depart and allow her to escape into sleep.

Silas turned his gaze to Lyric, standing there so stoically, when he knew her heart was breaking.

And he had been the one to shatter it.

All these happy couples had come out of the house party held in the sisters' honor. Lyric was the only woman who had not received an offer of marriage.

Their gazes met, and he saw the tears swimming in her eyes, tears he had put there due to his selfishness.

Why couldn't he say the words? Why couldn't he express to her how he felt?

If he didn't now, he would lose her forever. Somewhere down the line, a gentleman would see the jewel she was. That man would sweep Lyric off her feet and love her completely.

While Silas rotted at Chase Oaks, swimming in regret.

He wondered what Uncle Oscar would think of him now. Silas was behaving badly, ruining his own life and making Lyric miserable.

Could he summon the courage to voice his true feelings?

He stood on a precipice. He might fail utterly if he spoke now, Lyric rejecting him for good. Yet if he didn't, he would live the rest of his life in regret. Silas might not believe he was good enough for Lyric at this moment, but if she gave him the chance, he knew he could grow to become the man she needed.

The man he wanted to be. For himself.

For her . . .

Clearing his throat, he loudly said, "Excuse me."

That got the attention of everyone in the drawing room. So many pairs of eyes upon him. Sweat beaded along his hairline, but he plunged ahead. Because he did love Lyric more than he'd ever thought possible.

And he had to tell her—before he lost her.

"Many of you in this room know my reputation, that of a rogue," he began, gazing out across those gathered in the drawing room. "I will openly admit that I have sown more wild oats than any man present. Except for Lord Carroll, of course."

Nervous laughter sounded. Silas couldn't yet meet Lyric's eyes, though he knew she bore a hole through him now.

"My parents had the typical *ton* marriage, arranged by their parents, with no say in the matter. They did their duty. My father sired his heir. He and my mother led their own separate lives, promptly forgetting about me. I was the son who was supposed to bring the family together."

Silas swallowed painfully. "Instead, I was ignored my entire life. I never knew the love of a parent. I sought attention from others. Craved it, in fact, when what I was seeking all along was love. I never recognized it, though. I truly did not believe in its existence."

He looked directly at Lyric now. "And when it happened finally, I was too blind to see it for what it was. Even when I realized what had struck me, I couldn't make the final commitment to the woman I loved."

Audible gasps sounded as he walked toward Lyric. She had gone white and visibly trembled.

Taking her hands, he said to her, "My parents, the people who should have loved me the most, never did. I thought if they couldn't, how could anyone else? I never felt worthy of anyone, Lyric. Least of all you."

His fingers squeezed hers. "Yet you loved me. Openly and unconditionally. Because you have known love with these Strongs surrounding you. Your family has been a guiding light and shining example to you of what the power of love can do. You have seen your cousins—even your aunt—wed for love. You wanted a love match for yourself, but I was too stubborn to recognize or even admit that I loved you, Lyric."

Silas dropped to his knees before her, still holding her hands.

"When my uncle died, I promised myself I would be a better man, the one he always thought I could be. Uncle Oscar wanted me to find a wife. To find love. He longed for me to have children of my own and hold them dearly. From the moment I arrived at Shadowcrest and stepped from the carriage and caught sight of you, I loved you, Lyric. I truly did."

He paused, pressing a solemn kiss to each palm.

"At first, it was a physical attraction, but soon I was attracted to you emotionally. I told you that I cared for you. That I would be faithful to you. But you needed words I had never said. Words

I was too bloody frightened to utter."

He smiled at her, tears misting his own eyes now. "I have been a fool, my darling. I do love you. I love you so much it hurts. I think that is what caused me to be so afraid. I also understood you would settle for nothing except a love match, as those in your family have made. I did not believe I was a good enough man to be your husband, and perhaps that is why I could not speak those powerful three words."

Swallowing the emotion building in his throat, he told her "I understand now that a life without you would be no life at all. But it is not for me to judge if I am the right man for you. *You* are the only one who can determine that. If we are to have a future, you must be the one who speaks now."

Silas took in the face of the woman he would forever love. "My heart has spoken, and I have voiced what is in it. I want you as my wife, Lyric, and I will tell—show you—each and every day how much I do love you if you will give me the chance. I will cherish you. I want to build a life with you. I want us to have children and spend so much time in the nursery that the nursery governess will chase us from it. I want to hold you in my arms when we go to sleep at night and still be holding you when we awake each morning."

Pausing, he saw tears cascading down her cheeks and felt her trembling.

"I am sorry for the hurt I have caused you—but do not say no to me, Lyric. I simply cannot accept walking out that door without you. My life would be so empty, I do not know if I could go on. And I certainly couldn't stand to see you wed to another man when my heart cries out that we belong together. So, will you take a leap of faith with me? Will you believe that I love you and only you? Will you be my wife?"

She tugged on his hands, causing him to rise. "You know I love you, Silas. I will always love you. Even when we are at the end of our lives, our faces lined with wrinkles and our hair threaded with gray, our love will be strong. If I do not wed you,

Silas Chase, then I will be relegated to being an old maid, because the thought of being another man's wife is simply preposterous. Yes, my love. I will marry you and treasure you all the days of our lives."

His mouth seized hers in a kiss that spoke of his passion and the promises between them.

Breaking it, he said, "I love you, Lyric Strong. I love you." Then shouting with glee, he echoed, "I love you!"

Those gathered in the drawing room applauded as Silas took his betrothed in his arms again, kissing her once more, not caring that they were in front of an entire roomful of people. This kiss was not a light, polite kiss, which would put the seal of approval upon their betrothal. No, it was a kiss of fire and the pent-up passion which had lain unanswered.

Relief swept through him as Lyric answered his kiss with enthusiasm. They had been without one another for far too long, and need poured through them both.

When he broke the kiss, Silas gazed deeply into her eyes. "Thank you for forgiving me. Thank you for a second chance. Thank you—in advance—for all the happy years I know which lay ahead for us."

"Thank you for opening yourself up to me," she told him, blinking as tears filled her eyes. I know the words did not come easily to you, Silas."

"My feelings for you were always there, Lyric," he said. "The love, too, was present. I simply had to find the courage to give voice to those feelings. I have loved you for so long, and I feel liberated being able to say the words aloud. I love you, Lyric Strong. I love you now and forever. I want to marry you as soon as possible."

She stroked his cheek. "I want that, too, but I would like as many of my family present at our wedding as possible."

Allegra and Sterling joined them, Allegra wrapping her twin in a tight embrace.

"I knew you were meant to be together," Allegra told Lyric.

"I am delighted Lord Blankenship finally came to his senses."

Sterling also embraced Lyric and added, "I knew how much the fool loved you, Lyric. I would have blocked him from leaving Shadowcrest if he tried to do so before telling you of his great love for you."

"So, we are to be related by marriage," Silas said to his friend, slapping Sterling on the back. "Lyric tells me she wishes to wait for her missing family to return to Kent before we can wed."

"Allegra has told me the same," shared Sterling.

Silas looked to his newly-betrothed. "You shared the womb together and every day since then. Would you consider sharing your wedding day?"

Lyric smiled at him through tears of happiness. "It would mean the world to Allegra and me if we were married at the same time and place."

"Yes!" Allegra echoed enthusiastically. "Strongs always wed at the Shadowcrest chapel."

"I was going to leave for town tomorrow in order to purchase a special license," Sterling said. "I would like nothing better than to have your company in doing so."

He laughed merrily, joy filling every limb. "I would be happy to journey to town with you and for each of us make this purchase at Doctors' Commons."

"You can keep each other in line," Allegra said, laughing.

Sterling cradled Allegra's cheeks and kissed her.

For his part, Silas told Lyric, "You have nothing to worry about, my darling. We two rogues have met our matches—and this viscount's heart is spoken for until the end of time."

He took her in his arms again, heedless of those around them, and kissed the woman he loved.

EPILOGUE

Chase Oaks—July 1811

LYRIC AWOKE, ENVELOPED in her husband's warmth. As always, Silas' arm protectively rested around her, holding her close even while in sleep. It used to encircle her waist easily, but now she was so enormous that his palm was splayed across her belly, also protecting their unborn.

Something told her that today would be the day she would bring life into the world. They had not attended the Season because when it began in April, she was already six months along and looked as if she were due to give birth at any moment. The local doctor and midwife had all but guaranteed she would be delivering twins because of her girth. The fact that twins ran in the Strong family only supported their words.

Allegra, too, was with child. Most likely, she would give birth within the week. Wouldn't it be ironic if they had their babes on the same day, just as she and Allegra had been born the same day Aunt Dinah gave birth to Georgie and Pippa?

Warm lips grazed her nape as Silas began stroking her belly. His hand stilled, and she could feel his smile against her neck.

"They are active this morning," he said jovially. "Kicking away as if they hadn't a care in the world."

Already, Lyric knew her husband would make for a wonderful father. Many of the servants at Chase Oaks had been here when Silas was a child, and both the housekeeper and cook had regaled her with stories about him when he was a small boy. Yes, he had been full of mischief, but he was also full of kindness for the staff and others around him. Silas treated her not like a viscountess, but as a queen. True to his word, he told her he loved her each day, and he was eagerly awaiting the birth of their child—or children.

She turned in the bed with his help, facing him now, and they exchanged sweet kisses for a few minutes.

"We have yet to discuss names," she told him. "Do you have any in mind?"

"Although I am not the superstitious sort, I was loathe to talk over names with you," he admitted.

Her fingers lightly brushed his cheek. "Well, Allegra and I have done so. Aunt Dinah, too."

Aunt Dinah and her captain would welcome their babe into the world in two months' time. Because of her age, her aunt had said it most likely would be their only child together. The Captain said he would be happy with either a boy or girl, teasing that they already had so many girls anyway, another one would probably be easier to raise.

"What did you and Allegra decide upon?" Silas asked.

"She feels since I am carrying two babes, I have had to work harder these past few months. She told me for us to name them, and then she and Sterling would select their own name. While I have not thought of two male and two female names, I have come up with one of each," she revealed. "Allegra already knows what they are."

He kissed the tip of her nose. "Share these names with me. I am curious about them."

"While I do not know what your parents' names were, I know for certain you would never wish to have any child of ours named after them."

"Heavens, no!" he declared.

"You were close with your uncle Oscar, though. If one of these babes turns out to be a boy, I wish to name him after your beloved uncle."

He kissed her tenderly. "Thank you. It means the world to me, and it would have to Uncle Oscar, as well. What other name have you thought of?"

"Although I never knew my own mother, from all accounts, Aunt Dinah has said she was a lovely woman. Her name was Elizabeth. I would very much like to name a girl after her."

"Elizabeth," Silas echoed, smoothing her hair. "Elizabeth Chase. I rather like the sound of that."

Lyric opened her mouth to speak when she felt a whoosh come from her body. Immediately, she felt the dampness and knew what had occurred.

Her husband frowned. "What is it?"

"My water has broken. It is finally time."

He kissed her softly. "I will have a footman fetch the midwife at once. Can I do anything for you before I do so?"

"Just send my lady's maid and a couple of other maids. They will need to change these bed linens and prepare me for the birth."

She caught his hand and brought it to her lips, pressing a soft kiss into his palm. "You do realize this will be a prolonged process? That it may be nightfall—or even tomorrow—before I give birth."

His eyes widened. "I had no idea things took so long."

"Aunt Dinah has said the first time a woman gives birth is quite lengthy. The midwife has warned me of the same. Especially if I do carry twins, and we suspect that to be the case, it will be some time before they make their appearance."

"Whatever happens, I love you, Lyric. These past months of marriage with you have been the best of my life."

She saw tears glimmering in his eyes. "I feel the same, my love. Now, go."

Hours later, Lyric lay in the bed, her cries becoming hoarse since she had been quite vocal. Aunt Dinah had warned her and Allegra that childbirth pains were almost intolerable, but they should keep their focus on the results of the birth.

Another pain struck, and her moan turned into a scream.

Suddenly, the door burst open, and Silas rushed into the room. He came straight to the bed, dropping to his knees, taking her hand in his. He bowed his head, holding her hand tightly, smothering it in kisses.

"My lord, you simply cannot be present at the birth of your child. Or children," the midwife corrected.

He lifted his head, and Lyric saw her own agony reflected in his eyes.

Facing the midwife, Silas said, "My wife cannot go through this alone any longer. I must be by her side. I want to help."

The midwife opened her mouth to protest, but Lyric shook her head slightly. Instead, the woman said, "Very well, my lord. I will ask that you do not question anything and merely remain to support Lady Blankenship."

Another half-hour passed, the sharp pains growing in intensity, when the sudden urge to push overwhelmed Lyric.

She told the midwife, "It is happening. Just as you said it would. May I push? Is it time?"

"Yes, my lady. Bring new life into the world."

Gripping Silas' hand, she bore down hard with the next pain, hoping she would not break his bones.

"That's it, my darling. Push our babe out so he or she might meet us."

With the midwife coaching her along, Lyric did just that. She felt the babe slip from her body and looked eagerly as the woman cut the cord and lifted the infant.

"It is a boy," the midwife announced.

"Oscar," she said weakly, seeing the midwife swat their son's bottom.

The babe gave a loud, angry cry, and the midwife handed

him to a maid to clean up.

Another wave of pain caused dizziness within her, and she knew her task was only half-complete. Thankfully, it only took another few, intense pushes. Less than five minutes later, she had brought a daughter to life.

Both babes, cleaned and swaddled, were brought to her and Silas. He took Elizabeth, while Lyric held Oscar. She peered down into her son's face, his features so tiny and perfect. The babe opened his eyes and studied her thoughtfully, curiosity on his face.

"I am your mama," she told him. "And this is your papa and sister. You are twins, which is a very special relationship. You will understand one another as no one else can."

After a few minutes, Silas traded with her, pressing a gentle kiss to his daughter's brow before doing so.

She looked into her daughter's face, which so closely resembled her brother's.

"Welcome to the world, my sweet Elizabeth," she cooed to the babe.

After several minutes of bonding with her daughter, the midwife said it was time to hand over the twins to the wet nurse for their first feeding.

"Should we hire two wet nurses since there are two babes?" Silas asked worriedly as the midwife took both infants and passed them along to the wet nurse, who left for the nursery.

"One should be adequate, my lord," the midwife replied reassuringly. "Your maids have brought clean linens, my lady. Allow his lordship to assist you from the bed."

Silas helped her rise so that the maids could remove the soiled linens and replace them with fresh ones. She had given birth in the bedchamber set aside for the viscountess, a room she had never slept in, since she spent every night with her viscount. Knowing she didn't possess the strength to go anywhere, she told her husband she would sleep here tonight.

Silas dismissed the servants once the job was completed, and he gently ministered to her, bathing Lyric and then placing her in a fresh night rail her lady's maid had laid out for her.

"You did so well, my darling love," he said, kissing her tenderly. "I know you are exhausted. You should get some rest."

"Do not leave me just yet," she said.

"I will never leave you, my love."

He carried her to the bed and placed her gently upon it. Then a knock sounded at the door, and he went to answer it. Their butler handed Silas a letter, saying, "This came from Carrollwood, my lord."

"Thank you," her husband said, closing the door and bringing the folded note to the bed.

"Open it," she said. "Read it aloud."

Perching on the bed, he broke the seal, unfolding the letter. Silas slipped one hand about hers and began to read.

Dearest Lyric & Silas,

I am thrilled to share with you that Allegra has given birth to a healthy boy. Her labor began in the wee hours this morning and progressed for some time. Our son came into the world at three o'clock this afternoon. I would not be surprised if you heard his lusty cry all the way to Chase Oaks.

Allegra came through the birth well, and she hopes Lyric will do the same. As agreed, we will wait to name our son until we hear from the two of you.

I pray all is well and that we will be able to come together soon and introduce our bundles of joy to one another.

All my love,
Sterling

Relief swept through Lyric. "I am so glad to hear Allegra is fine, as is our nephew. If the messenger is still here, pen a quick note to them, Silas, and let them know about little Oscar and Elizabeth."

He kissed her brow. "I will do so now. I will only be gone a few minutes, and then I will sleep with you here. Close your eyes now, my love. I will stay with you until you do fall asleep."

Her husband kissed her again, and Lyric drifted off, dreaming of the good years still ahead.

About the Author

Award-winning and internationally bestselling author Alexa Aston's historical romances use history as a backdrop to place her characters in extraordinary circumstances, where their intense desire for one another grows into the treasured gift of love.

She is the author of Regency and Medieval romance, including: Dukes of Distinction; Soldiers & Soulmates; The St. Clairs; The King's Cousins; and The Knights of Honor.

A native Texan, Alexa lives with her husband in a Dallas suburb, where she eats her fair share of dark chocolate and plots out stories while she walks every morning. She enjoys a good Netflix binge; travel; seafood; and can't get enough of *Survivor* or *The Crown*.